KING'S COUNTRY

LARGE PRINT

MARIE JOHNSTON

LE PUBLISHING

 Created with Vellum

I've been the wicked witch of King's Creek since I was eight years old, from my angry red hair down to my ball-busting boots. With a mean drunk for a daddy who left nothing but insults and unpaid bills in his wake, was there ever any other fate? Now his passing has left me one bad turn from losing my land to the neighbors my family's been feuding with for generations.

So of course it's Dawson King who comes to my rescue in the middle of a snowstorm. But I don't care how good he looks in a pair of Wranglers, or how much he spoils my horse, or how great of a cook he is. The Kings already have everything—money, looks, and charm. Dawson's not getting my heart too.

I'm living my dream, I admit it. I took over the family ranch from my dad and grew it into the envy of Montana. I have the best views, the best employees, and the respect of the entire town. The only thing I don't have is someone to share my dream with. So when my neighbor breaks her leg and nearly freezes to death, I all but kidnap her back to my place to recover.

We grew up less than a mile apart, but we couldn't be in more different places now. Bristol's had nothing but pride for so long, it's hard to get close to her—and I want to get *very* close.

I don't care if the whole town loves me, I'm only interested in earning the love of one woman. But for a guy who's got the world at his feet, Bristol's heart might be out of my reach.

ristol

BITTER WIND CUT around the collar of my old Carhartt jacket, sending shivers racing down my body. My teeth chattered, but I tucked my chin into my jacket and encouraged Bucket forward. My bay's full name was ShitBucket, thanks to Pop, but I'd shortened it.

God. Pop. What would life have been like if he'd been able to crawl out of the bottle? What did it say about me that part of me was relieved I didn't have to endure his need for control and the daily tongue-lashings anymore?

I blinked back tears and squinted into the wind. Bucket's hooves crunched through old snow into the dried, brittle grass underneath. Daisy, my rescue dog, trotted next to us, her tongue lolling out. The pound had thought she was a mix of Australian shepherd and rottweiler, but I'd only cared that she wanted to herd cattle and, more importantly, that she had been free. That she'd turned out to be a damn fine dog was one of the few good things that had happened to me.

Bucket was another. And I was risking them both in this weather, but the four-wheeler wouldn't start. Again.

Another gust of wind bit into my skin. It was bringing an early March storm. I couldn't remember which month was in like a lion, out like a lamb. March? April? Hell, in Montana, it could also be May. But this month had been all lion and I'd had two heifers calve early. One had lost her young.

Stress clenched my jaw. What the hell was I going to do?

I'd been asking myself that for as long as I could remember, but with Pop's death had come open books to the actual state of the ranch.

It was worse than I'd thought. I couldn't believe we hadn't lost everything already. The only reason we hadn't was because Pop had been so hard to deal with, it'd been easier for businesses to ignore him. They wouldn't feel the same way about me.

Well . . . maybe a little. But since I didn't touch alcohol, I also wasn't fueled by liquid courage that stole all the fucks I had to give about what people said to me.

I had that going for me and it happened to be my biggest weakness right now. The mailbox was already full of notices. We owed for feed, we owed for equipment, and we were overdrawn. Not we. Me. Pop had put everything under Cartwright Cattle and now that he was gone, it had fallen to me, debt and all.

Our cattle weren't healthy. They routinely got injured because Pop had been too stubborn to move fencing to block bad areas the cows were drawn to, which only led to them getting stuck in mud, breaking a leg, or calving in the toughest spot for a human to reach.

I was missing one now. Dammit, Pop. He'd let the bull in the cow pasture too damn early. I'd talked him into spring calving. We didn't have enough bodies or resources to keep calves healthy in the cold months, and what we lost in income for lighter calves in the fall, we'd make up for in lower feeding costs and less wear and tear on bodies. Mostly *my* body, out feeding and tracking down calving cows in bitter temperatures. We could turn calves out to pasture sooner after they were born, saving manpower and feed. April, even early May, would've been better to aim for. Sure, sometimes nature had other ideas, but for the most part, cows were less likely to give birth out in the middle of nowhere before impending storms.

Pop had been resistant and last year, after a spat between us, he'd turned out the bull too early. He'd probably thought he'd be around to deal with the fallout—even though he would've been in a drunken stupor. But he'd died, and it was only me now.

My phone vibrated against my chest. I should ignore it. It wasn't like anyone was calling to offer their sympathies for Pop being gone. The only other person who mourned his death was the owner of the liquor store and he'd been a selfish bastard who had fueled Pop's addiction no matter how often I'd asked him to turn Pop away.

I yanked off a thin glove and pulled my phone out. It was the one luxury I'd managed to squirrel money away for. It wasn't fancy, but it was smart and I could pay ahead for the data I used. Sometimes I had enough to splurge for a movie, but Pop had sniffed out extra cash more often than not.

Marshall's name flashed across the screen. I groaned. Dammit. I was late, and since I hadn't found the wandering cow, I likely wasn't going to make our date.

"Hey," I answered, turning my head to minimize wind interference. Bucket was sauntering slowly enough I didn't have to watch where he was going.

"Goddammit, Bristol, where the hell are you?" His tone wasn't as irate as Pop's usually had been, but familiar anxiety twined its way around my insides.

"Marshall, sorry. There's a problem on the ranch."

"There's always a problem on the ranch." He paused for a beat but I had nothing to interject. He was right. "You aren't even on your way to town, are you?"

I swallowed. If he was pissed already . . . "One of the cows I planned to get in before the storm is missing." I'd missed the last meet-the-parents meal and Marshall could be persistent.

"For fuck's sake, are you telling me that you can't make another dinner with my parents? We've already canceled once."

"*You've* already canceled once." My jaw set as humiliation chased away some of the cold. I'd shown up to dinner at Hogan's, the local steakhouse, in my best jeans and the nicest shirt I owned. Marshall had blanched and asked if that was what I was wearing. Then he'd called his parents and said that I had the stomach flu.

"Bristol . . . we talked about this. We might not be from King's Creek, but even my parents know your dad's reputation. You can't show up to a nice dinner in your work clothes looking like you don't give a damn."

I ground my jaw together. Those were my best clothes. My only set of nice clothes.

"They're already put out, having to drive an hour to get here when the weather sucks." He blew out a gusty sigh. "When are you gonna arrive?"

"I don't know." I glanced around the bleak landscape. A few flakes fluttered in the wind. Shit. I had to find her.

"Are you telling me that you're putting a cow before your boyfriend?"

If you were a good boyfriend, you wouldn't have to ask. I brushed that thought away as fast as it formed. Marshall was a good man. Unlike a lot of the men in King's Creek, he thought I was worth more than a quick fuck and a brag that they'd bagged the prickly Bristol Cartwright. I'd learned the hard way that dating in my hometown was only a trial in failure.

"Marshall, if she calves and one or both die, that's a lot of money." And more lives added to my conscience. These animals were either raised for food or to breed more animals for food, so having them suffer and die for nothing was a waste on so many levels. It hurt my heart more than I cared to admit.

"Bristol." There was the patronizing tone that I'd worked hard to ignore the last couple months of the six months we'd been dating. "This was an important night for me."

"And this is an important job to me." I bit my tongue before telling him that if he cared about me at all, if he'd been listening to me at all, he'd know how critical this was. Too many people already made comments about how I was just like Pa.

"It's your job. These are my parents and they drove an hour to meet you—again. If you don't get here in the next half hour, I can't do this."

It wasn't like I could invite them to my place, tell them to make themselves at home, kick back, and I'd be in shortly. My home wasn't presentable, which hadn't been an issue. Marshall hadn't expressed interest in seeing my place, or staying the night. He'd always invited me over to his house in Miles City. I'd spent good money on gas to get there when the funds should've gone back to the ranch—or to buy a new set of clothing that would've passed the parent test.

Which brought up another issue. I still didn't have any nicer clothing than before. Putting Pop to rest had emptied my bank account, and since no sympathy cards had flooded the mailbox, much less any filled with money, I was on a tighter budget than normal.

These cows and their calves were my future. Without them, I didn't have a ranch or a way to bring in money. With them, I could slowly build the ranch up to be self-sustainable. I could grow it until it sustained me. What I couldn't do was throw my livelihood away over one man's hissy fit.

Marshall would have to understand. He'd see my side. He'd support me.

Right?

"Marshall—"

"Fuck, Bristol. Are you kidding me? You're choosing a cow over me?"

"I—"

"No, if you can't tell me that you're on your way here right now, then I'm done. Done, Bristol."

I blinked against the onslaught of his anger, against the urge to shrink into my coat, turn Bucket around, race to the RV I was living in, and hide.

"Bristol?"

I squeezed my eyes shut. The grind of Bucket's hooves on the ground centered me. This was the right decision. "I . . . can't."

"All right, then." He bit out the words and ended the call.

I stared at the phone and bit my lip, momentarily considering turning Bucket around and racing home.

Then what? I'd show up and he'd be pissed that I was wearing cowboy boots and had hat hair? Then I could be publicly shamed once again.

"Shit." Nothing was happening until I found my cow. The task took my mind off the unexpected breakup.

It shouldn't have been unexpected. I hadn't even thought of Marshall when I'd saddled Bucket and headed out. Selfish like Pop. Wasn't that what people said?

Daisy whined next to me.

"Follow the fence," I said as if the dog could understand me. Daisy might. She was a smart creature. "There must've been a hole she escaped through. Let's find it."

The phone buzzed. I glanced down and scowled at the screen.

I can't believe you.

He'd dumped me. He'd gotten the last word. Why the message?

Bucket started up an incline that normally wouldn't give him problems, but the crunch of snow under his hooves filled me with anxiety. He shouldn't be out in this. I needed to make a decision between the cow and my horse, and the cow wouldn't win. I couldn't do this job without Bucket. He was a good ranch horse.

My phone buzzed again. Another message or just the reminder buzz?

After this hill, the rest of the terrain wouldn't be that bad. I'd moved all the cattle out of the pasture with the nasty ravine before Pop had died and before winter had set in. Pop had been too sick to get out of the house to know what I'd done. He'd refused every other time and my asshole neighbor Dawson had gladly called to berate me about the poor cows that had found their way into the ravine and hadn't survived the trip.

He might've texted that message, but I knew Dawson well enough to infer the tone.

If he knew that I'd lost a cow ready to give birth, he'd have more choice words to give me. The guy had no inkling what it'd been like to ranch with Pop and I doubted he cared. He only cared that I was a Cartwright, and apparently that was enough to earn his hate.

The phone kept buzzing, but Bucket was close to the crest, his powerful body bunching and heaving to keep from slipping down the incline. I should stuff the phone back into my pocket and hold on with both hands. I should turn him back around and find a safer way down. My search for the cow was done.

And yet, my heart ached. Gritting my teeth, I clutched the phone in one hand and the reins in the other. "Come on, boy, you can do it."

Daisy ran ahead and danced in a circle like she was cheering Bucket on.

Montana winters were brutal, but the last few years, there'd been stretches where temperatures reached nearly forty degrees. All it did was melt the top layers of snow and make it hard to get through the pasture on horseback. I should've thought of that before I risked cutting up Bucket's legs.

"Almost there."

Bucket's sides heaved. If I had oats to spare, I'd rain them down on him when we got back. He deserved spoiling and I couldn't do it nearly enough.

My fingers were stiff and the phone vibrated again, falling out of my hands.

I gasped and scrambled for it at the same time Bucket lunged over a particularly bad spot. He landed and bounced me in the saddle. I yelped, startling him just as he was primed for another lunge. He heaved and landed off-kilter by a section of fence that was loose. Barbed wire sprawled onto the land bordering mine.

Already thrown out of his calm, Bucket spun, tossing me from my seat. I was an experienced rider, and had it not been for Marshall and that damn phone, I would've been ready. But I went airborne and tried to right myself before landing in a mess of barbed wire. Agony exploded through my right leg and the rest of my body slammed into the unforgiving ground.

Crying out, I rolled and pinpricks of pain stabbed through my legs. I gasped in breaths and forced myself to focus through the blaze of pain.

What the fuck had happened?

My brain registered it before I recognized it.

I'd broken my leg.

Son of a bitch. I blinked and carefully raised my upper body, my breath coming in panicked pants as fire engulfed my lower body. I'd landed on the line of barbed wire that was supposed to be attached to the top of the fence posts. My jeans had taken the brunt of their angry stabs, but each move drove the barbs deeper.

Shaking, I looked at my leg. My vision was blurry. I didn't know if the tears were from the pain or the cold, but I sniffled and forced myself to concentrate.

How did I get out of this?

"Bucket?"

A soft nicker met my ears. He hadn't run off. But he was on the other side of the fence. Maybe I could crawl to him and drag myself onto his back.

The wind howled and more flakes danced in the air, zipping by me like they had better things to do. Daisy ran around me, whining and sniffing my face.

"I'm all right, girl." The wind stole my words. I wasn't all right. I was in the middle of nowhere, tangled in barbed wire, with a broken leg and a storm on the way.

The cow wasn't the only one in trouble.

Dawson

I STOMPED into the house and let the warmth of my favorite place in the world swallow me up.

"Shit weather's on its way," I said to no one. The house was empty. Should I bring one of the barn cats inside?

I shook my head, answering my own question. There was no reason not to— other than my brothers giving me eternal crap for spoiling cats.

I couldn't help it if they liked me so much.

I tossed my jacket on a hook. The mudroom off the garage wasn't nearly as full of winter weather gear now that Xander and Savvy had left. Once the weather wasn't so far below zero, they'd taken off to find their own piece of paradise and do a little traveling.

The house was quiet once again.

I set my gloves and hat on the bench and toed out of my boots. I was prepared to get snowed in. The guys who worked for me had wrapped everything up. Our calves had all dropped. I could relax through this storm for once. Tucker had put the cow we'd found wandering through the back forty in the barn. It was going to drop any day, but I could keep an eye on it so Tucker and Kiernan could hunker down at their homes.

I shook my head again. I'd have to let the fucking Cartwrights know I had the cow in our pen and he'd—

I let out a sigh. Danny was gone. I'd rarely dealt with him, and Bristol and I were more than happy to communicate through curt text messages. But I'd call her for this one.

The haunting image of her from her dad's memorial service snaked through my mind. Shoving away the guilt, I dialed her number, primed to give her a piece of my mind. The cow had dug into one of my bales and chomped away.

After the fifth ring, I hung up and tried again. For all of Bristol's prickly ways, not answering my calls wasn't one of them. Her land bordered mine, and we had to deal with each other. We sucked it up, and I stayed as professional as my *get your shit together* tone would allow.

No answer.

I punched out a message. *Found one of your heifers.* I hit send.

Dammit. It was about to storm. I tapped out another one. *She's safe in my barn.*

That was all I could do. It wasn't like a

Cartwright to let us do much for them. They'd accuse us of screwing them over anyway.

I went to the kitchen and opened the fridge door. I had hamburger, roasts, steaks, vegetables, pasta in the cupboard, and potatoes on the counter, but cooking for one got old fast. While my brother and his wife had been here, I'd indulged way too often in my favorite hobby. There'd been three of us and I'd still had leftovers for me and the guys. I had to pare it down to just me riding out a storm. Maybe I'd just make some spaghetti.

With meatballs. Mozzarella-stuffed meatballs.

I was digging out a pound of hamburger when barking intruded on my recipe formulations. I shoved the food back in the fridge and straightened. Claws skittering up and down my porch filtered into the house. My old cattle dog had died a couple of years ago and I should've gotten around to replacing him, but I hadn't.

Going to the front window, I peered out. Bristol's dog was going batshit on my porch, racing up and down the length, hopping at the windows and rising up to her hind legs at the door like she was going to barge in. "Daisy?"

The dog must've heard me. She spun around and went crazy barking. Every few barks, she'd pause and gaze toward the pastures.

Something was wrong.

I ran to the mudroom and got back into everything I'd just gotten out of. As I jogged outside, my boots crunched against old snow and ice that hadn't gotten a chance to melt yet in our cold March temperatures.

Daisy raced around the house and stopped when she saw me. She turned one way, then whined and looked back at me.

"What's wrong?" As if she could tell me.

I dug into my pocket and fished out my keys. This wasn't the weather to take a horse out in. The guys and I maintained painstakingly manicured trails through the pastures so we could use wheeled vehicles, whether it was the Ranger or the pickup. I went for the little Ranger. It had a cab and was more versatile in the pastures than my pickup.

Daisy didn't wait for me. She ran off.

"Dammit. Wait." I sprinted for the Ranger, slipping and sliding, but made it without falling. I fired up the engine and hoped I could find the dog.

She raced through the pastures, not waiting for me to stop and open gates, then stop on the other side and close them. I sped after her.

I bumped and jumped over the pastures, pushing the speed of the small engine. After we crested one rolling hill, I spotted Bucket. My stomach bottomed out. He was saddled, but there was no rider. There was bad weather coming. Where the hell was Bristol?

As the Ranger struggled up a particularly nasty hill, my gaze was on Bucket—was there any logical reason that

Bristol wasn't around?—when Daisy's barking caught my attention. Bucket trotted away from the noise but I barely noticed.

Bristol was on her side, her body curled in on itself.

Fear drove adrenaline through my veins. I stopped as close as I could to Bristol. A section of fence had fallen, not a surprise with the shoddy work Danny Cartwright had done with his land. But somehow Bucket had bucked Bristol right into the mess of it. She hugged herself tight, her stocking hat tugged so far down it was hard to see her brilliant red hair.

"Bristol?"

I don't know if she nodded or just shivered. I gingerly stepped over the fence. It was twisted around her legs. The headlights of my Ranger lit the rusty blood staining her jeans where the barbs had stabbed her.

"M-m-my l-l-leg."

"Broken?" How'd a rider like her gotten

thrown? It didn't matter. My mind worked over everything I needed to do. "Which one?"

She extracted one hand to tap on her right leg, then tucked it back into the warmth of her body. Sitting in a heap of metal on top of ice, injured, she had to be freezing. Freezing to death.

"Wait here." I went back to the Ranger. Bristol had to be in bad shape if she didn't bite my head off asking about where else she could go. I searched the little toolbox for what I needed to free Bristol from the wire.

I went to work. She stayed still as I cut around her. I cut as many points as I could, but I still had to remove it from her body.

"Bristol, this is going to hurt." The animosity we'd nurtured over the years was tabled. She needed help and I was the only one to give it.

"D-doesn't matter. D-d-do it."

Not many points were actually still

stuck in her, but even I winced as I yanked them from her body.

She drew in a shaky breath, but I wasn't done.

"I have to move you, and you're lying on some wire. Can you sit up?"

I knelt next to her, cold leeching through my jeans. How fucking cold was she? She struggled to a sitting position, trying her best to keep from jostling her right leg, but her already ashen face was bled of more color.

She moved her arms to brace herself, one hand without a glove.

"What the hell happened to your glove?" How could she go out in this weather so unprepared?

She flinched and I immediately regretted the heat in my words. She'd been through a lot today and didn't need my shit. "I w-w-was trying to warm up my hand before t-t-trying to get up again."

One glove was missing. Obviously she

hadn't meant to lose it. "Here." I took mine off.

She shook her head and squirmed to try to stand again.

I kept my hand on her shoulder. "I can wrestle the gloves on you and waste more time."

"F-fine." She put them on and I didn't miss the beat of relief that passed over her face. "G-grab Bucket."

"He's fine."

"G-get him." Her jaw was rigid and she wouldn't budge. I'd have to wrestle her if I didn't get her horse first.

"Don't move while I grab him. And put this on." I shrugged out of my coat and draped it around her shoulders. Her own jacket was way too thin for this wind.

The wind batted against my shirt. It was frigid, but I was moving and we'd be in the Ranger soon enough.

I jumped the fence and walked slowly toward Bucket. He watched me warily, but I was familiar enough. I always snuck him goodies when I was out on Gold Rush and riding past his pasture.

Bucket allowed me to take the reins. As I aimed for the hole in the fence and hoped that Bucket was comfortable enough with the rumble of the engine to let me tie him to the Ranger and lead him back, I spotted a rectangular black object on top of the snow.

She'd lost her phone. Bristol had been in more trouble than I'd thought. I picked it up and the screen sluggishly flashed on to show a series of messages from "Marshall" berating her, and then my missed calls.

Whoever Marshall was, I didn't like him. I didn't care how obstinate Bristol was, she didn't deserve a series of text bubbles telling her she was trash.

I secured Bucket and went back to Bristol with my hands tucked under my armpits. "I have to pick you up."

"I can stand."

"Bristol."

"I can stand." Her green eyes flashed.

There was only so much help she would accept. As stubborn as her daddy.

"All right. Stand, then." I put my hands under her armpits and lifted.

A pain-filled cry echoed around us and she sagged, her right leg limp.

"Shit." I snugged her against me with my arm around her and half carried, half limped her to the Ranger. The only reason I didn't swing her into my arms was so she could have some control over how her leg dangled. If I carried her, it'd get bumped around.

Once I had her loaded, I patted the back platform and Daisy jumped on. I took off, going only as fast as Bucket would follow. He had no problem with the Ranger, probably because I was the treat guy. Eternity came and went with only Bristol's ragged breathing. I wanted to pull up next to my pickup because she needed a hospital, but I knew she'd argue about Bucket.

"I'll put Bucket with the other horses, and then we're going to the ER."

Indecision crossed her face, but she had to realize she didn't have a choice. "Okay. Thanks."

"It's what neighbors do." I got out and untied Bucket. I shouldn't have slipped that dig in, but for years I'd tried to extend an olive branch to her and she would slap it down on a good day. Most days, she'd send that branch back smoking from her whip-sharp words. She didn't hold back on her opinions.

Once Bucket was unsaddled and settled, safe enough for the storm, I started the pickup, flicked the heat to high, and pulled it close to the Ranger. I wasn't going to worry about parking the Ranger in its spot by the shop, or even getting it inside the shop. Bristol needed medical attention *now*.

She was already trying to get out of the Ranger on her own.

"We should splint it," I offered.

"Let's just go."

Damn woman. I rushed to her side. Her jeans were stiff with horse sweat and blood—blood that should've been in her white face.

We didn't say a word until we got to town. Her features were etched with concentration, and from the way she bent over her leg and held it off the vibrations of the floor, she was probably trying not to vomit from the agony.

"I found one of your cows," I said. We rolled past the buildings on the edge of town. The lumber yard, a dollar store, and a gas station. I turned onto the main road that'd take us to the small hospital that served King's Creek.

Bristol's sharp inhale had me looking over. Hope shone in her eyes. "Is she all right?"

"I put her in the barn." She'd know that there was nothing like a storm to bring on labor. One of the top ten of Murphy's Laws of Ranching.

Relief made her body sag as much as it

could when she was in so much pain and trying to keep her leg stable. "I was out looking for her."

"Wouldn't have to if that section of fence had been fixed better last fall."

Her expression shuttered and she stared out the window. For the second time today, I regretted saying something to hurt her. I never tried to hurt her. I was usually just trying to make a point, but tonight that seemed like more of a dick move than usual.

The clinic came into view and I drove to the ER entrance. It was a small five-bed hospital, with an extra room for the ER that I'd been in more than a few times when I'd been younger and doing stupid shit. I still had the scar from a broken arm I'd gotten diving off the top of the barn when the snow hadn't been nearly deep enough to land in.

"I'll get a wheelchair." I killed the engine and ran inside. One of the nurses behind the desk rose, her face brightening. We'd gone on a few dates until it was clear she wanted more than I did.

"Dawson," Emma said.

She might be happy to see me, but I wasn't happy to be here. "Hey, Emma. I've got Bristol—I think she broke her leg."

Emma blinked. "Bristol. Cartwright?" The whole town would be surprised a King and a Cartwright had ridden in the same vehicle.

I didn't answer, grabbing a wheelchair by the door and speeding out before I had unfolded it.

The passenger door was open, but Bristol's head was on the headrest, her eyes closed as she breathed through the pain.

Emma was behind me. A younger man trailed her. "We've got her, Dawson, thanks."

I ignored the dismissal and helped Bristol get out, landing on her good leg and pivoting to sit in the chair. We all wheeled in while Bristol shrank lower in the chair, holding her leg like it was levitating on its own.

"What happened?" Emma asked.

"Slipped on ice," Bristol rasped.

I bit the inside of my cheek but didn't say anything otherwise. A fall from a horse was different than slipping on ice, but with Bristol it was a matter of pride.

I trailed them and was about to follow them to the room when Emma turned. "You can go now." A smile played on her lips. "Your role of hero is done for the night."

My feet were rooted in place. The kid and Bristol disappeared behind a door and I craned my neck like I could see through wood. "I'm not leaving." The words were out before I'd thought about them.

Emma's dark brows popped in surprise. Her silky hair was twined up in a messy bun and she wore a wide headband to secure the strays away from her face. She was attractive but any interest had died before we'd done anything that required removing clothing.

"Okaaay. Are you two dating?"

I scowled. "*No*. Why?"

She cocked her head like she was trying to figure me out. "Then you can wait in the waiting room, but I can't tell you anything without her approval."

Shrugging, I dropped into a chair. "She'll need a ride home."

Emma stared at me for a second, then sat next to me. "She's going to need more than a ride home."

"What?"

Emma glanced to the door, then to the desk. The other lady that had been there was gone, maybe getting Bristol's information. "She obviously broke her leg and the blood—"

"That's from barbed wire."

Emma's sympathetic wince was quick. "I don't know if she has anyone to help her"—the whole town knew she had no one—"but whether she'll have to use a wheelchair or crutches, she's going to need help."

"I'm shocked she didn't insist on driving herself." Her broken leg made it impossible.

"I'm shocked she let you help her," Emma said wryly, then her expression sobered. "Look, when I was in high school, I broke my leg. It makes doing the essentials tough. You know what I mean." She patted my leg. "I've gotta get in and help the doc."

"She can stay with me," I blurted. I'd seen Bristol's house. The trailer she'd grown up in. It'd been in rough shape when I was a kid. I'd be surprised if it survived this storm.

Emma gawked at me. "Seriously?"

"She's a pain in the ass, but I don't hate her, Emma."

"The King–Cartwright feud stops for a broken leg? I'm glad there's limits."

I shrugged. The words *it isn't my feud* dangled on the tip of my tongue.

CHAPTER 2

ristol

"No. Absolutely not." I stared at the nurse who was clearly infatuated with the frustrating man waiting to take me home—to *his* home—in the waiting room. Emma had informed me of his offer like I'd won the King's Creek lottery. *You get one night under the Kings' roof with the great Dawson King!*

"How about I let him in and you two can hash it out?"

The doctor had come and gone, barely sparing me a glance. He'd done no more than he had to, putting the cast on and sloughing the rest of the work onto Emma. When Pop had died, he'd left a lifetime of unpaid medical bills behind. Ones he'd never planned on paying. Pop's rough voice rattled in my mind. *They can't refuse treatment. Assholes.*

Dr. Jangula probably assumed I was the same. Unfortunately, I had no clue how I was going to pay.

My jeans had been sliced and diced and I had on nothing more than paper shorts from the lab-slash-X-ray department. My pale legs were covered with a warm blanket Emma had brought in. She'd had the young aide grab two more when she'd seen how badly I was shivering.

"Why's he still here?" I snarled. Now that my leg was secured against unwanted movement, the pain wasn't as bad. I was only nauseated and not outright gagging. My legs were covered with bandages, and the small cuts and abrasions burned like tiny brands, but at least that pain was diffuse and not concentrated in one spot.

My fingers and toes weren't as numb as when Dawson had found me. I'd narrowly escaped frostbite and wasn't shivering thanks to the warmed blankets Emma had brought. Dr. Jangula's bedside manner sucked, but I was patched up and had gotten a tetanus shot. There was nothing left to do.

Emma's gaze softened. "Dawson's a good guy."

Ugh, I didn't need this. Dawson was the golden boy and I was the town's very own wicked witch. The one whose mom hadn't bothered to stick around long after birth. "I don't need him."

Emma pursed her lips and she eased onto the edge of the bed. "Bristol, do you have anyone else to call?"

"I lost my phone in the fall." My empty excuse fell dead between us. She knew I was full of shit, and I didn't care to have one of Dawson's lovers witness my low point.

I'd run into Emma and Dawson on a date. She'd been dressed exactly how Marshall wished I would've dressed the night I was supposed to meet his parents: silky leggings and a glittery shirt that was flattering and elegant, her ankle boots only pulling the look together. Emma was everything I wasn't. She was smart, had a successful job, and would make the parents of whomever she settled with proud.

I was *not* envious of the girls Dawson dated. There were too many to count.

"Is there a friend you can call?"

My cheeks burned, the warmest they'd been all day. I didn't bother to shake my head and confirm her assumption that I had no friends. The whole town knew I was a loner.

"Boyfriend?" she asked softly.

"None of your business," I mumbled, the conversation with Marshall pinballing through my brain.

"Well, Dawson's willing to help. I say you hear him out. Can I bring him in?"

"No." At her steady gaze, I sighed. "Fine. Then I can tell him to leave."

She nodded and left. I combed my fingers through my hair. It was a tangled mess. *I* was a tangled mess. I had on a worn Montana State sweatshirt I'd gotten from a thrift store in Miles City. Marshall had scoffed at secondhand stores, so I'd only stopped there before going to his place.

Dawson swaggered through the door, his expression guarded, like he expected me to attack. He had on a black stocking hat with the King's Ranch logo and his hands shoved into his dark brown coat. How his brown coat hid all the grunge that came with working on a ranch and mine only looked dirtier, I didn't know.

Emma closed me in with him. The small

exam room shrank even further around his broad shoulders. I wasn't short, but he towered several inches over me.

Dawson's brown gaze was serious by the time it collided with mine. He didn't start with small talk. "Why can't you stay with me?"

"Because I don't need to."

He cocked an arrogant brow, and it only added to his rugged manliness instead of making him repellent. "The snow's started. I have your horse, your cow, and your dog. You might as well stay."

I gave him a tight smile. "Are you going to put me in the barn too?"

"I have nice straw, what can I say?" He rolled his eyes. "I don't know what cave you think I crawled out of, but I have a big house. You won't even have to see me that much."

I gestured to my cast. "All your bedrooms are upstairs."

"Not mine." Grief hid in the depths of

his whiskey eyes. "I have Mama and Dad's old room downstairs," he added softly.

The reminder of his mom peeled open the haphazard bandage I'd slapped over my heart years ago. Sarah King had been one of the best people who roamed the earth, and one of my dad's stupidest decisions had stolen her from us.

"I don't want to sleep on a couch." Dawson's couch was probably nicer than the salvaged mattress I had in the RV, but I didn't want to sleep under the same roof as him. If only the trailer were more inhabitable.

"I'll stand at the end of the stairs so when you fall hopping up them, I can catch you." His tone was dry. "You can use my bed."

Heat swamped my body. There was no reason on God's green earth that I needed to be near or in Dawson's bed. I didn't care if it was for convalescence. No. "I'll be fine at home."

That wasn't true. I had no goddamn clue how I was going to stay in my RV and do what needed to get done, but I'd figure it out like I had all my life.

"Bristol."

"Take me home." I sat up and scooted my legs over, biting back a grimace. My right leg was killing me and my cuts screamed. "Never mind. I can call for a ride."

"And pay them how? I didn't see a purse on you."

"I can call . . . someone else."

"Like a boyfriend?" His voice was stilted. Odd.

I gave him a careful glare. "Yeah, like a boyfriend."

He pulled out my phone and handed it over. The screen blinked on. The barrage of messages from Marshall would've been easy to see. My cheeks burned. Would there be a time I wasn't ashamed around Dawson King?

I snatched the phone away from him but had nowhere to put it. I slapped it facedown. "Reading my stuff?"

"Didn't mean to," he said softly. "I saw it when—look, I'll bring you home and maybe you'll come to your senses before we get there."

"Fine." I sounded like a petulant child. Pop used to hate when I said *fine*. "Let's go."

"You need to get dressed."

"I am dressed."

He frowned and it did nothing to detract from his good looks, like the square jaw. The dark lashes around eyes that didn't miss a single detail. Or the silky hair sticking out from under his hat. Dawson King was the hottest man I'd ever seen, and I hated him even more for it. "You need more than that." He spun and left the room. Probably to go find equally hot Emma.

By the time he got back holding a foam-green pair of scrub pants, I was in my ratty winter coat, grateful that I hadn't gotten blood on it. I pulled my stocking hat out of the pocket and stuffed it on my head.

He dropped the pants on the bed and left the room. I slipped the scrubs over my good leg and then wiggled around to get them over my cast. Pain screamed over my skin as wounds opened.

There was a soft tap at the door and Emma popped her head in. "Oh goodness, let me help you with that."

"I don't need—" I gave up. My chest was heaving and I hurt. Who the fuck cared anymore? At least she wasn't Dawson.

"I'm glad you finally agreed," she said as she slid the pants over my cast. "Recovery will be so much easier with an extra pair of hands."

I didn't reply. I hadn't agreed, but the less I had to fight everyone, the better. Recovery was the first and last of my problems. Running my ranch and limping through the financial storm to come was the mountain between.

"Going to the bathroom sucks with a

broken leg," she said as she tugged the waistband over my cast.

My gaze jerked to hers. "What?"

Emma's kind gaze rose to meet mine. "Going to the bathroom? Anything in the bathroom, really. And getting food. It's hard to carry anything with crutches."

I looked around. I hadn't thought about crutches.

"I gave them to Dawson," Emma said. "We'll use the wheelchair to leave. But if you think you need your own wheelchair for the first couple of weeks, just let us know and we can get you one."

Another thing I couldn't pay for. A wheelchair would be useless anyway. Did it come with snow tires? If not, I wouldn't even get to the RV Pop had dumped a hundred yards from the cesspool he'd lived in. With this damn cast, I couldn't even drive.

What the hell was I going to do?

I wanted to scream, but showing any emotion was as pointless as wishing for more money. Nothing good ever came of it.

Emma helped me stand, pull the pants up, and then pivot me until I could drop into the wheelchair.

Sweat dotted my brow. I pulled my hat lower and Emma wheeled me out. "I need to grab the pain meds the doctor prescribed. It'll be enough to get you by until you can get to the pharmacy."

"I don't want pain meds." I avoided looking at Mr. Tall, Dark, and Stubborn in the waiting room.

"Bristol—"

"No."

Emma bypassed the nurses' station, skipping the medicine. Dawson made small talk with her on the way out.

"How much snow do you think we'll get?" she asked Dawson.

"The news said six to eight, but you never know," he replied. "It's hard to tell in the country. It all blows around."

I ached to add to the conversation, but

personal experience told me that my opinion was never welcome. Snow did blow all over the country. Amounts mattered but so did wind and the direction it blew. Would there be ice? The duration? So many things. But I kept my mouth shut.

Dawson had his pickup running. A wave of heat hit me when he opened the passenger door and Emma wheeled me closer. I pulled myself up, ignoring any and all pain, and lifted myself in.

Emma made sure everything was tucked in. "Take care, Bristol."

As she shut the door, I looked straight ahead, wishing the earth would open up and swallow me. A beautiful couple was helping poor old me. They could gossip later about how all my medical bills were overdue just like Pop's.

Dawson got in on a wave of cold wind. "You could've said thank you."

"She was doing her job." No one cared if I thanked them or not. They expected me to snap at them like Pop and half the time I did. "I'm sure you'll thank her thoroughly later."

Dawson's brows dropped and he gave me a *What are you talking about?* look. "I'm not dating Emma."

I rolled my eyes toward him. "I've seen you two."

"That was only a couple of dates."

"Not my business and not interested." I was *so* interested. Why had they broken up? They seemed to get along. I didn't talk to my exes. They were all assholes and had treated me like a conquest. If it wouldn't get me into legal trouble, I'd go back and nut punch every one of them.

"Manners aren't just for people who've dated."

I rested my head back and crossed my arms. The seat was back as far as it could go. I shifted my leg and the bulky cast. "As if people care whether you say thank you or not." I snorted. "They probably say it for you."

"Why would they do that?"

"You're a King. You and your family walk on water. They gossip about who you're seeing, what you buy. They gush over who your dad and brothers married. The town adores you, all of you. People love to hate me."

I snapped my mouth shut. What had happened to my verbal filter? I tried not to say much around anyone. I didn't need to add to their ammunition or confirm their preformed opinions. Around Dawson, all my filters dropped. Was it because we'd started out life as friends?

"People don't love to hate . . ."

I stared at him and he clamped his lips shut.

"All right, I'll give you that. But you can still say thank you."

My filter failed me again. "Why? So Emma can go tell her friends about how my jeans are so old they practically fell off when she cut them? But that the doctor didn't care because my family owes the hospital so much money, and if he got a little pleasure from ruining my clothing, so be it? But 'Oh,' she'd say. 'Bristol has some manners.' Is that how it would go?"

Dawson's brows rose but his gaze stayed glued on the windshield and deteriorating road conditions. Swirling snow masked the pavement underneath. "One, I'm sure Emma has to adhere to some confidentiality rules and all that. And two, you're really jaded."

"If your grandparents hadn't screwed mine, then we would've been King's Creek royalty instead."

His jaw clenched. He couldn't argue the facts. "Look, I get that my mom's parents sold your grandparents some land and then later oil was found on it, but keeping mineral rights when selling land isn't criminal. It's common practice. As for 'King's Creek royalty,' I can't help it's named after Dad's great-great-grandparents."

He'd skipped over a critical detail about the land sale, but I stuck on the royalty argument. "Your mom's side became filthy rich by wielding those rights like a broadsword cutting across my family's land. Then when your mom married a wealthy rancher, it was like a redneck fairy tale. One that I'm reminded of every damn day. So excuse me if a lifetime of being treated like shit because of my last name makes me a little jaded."

"It's not because of your last name. It's how you act."

I twisted in my seat. He couldn't look me in the eye without going off the road, but I had to make my point. "They judge me on how Pop acted. I never had a chance. I owe them nothing, not a smile, not a goddamn thank-you. And I especially never thought I should have to drop my pants just because Pop couldn't pay his—"

Dawson's head whipped toward me, his golden eyes blazing. "Who the fuck tried that?"

His rage pushed me back in my seat. I cringed. He wasn't angry at me, but I'd been yelled at too many times for my mind to leave my heart rate alone when someone's voice rose.

"Bristol." His voice cracked like the cold wind. "Who tried to get you to sleep with them over your dad's debts?"

"I took care of it," I mumbled. "But I'm sure it just gave the town another example of how difficult I am to work with."

His eyes narrowed as he glowered out the window. "It was Buck from the Car Garage, wasn't it?"

My mouth dropped open. "How'd you know?" Buck wasn't the only one, but a fist in the nose had made him the last.

"He was spouting off about some night with you. His story was so full of holes I called him on it." He slid his gaze toward me for a heartbeat. "Said you punched him cuz you were clingy and he wanted to end it. I said that if he looked up clingy in the dictionary, your picture would be under antonyms and then I recommended he look up the definition of antonym."

I stifled a giggle. "He wouldn't know how to spell either word."

He chuckled and we exchanged a grin.

I swallowed hard and turned to the passenger window. My place was coming up. The snow was falling heavier. I hoped Daisy stayed at Dawson's. He had a nice barn that wasn't full of old hay and drafts. Bucket likely wouldn't want to come back home. Dawson wasn't as smart as I thought he was if he assumed I didn't know he snuck Bucket corn on the cob every year.

Words clogged my throat as Dawson turned into the long drive that would take him to the trailer house Pop had lived and died in.

I couldn't go there. I couldn't.

But the RV didn't run, therefore I couldn't take it anywhere to empty the sewage. Its bathroom was little more than a mirror and storage. How would I run the generator and get back and forth to use the trailer's bathroom?

Panic clawed at my chest the closer he

got. There was no way I could stay there. No way I could live there. Yet I couldn't bring myself to tell Dawson that I lived in the RV during the winter and the hunting cabin in one of the pastures in the summer. How would I do this snow with crutches? A band tightened around my chest.

Dawson parked and I didn't move. I stared out the window at the trailer with its boarded-up windows, its saggy roof, and its peeling paint. The place was decrepit. Should be condemned. One match would solve the problem, but I needed its plumbing.

Several moments went by. Dawson put the pickup in gear and drove off without saying a word.

~

Dawson

.   .   .

MY ONLINE SEARCH came up with several
ideas that Bristol was going to fucking
hate. Her leg was in a long, bent-leg cast.
Emma had said that the doctor didn't
think Bristol would need anything more.
The cold had kept the initial swelling
down, but I also thought the doctor hadn't
given a shit whether Bristol did fine
or not.

What Bristol had said on the drive home
resonated. Did I treat her the way I did
because of what my family thought of her
family? Had I been unfair? The questions
plagued me. She was blunt, opinionated,
and had a knack for finding any topic I was
a little bit sensitive about. I tried to recall
our interactions over the years, but they all
ended with me being an insensitive bastard
to her.

My chest tightened and I huffed out a
cough. It was heartburn. Had to be. Bristol
had earned every snarky remark.

Hadn't she?

Those questions had led to the shittiest

night of sleep ever and it wasn't because I'd slept on the couch.

I'd started my morning trudging outside to check on everything and feed the dogs. Daisy had even stuck around, sleeping in the barn with Bucket. Then I'd researched.

Tibia fractures like Bristol's should heal fine as long as she rested and didn't try to do too much too early. I'd feel better if she got a second opinion, but no doubt she'd refuse.

Her cast couldn't get wet, so that'd make showers and bathing difficult. Several inches of snow were on the ground, so running anywhere for a bath chair was out until the roads were cleared. I could find something for her to use.

I'd heard her clomping to the bathroom. She never asked for help, and if she fell, she got herself up and didn't say anything. Last night I'd gotten her a water bottle and some acetaminophen. Hopefully she'd taken it. Her adamant refusal of the pain meds at the hospital had surprised me—and it hadn't.

After living with a raging alcoholic, who could blame her?

I read up on tips for using crutches. Shorts or loose pants were easier—

Damn. Bristol didn't have any clothes. I had plenty of shirts and she was tall enough that she wouldn't drown in the couple pairs of flannel pants I had. Whether she'd actually wear them was a different story. I couldn't help with the other stuff. Had Kendall or any of my sisters-in-law left things that would work?

Nothing would. Eva was shorter than Bristol, and Bristol had a lean, athletic body that I absolutely had not checked out the few times I'd crossed paths with her in the bar. She had strong legs from growing up on the back of a horse and well-defined muscles from throwing bales and doing chores. Much of the time, she'd been the only help her dad had on the ranch. Even when he'd hired someone, the quality of Bristol's work had far surpassed anyone else's.

Hell, I knew who'd come out on top of a ranch rodeo. Tucker and Kiernan would lose any event in the cowboy's version of driveway basketball.

My stomach growled. I hadn't eaten supper and neither had Bristol. She'd been ready to drop when we'd gotten home last night. The way she'd stared at her trailer . . . I'd never seen anyone so despondent, like the hope had gotten sucked out of her. But she hadn't fought me when I'd driven away, saving me from feeling like crap for dropping her off to be alone in a storm with a broken leg.

I popped up and went to the kitchen. I had eggs, sausage, and leftover bread that'd make excellent French toast. I went to work, keeping an ear out for Bristol. When I was wrapping up, I finally heard the toilet in the master bathroom flush. I loaded food on a tray that I'd found tucked deep in a cupboard. Mama had used it when me or my brothers were home sick.

I went to the bedroom door, tray balanced on one hand, and knocked.

"Yeah?" She sounded more cautious than annoyed.

I opened the door. "Hungry?" She was perched on the edge of the bed, but the bed was made. "Didn't you sleep under the covers?"

"I, uh . . . it's your bed." She lifted her hands like she'd have to decontaminate herself.

"I wash the sheets after every three women." When a flush added some much-needed color to her cheeks, I pushed it even further. "And I jack off in the shower to keep the cleanup to a minimum."

"Dawson," she snapped, but her lips twitched. When was the last time I'd seen her smile? When we used to play together as kids, she was always grinning. There was last night in the pickup, after she'd made the highly accurate joke about Buck. Her smile had chased away the pain in her eyes and her face had glowed in the dash lights.

With her hat smashed on her head, she looked like one of the guys, joked around like them, but her smile didn't make me feel like I was with just one of the guys.

"Look, not that I have to explain myself, but I don't bring women here unless it's serious, and I haven't had a serious relationship in a long time." The last time was in college, and McKenzie hadn't wanted a thing to do with ranching. Thus, the reason I was single. Women might want a cowboy, but they didn't want the cowboy life. "I shower before I go to bed, so the sheets should be minimally disgusting, but I'll change them later today."

She pushed a bright lock of hair behind her ear. "My leg was throbbing, so I had to prop it. It was easier to do on top of the comforter." Her tone hinted at an apology but that was the closest she'd come. She didn't owe me an apology either. I should've taken the time to change the sheets.

"Weren't you cold?"

She shrugged.

I'd get her more blankets. I lifted my chin. "Get back in. I brought breakfast."

"I thought I smelled . . ." She stared at the food, then at me. "Did you cook?"

"Yeah."

"Why?"

"Because I like to. Come on, get comfortable."

She grabbed all the extra pillows and sat back. I set the tray over her and she stared at the food but didn't touch it. "That's a lot of food."

"I like to eat."

Her gaze stroked up and down my body, as hot as a brand. Her hair was finger combed at best and she never wore a lick of makeup, but she'd always been sexy as hell. Being in my bed made that observation a lot more uncomfortable.

I spun away before I did something stupid like check out the creamy flesh of her legs. "Yell if you need anything. After you eat, I can change the bedding and find some clothes for you."

"You don't have to do all this."

I stopped at the door and looked over my shoulder. Her stark features were stricken and she hadn't taken her eyes off the food.

The woman didn't like to accept help, that was clear. Only this time I wasn't offended. "You're doing me a favor. If I didn't have a ranch to run, I would've gone to culinary school. I like to cook, but cooking for a party of one isn't always feasible."

She nodded, but didn't relax. Her gaze went to the window. The blinds were drawn. She couldn't see the blowing snow. "My chores . . ."

"What needs to be done?"

"No, you can't—"

"I think we've established that I'm helping you and I don't expect you to suck me off or whatever Buck thought you should do. Tell me what you need done and I'll get it done, it's as simple as that."

She dropped her gaze back to the tray of food that was cooling off. "I can't repay you," she said in a ragged whisper.

I let out a long breath. For a person who'd never accepted help in her life, this had to be uncomfortable. I thought of ways she could repay me—all nonsexual. She didn't have money. I didn't have to peek into her bank account to know that. She had her own ranch to run, so that left out working for me when she was healed. I didn't need money or help, but there was something that had rubbed me raw for years.

"How about you just answer one question."

She lifted her guarded gaze. "All right. What?"

"Why didn't you come to the funeral?"

I'd looked for her. She'd been my closest friend, and Mama had loved her. So damn much. Not only had Bristol been a no-show, but that'd been the end of our friendship. I lost Mama to a crazed meth head looking for money for a fix. When he couldn't find what he needed, he'd beat Mama to death. I'd lost her. Then I'd lost my best friend.

Her chin quivered and a horrible realization dawned in my ignorant damn head. The way she'd quit talking to us after the funeral. How untouchable she'd seemed since. The way she'd stared at her place after she got out of the hospital. Her home had been a prison and Danny the warden.

I'd resented her all this time. Blamed her for turning her back on Mama, on me, when I'd needed her. She'd been a kid. I'd been ten when Mama had died. Bristol had been almost two years younger than me.

"I wanted to," she whispered. "I wasn't allowed to."

I nodded, the grim confirmation humbling me to my bones. "I'm sorry. I should've known." I'd known what her dad was like. The trouble was, I'd assumed that was what she was like as well. But she'd been an eight-year-old girl without any power or control.

"I miss her," she said softly, with such yearning that she must've been wanting to say that for years.

"I miss her too. I'm making meatballs for supper tonight." I left the room before I did something stupid like break down in front of the strongest woman I'd ever met.

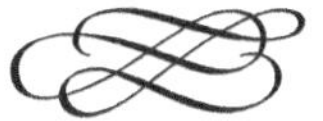

ristol

HIS SCENT SURROUNDED me and the problem was that I didn't want to get away from it. For the last week, I'd slept in his bed, cleaned up in his bathroom with his products, and worn his clothing. I would be the envy of the county if anyone knew I was here. Maybe the town did, depending on how confidential Emma had kept things.

I'd also eaten his food. If I had to stay

here much longer, I'd need to get fitted for a new cast and I'd have to keep his pajama pants. I could say without a doubt that I'd never eaten so well in my life.

Dawson wasn't lying about loving to cook. The first three days of the storm, he'd made cheese-stuffed meatballs and spaghetti, then braised pork chops with risotto, and a roast that was so tender it had practically melted in my mouth. I hadn't thought meat could do that. We'd been eating leftovers since.

The storm cleanup was done and warmer temperatures were melting the worst of it. Dawson gave me updates on my place. He'd moved snow in my driveway and around the barn. Bucket was still on his property, same with Daisy, and the cow too, but she hadn't calved yet. He'd had his guys checking on my cows and taking care of the calves.

I hated how much I needed their help, but this wasn't just about me. There were a lot of creatures depending on me, and

Dawson and his crew were keeping them all alive. Several would've died these last few days had I been left on my own.

I peered into the mirror. My hollow cheeks had filled out. From rest or food? This winter had been brutal for me. I'd kept the generator by the RV running as much as possible, but with poor insulation, it'd been a cold winter indoors too. I rarely ventured to Pop's trailer for a shower. Using it to go to the bathroom was almost more than I could take. Half the time, that was why I went to Marshall's. A clean bathroom and heat.

I glanced at my phone. Marshall had messaged. I'd told him to leave me alone, that I'd broken my leg and didn't need his BS while healing. His messages were now filled with concern, but compared to what Dawson had been doing for me, they seemed like weak platitudes.

Besides, Marshall's bathroom had nothing on the master bath in this place. Dawson's bathroom had both a shower and a bathtub. A deep and long bathtub fit for a King. They were all tall men. Had the bathtub been Gentry's idea or Sarah's when they'd built the house?

Dawson's question had shocked me, but I'd been glad to answer. Grateful to clear the air after so many years. Of course I would've gone had I been allowed. The Kings should've known that. And Dawson did now. Finally. It'd taken long enough, but the realization had dawned like a summer sunrise in his eyes before I'd answered. I couldn't explain why that was so important.

Grabbing my crutches, I hobbled out of the bathroom. My feet were in his white athletic socks, his sweats were tied around my hips, and his shirt hung off my shoulders. He was gone most of the day, like I would be if I could move freely. For now, I could go from the bed to the living room, where he had a TV. He had streaming services and I didn't bother to tamp down my excitement.

I reached the couch and stared at the pile of blankets and pillows piled on the end cushion. Was he sleeping out here? Why? There were four bedrooms upstairs, one for each of the King brothers.

Was he afraid I'd fall? Or need something? Didn't he trust me not to run off with the silver?

I'd have to ask. It'd probably sound accusatory and he'd say something sarcastic in return and we'd return to our old ways. Then he'd kick me out.

I'd soak up Netflix until then.

I plopped down and propped my leg on pillows. The pain was more manageable. I took the acetaminophen Dawson had left me and that was it. My wounds were scabbed over but Dawson swore that a little blood on his sweats didn't bother him.

I couldn't picture him in sweats and a T-shirt. He'd been using the upstairs bathroom, only grabbing what he needed and rewashing it so he wouldn't disturb me. Dawson was shockingly considerate.

That he was thoughtful wasn't a shock. That he was doing all this for me was.

It made hating the Kings harder than it already was.

I relaxed into the cushions and flipped on the TV. So. Many. Choices. I skipped the TV shows. I wouldn't be holed up with Dawson long enough to binge whole series.

Could I get a movie in before he got home?

I found a wannabe Hallmark romance about a normal girl falling for a prince and clicked. Just the unrealistic plot I needed.

A door opened in the back of the house and Dawson's voice drifted down the hall. "No. Sorry. I'll tell her you said hi."

After a few minutes, he appeared. His hair was pressed down from his hat and his cheeks were reddened from the chill in the air.

He stopped when he saw me. "I think your dog thinks I kidnapped you."

"You kind of did, and she's used to being

inside with me." We kept each other warm at night, and sometimes during the day.

Dawson looked at me for a moment, then backed down the hallway. I'd paused the show, wondering what I'd said wrong, when the clack of claws on the floor preceded a bounding dog.

A laugh burst out of me and I held my arms out. Daisy landed on my chest, licking my face and wagging her tail.

"I missed you too," I muttered. I ignored Dawson as he stared at my reunion with Daisy. I was giggling like a little kid from Daisy's exuberance. "But I'm not sure Dawson wants you on the couch."

He snapped his mouth shut. "As long as you clean up the fur. But my bed is off-limits."

I laughed and hugged Daisy. She'd been my companion for the last couple of years, and until now, I hadn't realized how much I'd missed her. Knowing Dawson was spoiling her hadn't been good enough.

Dawson strolled into the living room

and sat on the other side of the couch. Daisy settled on the cushion between us. "What's on?" he asked. I was about to tell him it was nothing he'd like when he said, "Oh, I've seen this one."

My eyes widened.

"What?" he asked, feigning innocence. "I needed something wholesome after *Tiger King*."

"Never seen it."

"How morbidly fascinated-slash-depressed about the human race do you want to be tonight?"

I laid my head back. "I'm good with a campy romance, where the leads fall in love before they even kiss." I pushed play and ran my hands through Daisy's fur. "How are you done for the night?"

"Kiernan wants a day off next week so he offered to work later tonight and tomorrow."

"You've got a couple of good guys." Our conversation was light, safe, and I should stop right there. "The guys Pop hired rarely were. If they were decent people, then they got sick of Pop's shit and left pretty fast."

Dawson ran his thumb across his lower lip. "I can't forgive him for hiring the guy that killed Mama."

His words made me flinch. I didn't bother telling my side. Minds were already made up.

Instead of answering, I stared at the girl on the TV screen. She had flawless bronze skin, long dark locks, and a smile that would be visible from space. She giggled nervously at something the prince said.

"When did his drinking get bad?"

I never talked to anyone about Pop's drinking, other than to tell bar owners to cut him off. Otherwise, people told me all their opinions about Pop and his drinking. Normally I wouldn't answer, but the tone of Dawson's question was neutral. "It was always bad. But alcoholics can go in spurts. He'd try to clean up, try to get on top of it, but he never got professional help. The idea of showing up at an AA meeting where people knew him was terrifying."

"He could've gone out of town."

"That much effort, more than dropping in on a quick meeting in town? It would've meant admitting he had a problem." I ran my lower lip between my teeth. It was freeing to talk about Pop, and I couldn't believe I was telling Dawson, yet I couldn't help but feel that he needed to hear it the most. Him and his brothers. The ones Pop had hurt the most. "Then he got sick and the bills piled up higher. What do you do when the thing that hurts you the most is the only thing that makes you feel better?"

I kept my attention on the show, but Dawson's gaze burned into me. I was exposed. Raw. Telling Pop's secrets was safer than divulging my own. Like confessing that I was terrified every day that my life would swallow me whole and spit me out—and there'd be no one to find me.

"That's deep, Cartwright."

I scowled and flung a throw pillow at him.

He chuckled and plucked it out of the air. "All kidding aside, that sucks. About your dad. For all his faults, I know he really had a thing for Mama."

Pop had clung to the scorned-lover role like he was on a life raft going over a waterfall. He'd never dated Sarah King. Before he'd ever gotten the nerve to ask out the girl he'd grown up with but whose parents his had fallen out with, Gentry King had swooped in. She'd gotten pregnant and the rest was King's Creek's proud history.

Had it not been for those damn mineral rights, Pop probably would've asked Sarah out and who knew what life would be like? My mom might've met a man who loved and respected her. Instead, she'd been removed from my life as thoroughly as a ruptured appendix.

"Well," I said, not wanting to let the lighter tone of our conversation die, "your dad had to do something while waiting a couple decades for his new wife to be born, so . . ."

"Bristol Cartwright, did you just diss my dad and his much-younger wife?"

I chuckled. Gentry's wife had been nothing but nice to me. All the King wives were awesome to me, but then none of them were from around here. "How is Kendall?" I kept my voice light, like I wasn't invested in the answer. But it wasn't often someone was nice to me for no reason.

"It's weird. She's like a sister, but she's my stepmom."

"You have a lot of sisters now."

His lopsided smile was adorable and my belly flipped. Must be hunger pangs. I wasn't the type to get all girly over a guy. "They're great."

Every single one of them was probably legitimately great. They'd all talked to me at one point or another and none of them had been rude or dismissive. They had to know about me, but they still smiled and said hi when I saw them around.

"The house is sure quiet when they're not here. It's weird after all these years."

"All these years?" I said wryly. "You're not even twenty-nine."

"Three months and twenty-three days."

"You have a countdown?"

His jaw jumped. "Yep."

Whatever. Age was just a number. I'd felt like I was forty since I was fourteen. We watched the show. Had I said something wrong?

My phone buzzed. Since it wasn't Dawson telling me a cow was in trouble, I ignored it. I had no one who wanted to get ahold of me.

Dawson didn't ignore it. "Did you tell Marshall to shove it?"

The same humiliation I'd felt in the hospital flared up. He'd already seen the messages, but I almost spilled the rest of the details. "If you want to know about my dating life, tell me about yours."

He blew out a breath and ruffled his hair with a hand. The effect made a few chunks stand out. Sexy and adorable. Staying here might be more dangerous than I'd thought. A handsome Dawson who swaggered through town like he was an untouchable bachelor was one thing. This Dawson, the one who watched sappy movies, let my dog inside, and joked around, could hurt me more.

What was I thinking? He wouldn't fall for someone like me. I'd seen the girls he dated. I'd gone to school with them. They were the cheerleaders, the valedictorians, the nurses who helped bitchy patients. The women on the town council who actually contributed to society.

I was broke as hell and he'd dug me out of a ditch. Okay, it'd been a pasture, but close enough.

"My dating life isn't nearly as exciting as people assume." I didn't think he'd say more, but he continued. "I dated who everyone thought I should in high school, but I wasn't into the same things they were." His devilish smile flushed searing heat through my body until I squirmed. It should be impossible to get turned on with a broken leg. "But I was still a guy and wanted to experience guy stuff, right?"

"And you're not anymore?"

He ran a hand through his hair again. Different parts stuck up. "Oh, I'm a man." His voice dropped and he eyeballed me. "But not many women can handle this."

"Give me that throw pillow back. You need to be hit."

He laughed and stretched his legs out like mine, minus the big cast. "No. I go on dates and we talk and it's just . . . there's no chemistry. It's like I'm sitting there while we're talking and I can just hear their complaints about why I'm gone all day. Why do I drag so much mud in the house? Why don't I take weekends off? Why can't I travel in the winter? My college girlfriend asked me all that. The neon-pink writing was on the wall." He glanced at me. "Do you get that from guys?"

Commiseration kept me from holding back. "That's why Marshall dumped me. I missed dinner with his parents because I was looking for that cow."

"You were saving a life and he was pissed?" Disgust dripped from his voice.

"I'd already messed up the first dinner we'd planned and they're not from here, so . . ."

"Messed up how?"

I wrinkled my nose, wishing he'd missed that. I gave him a version of the truth. "He hated what I was wearing."

Dawson stared at me. "Please tell me you told him to fuck off."

"No. He's a nice guy and his parents had to drive up from Miles City."

Dawson's expression changed to doubtful. "Nice guys don't send messages like his."

"He's nicer than anyone I've dated. At least he didn't brag all over town that he'd banged me in the back of his pickup." I seriously had no filter around Dawson. "There's two minutes of my life I'll never get back."

He snorted. "I know who you're talking about and I'm surprised he made it that long."

"As if most guys make it longer?"

"If they can't, they better damn well fill the rest of their time pleasuring their lady."

I coughed out a laugh, but my body thrummed. The easy confidence in his voice told me that Dawson was good for more than two minutes and filled up *a lot* of extra time to boot. "Well, not many have tried." And like climbing Mount Everest, not many had succeeded.

"I haven't slept with all the girls I've dated. I don't know why people think I sleep around."

I sent him a dubious look. I went into relationships knowing that whomever I dated wouldn't marry me, and he definitely wouldn't live out at the ranch. There wasn't any other point to dating.

He spread his hands out. "I haven't. I know you've seen me out with women, but they weren't all a roll in the hay."

"Hay's itchy."

He grinned. "Tell me more."

"No." I couldn't bite back my smile. Credits rolled on the movie I'd hardly paid attention to. The conversation had been more enjoyable than having internet access. Dawson hadn't touched me but tonight he'd outdone all of my previous dates.

Dawson grabbed the remote. "The roast was frozen, so it isn't done yet. Want to watch the sequel?"

"Sure." I stuffed my hand into Daisy's fur, ignored Marshall's messages, and marveled over a Friday I'd never forget—and the sad irony that experiencing this would only make going back to my life that much harder.

Dawson

WATER PLOPPED IN AN UNEVEN RHYTHM. Snow melted off the roof of the shop, dripping off downspouts, and icicles shrank under the spring sun.

April had arrived and, with it, seasonably warm temperatures. And mud. Mud everywhere.

I parked the Ranger by the shop closest to the house. Tucker pulled up next to me, his once-red pickup now Montana-clay brown.

Tucker jumped out, removed his ball cap, and wiped an arm across his brow, leaving more grit behind. "When do you think Bristol's going to be back to work? I know it's only been a month, but just so we have an estimate."

We were all running. We had our normal spring work, like getting ready to plant corn for silage. We'd be doing Bristol's planting too. Bristol's herd hadn't quit calving yet and she had more calves that needed bottle-feeding than I ever had. Kiernan had pulled shifts to watch for cows in labor in the darkest hours of the night, but now he was on bottle-calf duty. Some simple planning and better nutrition would've prevented most of this, but I'd heard enough of what Bristol was willing to say and a lot of what she'd left unsaid. Danny had been impossible to work with in the last few years. Alcohol had eaten away at his mind and everything around him had suffered.

The guys and I were working overtime during a normally stressful time of year. "She has another couple of weeks on crutches at least." Then physical therapy I doubted she'd do. "Think I should find a high school kid to help out?"

"Wouldn't hurt to have an extra pair of hands for the smaller tasks. If it's only for a couple more weeks and then Bristol can jump in, that'll be fine, but we all could use a break."

I worked the idea over. Bristol was moving around better. She cruised on her crutches and tried to keep up with laundry and minor cleaning that she could do with one hand while leaning on a crutch.

She wouldn't like some kid up in her business. "He could help us and I'd be free to work on Bristol's land."

"About that." His somber expression was on the house. "I rode out to make sure we have all the Cartwright head accounted for. There's a nice tidy pile of firewood around the cabin and a fire pit that looks like it's been used in the last year. I think someone's staying there."

"Like right now?" It was nothing more than an old hunting shack.

He shook his head. "No, I don't think so. They'd have to have been there before winter. There's a small garden tilled out. The door had a lock, so I didn't force my way in. The lean-to and little fenced area would be perfect for a horse. Think Bristol's been living there?"

"There's no electricity or water." She couldn't have *lived* in that cabin. That was camping, not living. The trailer house wasn't any better, but it had heat and running water. An old AC unit hung crookedly out of a bedroom window. Did it work?

"There's that old well. And an outhouse."

Bristol was stubborn enough, and savvy enough, to live in the cabin during the nicer months. She wouldn't have had to live on top of her permanently angry dad, and it'd be cheap.

No wonder she soaked up the TV like it was a clear blue sky and she'd never seen daylight. "I'll ask her. If it wasn't her, she'll need to know anyway."

Tucker bobbed his head. "What about the trailer? If she's out for six weeks, someone should check on it before it goes up in smoke, if it hasn't flooded from frozen pipes by now."

"I'll offer." She'd say no. We hadn't talked about the trailer since the night I'd pulled away. "I'm sure she's itching to get in as soon as possible."

"You don't seem like you're in a hurry to kick her out." He cocked his head and evaluated me. "You like her, don't you?"

"Are you asking if I like her, like this is middle school and I passed her a note?"

"You couldn't talk about her before without swearing."

"I wasn't that bad." I didn't look at Tucker. He'd call me on my lie. But since he and Kiernan were adding the Cartwright duties to their plates and hadn't complained, I owed him more than a subject change. "I misjudged a lot of things about her. Her life hasn't been easy." I think it'd been harder than she let on. Harder than anyone knew. "And that big house gets too damn quiet."

I kept it at that. I didn't think about how I tossed my gear aside and rushed to the house every day after work. That I hadn't moved from the couch at night because that'd be farther away from where she was sleeping. Or how quickly I'd become addicted to our nightly routine of watching movies with Daisy snuggled between us.

"That wasn't exactly an answer, jackass. But if you don't hate her anymore, you'd better go save her from your grandma."

I spun around. Grams's black SUV pulled up in front of the house. "Shit." I sprinted across the yard, Tucker's laughter fading behind me.

"Grams," I called before she marched into the house like she owned the place. My family all knew I had an open door and they were welcome anytime.

This was just a really bad time. Anytime from now until my birthday was a bad time.

She waited at the bottom of the porch stairs, but she didn't look at me. Her gaze was on the figure sitting in the porch swing. Daisy darted across the porch and down the stairs to greet me. Grams's shrewd gaze watched her the whole way.

I stooped to pet the dog but kept my

gaze on Grams. Her mouth was turned down and her eyes glittered.

"I see you have company," she said crisply.

"Yeah, Bristol's staying with me for a while." I willed my grandmother not to make a scene. She'd come here to pester me about dating and getting married before I turned twenty-nine. This was the most she'd ever been involved in my life—she'd done the same when my brothers had been my age—and that was because there was money on the line. A lot of it.

The sun rose and set over piles of cash for Grams.

"Why would she be doing that?" Grams talked like Bristol wasn't on the swing, her body stiff, her jaw tight. Bristol's hair was up in a clip I'd found in the upstairs bathroom—left behind by one of my brothers' wives, or maybe Kendall. Her gorgeous red strands spilled over her head. I'd never seen the style on her before, and at least two hunks of her hair had escaped to trail down her neck like she didn't have much practice at getting either her hair or her clip to do what she wanted. Which made it all the more endearing.

Most likely she just didn't give a shit.

Getting to know the other side of Bristol over the last four weeks had become my favorite pastime. Ice-cold Bristol that gave as good as she got was sexy as hell, and I could finally admit it without feeling like a traitor. But the softer Bristol, the one with vulnerable emerald eyes and sudden smiles, made a guy go stupid.

"She broke her leg. I'm helping her out." I jogged up the stairs. "You coming in?"

Grams stood at the bottom, her gaze jumping between us and settling on Bristol. "How'd you break it?"

Well, she could've been ruder. As it was, I didn't trust where her line of questioning was going.

"I fell," Bristol answered flatly.

I wouldn't have to worry about Bristol handling herself. She was the third generation of Cartwrights that'd been on the receiving end of Grams's insults. But that didn't mean she had to deal with it.

"You fell and couldn't stay with anyone else to recuperate?" Grams asked just as flatly.

"Grams," I snapped. "Bristol is a guest in my home, here by my invitation." I cocked a brow as if to say *and you aren't.*

Grams drew herself up and gave me a cold, appraising look, managing to look down on me when I was at the top of the porch stairs. "We need to talk. Privately."

I was about to tell Grams she needed to leave when crutches scraped against the boards.

"Don't worry. I was just heading in."

"Bristol—"

"It's okay." She gave me a small smile. "I'll go in the bedroom so you two can talk."

Grams wasn't welcome inside if this was how she was going to act. I went down to meet her before she came up the stairs.

"That was uncalled for," I said.

"You do realize what birthday's coming up, don't you?"

That damn trust. Mama had created it with stipulations that my brothers and I each marry before we were twenty-nine, and that we remain married for at least a year. I didn't know why she'd thought my brothers and I needed prodding to get married, but that was what she'd done.

The other stipulation, what would happen if the trust's demands weren't met, was what stuck in Grams's craw.

"Of course I do, but that's not for months yet."

"Then what is she doing here? Don't you have a girlfriend who would be upset?"

"No. I offered." I skipped the girlfriend part.

"She has to know." Grams's derisive snort almost had me looking back to make sure Bristol couldn't hear the way Grams talked about her. "She's here making sure you stay single, or she's trying to marry you and get at least half."

Keeping my voice low, I hissed, "She doesn't know about the trust. You know we kept it in the family."

I wouldn't hurt her that way. Knowing all my brothers had married before they were twenty-nine to keep her family penniless would hurt her more than how the rest of the town treated her. Their marriages had all turned out to be true love, and maybe I'd hoped it would work out for me too, but unlike them, I didn't feel the pull to marry just because.

Grams shook her head. "She has to know. She wouldn't be here otherwise."

"I found her in the pasture, wrapped in barbed wire and freezing to death. She could've died. Are you saying she planned that?"

Grams had the grace to blanch. "How'd you locate her?"

I pointed to Daisy. "She didn't even have her phone, Grams. It was life or death."

"That may be, but I wouldn't put some kind of scheming past a Cartwright."

"You mean like selling land you suspected had oil in it, keeping the rights, then profiting two different ways on it?"

Grams's expression hardened. "Keeping mineral rights is common practice."

"The Cartwrights were your best friends."

"Then they shouldn't have told the whole town we were heartless crooks."

"Kinda sounds like you were."

"You forget that the quarter of land they've been living on right next to yours used to be in your father's family, until they conned Gentry's dad out of it."

"Maybe, but that was before Bristol's time. That was even before her dad's time." It was no wonder Danny Cartwright had turned out like he had. He'd grown up nursed with resentment and bitterness.

"She's still a Cartwright. Who's doing all her work?"

"I am. I offered." I skipped the part where Bristol had insisted she'd pay me back, including Tucker's and Kiernan's pay.

I wouldn't accept it. I could cover the cost. She couldn't.

"Hmph. Have you told your father yet?"

I clamped my lips shut. I hadn't told any of my family. A knowing gleam entered her eyes.

"If it's not a big deal, then why don't you call him? Tell him you've got the daughter of the man who got his wife—*my daughter*—killed staying with you." Her voice shook by the time she was done talking.

"Dad is old enough to keep the two separate." I hoped he was, since I should've been old enough to do the same years ago. "Bristol's not her father."

"You need to take this seriously, Dawson. If not for your mother, then for me. Do you remember how I sat in your room all night with you for two months after the funeral? Gentry trying to juggle his job at the company and taking over your mother's duties. Four scared and grieving boys. You seem to have forgotten what I've sacrificed. What I've lost."

I'd clung to Grams during that time. The most maternal this woman had been her entire life and she'd done it for me, for the rest of the family, so Dad could get some sleep while she soothed my nightmares. "I haven't forgotten," I murmured.

"Then tell your father what you're doing." Grams went to the driver's side of her vehicle. "Or I will."

She hopped in and pulled away. I was left standing with Daisy at my side. I waited until her taillights disappeared before I went inside.

Bristol was nowhere to be seen. I went to the bedroom but she wasn't there.

"Bristol?"

An object clattered from the hallway. The office door was open.

Inside, Bristol was balancing on her good leg and picking up a picture frame.

"I'm sorry. When you didn't come in, I got restless."

The picture was a family photo. The last

one we'd taken before Mama died. I kept it on my desk.

I went around the simple rectangular desk Mama had hauled from Billings and assembled in one afternoon and pulled open a drawer. Deep in the back was a framed photo I hadn't had the heart to throw or pack away.

I held it out.

Bristol accepted it and gasped. The picture was of Mama and Bristol when she was six. Mama had put pigtails in Bristol's hair and asked me to take a picture. I'd been so proud to use Mama's camera despite how crooked the picture turned out. Both girls were smiling. I'd never seen Bristol look so happy.

She pressed her finger to her lips and moisture glittered in her eyes. "I . . . I can't . . ."

She set the picture down, grabbed the crutch she had set aside, and clomped out.

"Bristol?"

"I shouldn't have been in your office, I'm sorry." Her voice was thick. Was she crying?

"Bristol." She was fast with her damn crutches. I caught up to her but I wouldn't grab her arm and throw her off-balance. "Bristol."

She stopped abruptly outside my bedroom and I nearly ran into her. "I remember playing in there with her. That's why I went in. It was a mistake."

"Tell me about it."

She still wouldn't look at me. "About what?"

"You and Mama. What did you two get up to in there?"

She crossed to the bed and swiped at her eyes before turning to sit. Setting her crutches aside, she scooted back so her feet hung off the bed. She was supposed to have the cast off in a couple of weeks. I'd asked her about a checkup, but she'd brushed me off.

"She used to let me draw on the other side of the desk as she balanced the books.

I'd ask her about running the ranch and she'd talk to me. Like I was an adult, you know. With respect. She . . . never yelled."

I snorted. "She never yelled at you. Four rambunctious boys were different." I pushed off the door and sat next to her on the bed. "She was like that with us too. We didn't get babied. I always wondered if that's why Aiden's been an old man since he was fifteen."

"He is not."

"He is too. He's serious as fuck. I don't think Kate knows how to remove the stick up his ass but I can guarantee she wants to see his wild side."

"No!" Bristol said like I'd spouted off scandalous info. "Kate is as straitlaced as they get."

"I think there's a wild child hidden in there. There's gotta be, or that's a sad marriage."

"But it's the mighty Aiden King. He was like a god at school."

I nudged her. "Are you saying my brother's hot?"

She rolled her eyes at me. They were dry now and that'd been my goal. She'd had enough sadness. "All of you know damn well how good-looking you are."

I leaned back on an elbow and faced her. "No, this is all new to me. Tell me more."

She shoved me over but I tickled her side.

She burst out laughing and scooted away.

"Bristol Jane Cartwright. Are you ticklish?"

She pushed loose strands of hair out of her face. "You remember my middle name, Dawson Preston King?"

"How the hell do you remember mine?"

"Your mama said it enough when I was around."

To keep the conversation from getting melancholy again, I circled around. "You're avoiding the question. You're ticklish."

"Am not."

I reached my hand out and she slapped it away. Oh, this was some good information to have. "What's wrong? I thought you weren't ticklish."

Her mouth formed a mutinous line.

"So you are?" I tried again and she slapped it away again.

"Stop it." She laughed.

I caught her hand and tugged her toward me. She rolled into me, catching herself on my chest. She was next to me, her torso over me, and those pink lips close to mine.

My gaze stroked over her face. "I like how you talk to me."

A pretty line formed between her brows. "How do I talk to you?"

"You tell me what you're thinking."

"You nag me until I do."

"I'm charming like that."

She grinned and I was caught in her beauty. The stress of surviving each day was gone and she was free to do things like smile and laugh.

I cupped her cheek, her warm skin as soft as I'd dreamed. "Bristol."

"Dawson?" She sounded as hesitant as I felt.

Her hand splayed over my chest, then her fingers tightened in my shirt. She was hindered in her movement with the cast or I'd have her draped over me.

I recalled our conversations over the last four weeks. People treated her like shit. The guys she'd been with had wanted nothing but sex, and Marshall sounded like a controlling asshole in his messages. Bristol was my guest. I didn't want her to think she was nothing more to me than a quick fuck. I wanted . . . I wanted to know if this chemistry between us was more than an old friendship or Bristol thinking she owed me for helping her out.

Uncertainty lit her bright eyes. I never wanted to see them full of shadows again. I wasn't kissing her, and thanks to the way she'd been raised, I'd bet half my ranch that she thought it was because something was wrong with her.

Before I could think of a suave way to tell her that I wanted her more than anything, but I wanted to take it slow so she knew I was serious, she pushed back. Her cheeks were flushed, but her eyes didn't flash with desire. She was angry.

"Don't tickle me."

"Not until you give me permission," I agreed.

Anger fled from her eyes and she huffed. "You think highly of yourself, King."

"It's called confidence. You'll ask me to do it a lot." I rolled up and captured her chin with my thumb and fingers, unable to stop from stroking her skin. "Don't doubt that I want to do more than tickle you, but I have to prove I'm not like the guys you dated before. And I'm not like fucking Marshall whatever his last name is."

As if on cue, her phone buzzed on the nightstand. "Moe."

"What?"

"Marshall's last name is Moe. He's a lawyer."

"He's a douche." Her lips twitched, but I pressed. "Seriously. Whether you decide to give me a chance or not, you deserve better."

If I expected a thankful smile and her gratitude, I should've known better. "What the hell, Dawson? Care to impart more worldly wisdom on poor ol' me?" She snatched her phone up and looked directly at me when she answered. "Yeah?"

Hurt slammed into me. I wanted to do the right thing. I wanted to treat her like she'd never been treated before—and she answered that asshole's call?

I rose and stormed into the kitchen as her tone softened and turned defensive. Fucking Marshall. Instead of weaving together the first threads of a relationship, I'd pushed her right to him.

ristol

DAWSON HADN'T DONE MORE than update me on my ranch for the last week. And I'd spent my time in his room, syphoning free Wi-Fi and streaming shows. One more week and I'd get this cast off. Then I could go home.

Bile rose in my throat as I thought about home and what it'd be like to sleep in the

RV for another month or two while my leg finished healing. I didn't mind the RV. It was small, but clean.

The trailer was so far from clean it should be in another zip code.

My stomach heaved as I thought about walking into that place again. As Pop had deteriorated, so had his living conditions until he'd quit taking the garbage out, washing dishes, or cleaning up after himself. One sink plugged and he quit using it. The washing machine broke? Then he didn't need clean clothing.

I'd done what I could. Snuck garbage out when he was passed out and couldn't yell at me to quit picking up after him like he was a child. Researched how to unclog sinks and fix washing machines. I'd kept a lot of appliances in the trailer limping along and I'd been militant about keeping the bathroom clean and clog-free, even if it meant wiping up another human's excrement.

I shuddered.

The mess had been hard to deal with. The smell lingered in my memories. A simple thought conjured human funk in my nasal passages. After I used the bathroom or showered, the stench lingered the rest of the day. I washed my clothing in town when I could gather enough quarters for a load or two.

So yeah. I'd be going back to that. After living in grandeur, I'd go back to the sewer I came from.

You deserve better.

It should be refreshing that someone else in this town thought so, but it was humiliating. Treating me with kid gloves, like he knew better than me. Both of us had been stuck in this little town and wallowed in the same dating pool. Life was different with money.

He could afford "better." He was *given* more because his last name was King. It was hard to get "better" without a damn cent and Cartwright for a last name.

My phone rang. Marshall. Again.

Answering had bolstered him. He called more than he had before. And I ignored him just as much as I had before.

He'd been so apologetic, telling me he had no idea I'd been hurt when he'd been messaging or he would've rushed right over.

He was a lawyer. My mind stuck on that. He had his own house, a good job, and he'd gone to college and law school. A guy like that had dated me.

Dawson King had almost kissed me.
You deserve better.

Marshall was better than anyone I'd ever dated. But he didn't watch silly movies with me at night. I didn't have to ask him to know he'd hate a dog in the house. His cooking was okay. Tastier than mine, but nothing like the heaven on a plate Dawson whipped up.

Fucking cheese-stuffed meatballs.

I hobbled out. One more week on crutches. Then I could go home. Didn't mean I knew what I would do as far as feeding cattle and repairing equipment went. I'd have to work cattle in two months. With what help?

Pop's usual method for hiring someone was to pick up some dude hitching a ride off the side of the road in Miles City. He'd find the rest in the bar, and if they didn't stab him on the way to King's Creek, then they must be trustworthy.

If the help was decent, they went running after a day or two of work. Pop had two broken-down RVs for them to stay in. I'd be in the cabin by the time we worked cattle. But when the help figured out that they might not get paid for damn hard work, they'd be gone and I couldn't blame them.

I went outside to the porch and sat in the swing. Would Emilia Boyd come interrogate me again? Was she that terrified that her precious grandson would fall for a dirty girl like me? Couldn't contaminate the bloodlines with a Cartwright.

Whatever. She was a liar and a cheat.

Her husband had been too. I'd believed my grandparents on that. Just like I believed they'd screwed over Gentry's parents to get the land the trailer sat on.

Had it been the same during their day? Emilia and DB and Gentry's parents living the good life while my grandparents could barely afford a roof over their head?

An engine caught my attention. Tucker and Kiernan were working in the shop farthest from the house. Probably getting the equipment ready to plant corn for silage. Someday I'd get to that point. I planted and harvested some of my own corn, but one bad weather event and I was screwed. But someday I'd get to the point where I wouldn't have to buy crap feed that might make the cows sick.

One season at a time. It was almost summer. The cattle would be put out in the far pastures—except the one with the ravine. They'd graze and I'd reroute the fence.

Ugh. That would be grueling work on

shitty land. But it had to be done. The unused oil wells took up too much good grazing land as it was.

The pickup pulled in. Dawson. I frowned as a familiar car drove in behind him.

My heart rate kicked up. Marshall?

I would stand, but I didn't want him to see me hobble down the steps. But I also didn't want him getting close to the house. I didn't know why.

No, I knew. Dawson's house had become my sanctuary. My fantasy. I could forget what was waiting for me on the other side of the fence line. Being around Marshall popped that fantasy, reminding me that I was lower on the social ladder than everyone I came across.

Dawson parked in front of the house. He slammed his door as he got out and caught my eye as he strode around the bed of the pickup. His chestnut eyes had a hard glint, but the force behind them wasn't directed at me.

Marshall got out, his face screwed up as he studied the house. I held my breath when his gaze landed on me.

Unlike Dawson's hard acceptance, Marshall's eyes contained repressed rage.

"Bristol, what the hell?" He held his arms out as he came around his shiny car. He'd be pissed the dirt roads had made his Lexus all dusty. "I was at your place and I ran into him." He jerked his thumb toward Dawson and disdain dripped off the "him."

"What are you doing here, Marshall?" Not just in King's Creek, but at my house? And now at Dawson's?

He gave me an *Are you dumb?* look. "I was worried about you and I rushed over as soon as I finished the Crenshaw deposition."

He hadn't rushed over. I hadn't expected him to, but damn . . . I really was a low priority. He'd been bragging about getting the Crenshaw case when I'd met him months ago. It wasn't urgent. "I told you I was fine. I've been fine for weeks."

"You weren't answering my calls and you ignored most of my messages or I would've come earlier."

So basically, it was my fault I got injured and he couldn't move beyond his phone to check on me? I'd almost had enough, but I couldn't resist challenging his reasoning. He was a lawyer after all, with a deposition that came before me. "And you waited until you heard my voice before you spared time to come to King's Creek?"

"After the way you shut me out after your accident? I thought you'd slam the door in my face." Stomping up the stairs, he loosened his tie and stopped in front of me. "You didn't tell me that you were staying with your neighbor. I thought you hated him."

"Hard to hate a guy who pulled me out of a frozen pasture, brought my horse and my dog back, and then took me to the hospital."

"Fuck the horse and dog," Marshall snapped and I flinched. "He shouldn't have wasted time before getting you to a hospital." He loomed closer. "Have you been with him the whole five weeks?"

Bootsteps hit the stairs. Dawson had remained quiet, but he was getting closer, and I was grateful. After Marshall's messages, I was a little raw. He would've left Bucket and Daisy.

I kind of thought he would've left me too.

I folded my arms across my chest. I'd ignored Marshall long enough. I'd held out a smidgeon of optimism that maybe he was the better I'd hoped for. On paper, he was a catch. In person, he was a controlling asshole, and staying with him would make me as miserable as I'd been the last few years. "I don't see how it's your business."

"Bristol, you are my business."

"I thought I was too ungrateful, selfish, and redneck for you to waste another moment on. How did you put it? 'Only an insensitive, uncaring ingrate would make

my parents drive up from Miles City twice.'
"

His face burned red. "I was justifiably upset—and I didn't know you were hurt. Come on, let's go."

He was bending to grab my arm when I jerked my elbow out of his way. "Don't touch me."

"What the—" He looked over his shoulder to where Dawson stood a few feet away. Marshall whipped his head back toward me. "Are you fucking him? Is that why?"

"Yes, Marshall. All night and day," I said sarcastically. "We've done it right here on the porch, in the bed of his truck, and in every room of his house. Which is none. Of your. Business."

"You've been fucking him all along?" He shook his head. "I should've known."

My brows shot up. "All of a sudden *my* character is in question? I never raised my voice to you. I never swore at you. I never belittled you in public. Did I cheat on you?

Go fuck yourself, Marshall. And wear something nice when you do it. I'd hate for your parents to be embarrassed."

Marshall drew back. He tightened his tie, one of his douche power moves, and his mouth curled into a sneer. "You're nothing but worthless trash—"

"All right." Dawson stepped forward, angling himself between me and my ex. "Get the hell off my property."

"Listen, you piece of—"

Dawson yanked his phone out. "Look, man. I get that you're a lawyer. It's the only reason I haven't hit you. Dicks like you would sue over a bruised ego. But what I'll do is call the cops and report a man harassing an injured woman on my property. I'm sure Bristol can show them all your messages when they get here."

Marshall backed up a step. He sniffed and adjusted his tie again. Then he spun and pounded to his car like a tantrum-throwing child.

Before he got into his car, he yelled, "You were a waste of time, Bristol!" Then he got in and kicked up gravel with a tight three-point turn and sped away. In a moment, nothing but a dust cloud suggested he'd been here.

I sucked in a breath. I'd been called a lot of names. The ones from Marshall's messages were the most inventive—they almost didn't feel like insults, certainly not the ones I'd grown up with. But being a waste of time? That hit home.

I grabbed my crutches and stood. Dawson edged closer like he was dying to help but knew I'd rip his arm off and beat him with it if he did. My pride had taken enough of a pounding.

In the house, I didn't quit until I got to the bedroom.

"Bristol." Dawson's voice was soft behind me, like an early warning that I wouldn't care for what he had to say.

"Lay it on me."

"Yeah, so, Marshall was pounding on

your door when I found him. I think he might've busted the latch."

I sagged onto my crutches. How much more today?

"I can go out there with you," he said. "I know how you are about the trailer, but we can check it over when we go over there. Get it done with so you know what you're going back to. Not that you have to go back, since you might be in a walking cast for a while."

His voice eased the vise around my chest. "Dawson Preston King, are you rambling?"

"Maybe. I don't want you to tell me to put something nice on and go fuck myself."

I snorted while choking on a laugh. "He probably does that anyway."

"A reminder's always good." The air between us grew heavy. "I can always go check the door."

Ah, hell. If the door had been busted open, Dawson would see the mess. My pride was already flayed open. Might as well expose it to the elements.

Dawson might've thought about kissing me, but after he saw—and smelled—for himself what my life was like, it'd confirm that *he* was the one that deserved better.

Dawson

GOD, the smell.

I forced back a gag. Running a ranch, I came across many smells that were unpleasant. Rancid. Rotting, even. But this was a stench that disturbed me on a visceral level. This wasn't from a bloated cow's carcass. This was from a person's *home*.

Bristol hung behind me at the bottom of the stairs, her arms hugged around herself. No wonder she hadn't wanted to come back.

"I, um, stay in the RV." She was trying to

sound strong, but her vulnerability was as clear as the blue sky above us. "I have to use the bathroom in here. That should be clean, but I'm sure being closed up for five weeks made, um . . . made the smell worse."

"No wonder you've been living at the cabin." I couldn't go inside. I'd only pushed on the door to the trailer to make sure it was broken and it had swung open, hitting my nose with everything that'd been marinating while Bristol had been at my place.

"How'd you know?"

"Tucker saw the wood pile and garden." I put my back to the trailer. More fresh air facing this way. "I was going to mention it, but I figured it was you with the garden and the fenced area for Bucket."

"I should've cleaned it all after Pop died."

It'd only been a couple of months since he'd died. How was she doing? I was used to pretending Danny Cartwright didn't exist, but he'd been her father. She'd lost her dad.

Fuck, where would my headspace be if I lost Dad?

I went back down the stairs, leaving the door open behind me. That place needed all the air it could get. "Bristol, you don't have to do this by yourself."

A furrow formed between her brows. "Who else would do it?"

She was so heartbreakingly alone. She'd been alone all her life. Except for when Mama had been alive and had taken her in like her own.

"I'm here. I can help. Me and the guys can do it. Now or another time. There's no timeline on grief."

She blinked. Goddammit, were those tears?

This woman.

I folded her into my embrace. She held her crutches under her armpits and leaned in to me. My sweater muffled a little sob. She sagged further. I held her tighter. And she just cried.

I didn't know how many minutes went

by. I could've held her forever, but at the same time, I wanted to cheer her up. Bristol needed more cheer in her life.

She stiffened and pulled away, but I didn't let her go far. She didn't look at me as she wiped her eyes with the sleeve of her sweatshirt and sniffled. "I should get inside and check it out."

"I'll do it. All we really need to do is make sure no pipes froze and that there isn't a fire hazard."

"The entire place is tinder."

"How long have you lived in the RV?"

"The last five years or so."

I looked around the yard. Besides the trailer house and the three campers—two pull-behinds and the RV Bristol lived in— there was the decrepit barn. An equally broken-down tractor, a four-wheeler, and a side-by-side ATV were next to the barn. I could see Bristol's work in the arrangement.

The campers and the RV were evenly spaced. The rusted-out pickup that Danny had used most of the time was parked parallel with the trailer house. And the tractors and ATV were parked in a neat line next to the garage. Every item was an eyesore, but arranged the squarest way possible.

If I went into the RV, it would be night and day different than the trailer.

"How long have you been living in the cabin?"

She shrugged, still not looking at me but squinting into the distance where the old hunting cabin was nestled between a couple of hills, not far from the quiet oil wells. "I started fixing it up about the same time, but I didn't start living there until Pop brought home one of his less desirable workers." She wrinkled her nose. "I think he finally got arrested for not registering as a sex offender."

"Jesus, Bristol. Did you have a gun?"

"There's a rifle at the cabin and a shotgun in the RV." She said it so plainly it was disturbing. Having a rifle or a shotgun available was common sense to a rancher. Coyotes or wolves after our calves. Rabid skunks crop-dusting the house. Badgers that could get us thrown off a horse. But for Bristol, being armed was a part of her personal life. Protection from guys who'd take her land—and her too.

Fucking Danny. But I couldn't say that. Not after she'd cried her eyes out because she missed her dad. "Wasn't your dad worried about you?"

She lifted a shoulder. "I was glued to his side. They would've had to go through him to get to me. Sometimes I think it was just luck I wasn't . . ."

Remnants of fear lingered in her expression. How many nights had she stayed awake, afraid for her safety? Worried that she'd end up like Mama, or worse?

"I don't understand how he could keep doing that to you." I couldn't forgive Danny's responsibility in Mama's death, and now I could add what he'd done to Bristol.

"It wasn't all bad. I know what he seemed like to everyone, and yeah, he was difficult for me too. But he used to read me books and he'd do all the voices. *The Three Little Pigs* was our favorite." The memory prompted a smile. "And whenever I got off the bus and ran to my room crying, he'd declare it peanut butter and jelly night and we'd eat in front of the TV and watch the news together."

Her watery gaze traveling over the trailer was a testament to the complexity of her life. A toxic dad she'd loved and grieved for. Today had been hard enough. I'd take care of the rest.

She wasn't going to like standing out here while I checked over the trailer, so I pointed to her RV. "You wanna take RV duty and I'll look over the trailer?"

Her green eyes gleamed with understanding. She knew what I was doing and appreciated it. " 'Kay."

I steeled my nerves and olfactory senses and went inside.

God, the smell. The aged odor of urine was the most potent. Had Danny been pissing himself when he was asleep—or awake and drunk? The carpet was matted and grungy. No shampooer could save it. The walls had a yellow tinge and fly crap all over it. Same with the windows.

Five years of not having Bristol clean up after him. This was what had happened to Danny.

Sympathy wormed its way into my chest as I tiptoed around piles of clothing that were too far gone for any washing machine. The worst of the garbage was cleaned up and Bristol must've been the one to do the dishes, but she'd had a hard time keeping up with her dad's filth. My guess was that he wouldn't let her. Pride was all the Cartwrights had.

But damn. To live like this? It wasn't normal. It wasn't how someone in their right mind would live. To ignore the smell and the mess and the grit and—I waved off several fruit flies that stirred up from the drain of the sink. Danny Cartwright had been sick. He'd been an alcoholic, but that'd been both a disease and a symptom itself.

I checked under the sink, surprised that it was fairly tidy. But then it wasn't like the trailer had a lot of cleaning products crowding its cupboards.

I passed the laundry nook on the way to the bathroom. There was enough space cleared on top of the dryer for the soap and fabric softener. Bristol's doing. The bathroom was where I could take my first full breath. The smell lingered in the stained flooring and the whitewashed walls, but everything was scrubbed as well as it could be. The porcelain in the sink was chipped, same with the tub. There were stains in the toilet made by humans and the hard well water, but it was clean enough to use without wanting a biohazard shower immediately after.

Bristol braved the rest of the trailer to come here? She used her energy to keep this space habitable, but the rest had been too much for her to face so soon after her dad had died.

Me and the whole town were a bunch of fucking assholes.

I get Danny Cartwright might not have accepted a lick of help from anyone. He might've turned kind offers into major insults. But Bristol had been written off with him when she'd been nothing but a child. As an adult, no one gave her a chance. No one understood the stress she was under every day just to live her life.

I'd seen enough. The trailer had stood this long, it'd wait a few more days. I'd deal with it later.

Outside, I sucked in a few lungfuls of clean air. The smell of cows and manure was a welcome relief after what I'd left behind. Bristol was still in the RV.

I hurried across the yard. Part of me was curious to see how she lived and the rest wanted to hold her again.

The squeak of the RV door broke the silence of the yard and the distant mooing of cattle. Bristol sat on the couch of her RV and stared out the window that faced her dad's place. Inside the RV was as I'd expected. Neat. A soft floral smell from candles that lined the counters. None of them had been burned, but their scents were enough to brighten the place. And I'm sure she'd gotten them cheap.

The RV was a couple decades old. The wood accents of the interior were darker browns, but Bristol had brightened the space with a few throw pillows and a couple of plaid blankets like the ones I'd seen in the discount bins for five bucks. They were both a decoration and useful.

"It's bad, isn't it?" she asked.

"Could've been worse." I shuddered to think about how it would've been without Bristol's efforts.

Several moments of silence went by with her arms crossed and her gaze stuck on the trailer across the yard. "I think he thought giving a second chance to an addict was never a wrong decision. It bit him in the ass over and over again, but I can't help but wonder how much he saw himself in them. The biggest issue was that those men he hired were never in recovery or trying to get into recovery."

Just like her dad.

"There's this whole population . . ." She sucked in a breath and gestured behind her where the other two campers sat. "The people Pop brought home lived in a similar way. Some days, I felt like I shoveled more shit from them than I did in the barn. But, still. People live like this. They fly under the radar of 'normal society.' " She used air quotes. "They don't qualify for assisted living, and even if they did, they wouldn't accept the help anyway. They're their own legal guardians and there's not much the rest of us can do."

Other than become their guardian, but that was a legal—and emotional—battle few could afford. "Your dad was sick."

She snorted. "It wasn't like he could go to a few sessions with a therapist and be cured. He barely hung on by a thread when I was younger. Add twenty years and he'd probably need therapy for a hundred." She shook her head. "It was lonely. Nothing I could do, but I was the only one there for him, and the rest of the world hated me for it."

I sank onto the thin cushions next to her. "It's too easy for people to take the righteous road. I'm guilty. I'm sorry."

"I wish I could've done more. Found a way to help." She tilted her head to look up at me. The light caught the spun-copper strands of her hair, lightening them to the color of a spring sunrise. "You're the only one who's taken the time to learn a little more about him than what was obvious."

Guilt sawed into me. It hadn't been soon enough to help her through Danny's last years.

"You've had a day," I said quietly.

She chuffed. "You mean Marshall breaking up with me when we weren't even going out because he'd already broken up with me?"

"As long as he stays away for good." I leaned back, going for casual. Nerves lit my gut like a rowdy frat party. What the hell? I didn't get nervous around women. But Bristol wasn't like other women. "Let me take you out. Get a nice meal, let someone else do the cooking and cleaning."

She went still. "You want to go out to eat with me? In town?" Her gaze dropped to her cast.

She didn't want anyone to see her using crutches? Or out with me? "I'm not going to lie—I can make a better steak than Hogan's, but since they get their beef from us, I find it acceptable."

"Hogan's?" she echoed. Her brows pinched. "All I have is my work clothes."

The work clothes that clung to her body and left me wanting to wrap my hands around her thighs as tightly as the denim? "There's nothing wrong with those."

"They're not nice enough for Hogan's."

"I think the saying is 'no shirt, no shoes, no service.' As long as you're dressed, they're not kicking you out." Her words to Marshall rang through my head. Fucking asshole. "I don't care what Marshall thought. Whatever you wear is just fine. I can't tell you the number of times I've worn my work clothes there."

"You can get away with wearing just your work clothes," she mumbled.

I wanted to argue but I took a moment to really listen. She was pointing out the double standard. The special treatment I'd get compared to her.

She was right. No one would blink if I walked into the steakhouse with dirt on my boots and dusty jeans. I'd get slapped on the back and asked if I'd had a tough day at work. Bristol would get sneered at and people would talk about how her daddy hadn't taught her any respect. I could afford all the nice clothes I wanted. Bristol had to prioritize work clothing.

"I'll wear my work clothes too. It'll confuse the hell out of everyone."

"Us walking in together will confuse the hell out of everyone."

I grinned. There was my in. "Sounds like you want to see their reactions. Whaddya say? Want to go out with me?"

CHAPTER 5

ristol

MARSHALL'S WORDS echoed in my head as I walked into Hogan's. *What are you thinking? You look like you dressed in a barn. What will my parents say?*

I wanted to bolt. I was strong, I could take a lot. But I also avoided inflammatory situations if at all possible. Dawson swaggered next to me. The young hostess looked like a teenager, and to her credit, she didn't bat an eye at me—or at Dawson. He'd only changed into clothing that didn't have the stench of the trailer lingering on them and showered. I'd grabbed a couple grocery bags of clothing to bring to his place.

I would be out of Dawson's hair in a little over a week and back at my place, but I'd avoided my RV for so long, I couldn't have passed up the opportunity to get my own things.

The hostess seated us in a booth along the wall. The maple wood of the seats matched the trim on the window next to us, which matched the tables scattered throughout the open floor of the dining room. The darker wood accents on the hanging light fixtures matched the hardwood floors. The place was small-town Western chic. The fanciest in King's Creek. I hardly ever came here.

I tried to be as discreet as possible on my crutches, keeping them from banging into the table as I wedged them into the booth. I ran my fingers along the cloth napkins. Not as hefty as the ones I used in the RV. Cheaper than buying paper towels all the time.

The hostess folded her hands and recited, "The special tonight is the roasted garlic butter filet with butterhorn buns and lemon pepper green beans with roasted slivered almonds."

My mouth watered with each word. My taste buds were getting spoiled. I'm sure the beef was divine, but I was also certain Dawson could grill one that was better. Just like I could see him roasting the garlic and whipping the butter for the top. But he never quit working and he hadn't gone out to eat in the five weeks I'd been at his place. Half the reason I'd agreed to come was because he wouldn't have gone out if I hadn't come along.

My skin prickled with all the eyes on us. Saturday nights were the busiest for Hogan's. Popular for dates.

Was that what this was, two friends

hanging out? Or did Dawson want this to be a date?

What did I want it to be?

"Hey, Dawson." The server appeared in crisp black slacks and a pristine white dress shirt. Skylar Dodd. She was older than me, but as the quintessential cheerleader who'd married the football captain, I knew of her. Her hair was tied up in a way that let all her dark curls escape. Her eyes crinkled in the corners when she smiled at Dawson, but they flared when she turned to me. Her gaze dipped to my button-up shirt and a brow quirked. It was a man's style, but in decent shape and a little dressier than the T-shirts and sweaters I often wore.

Since she owned the popular restaurant with her husband, who worked in the kitchen, I doubt she ever wore anything like it.

"Hey, Sky. How's Shepp?" Dawson asked.

Her smile was warm. "Ornery as always,

but he'll cook the best damn filet you've ever tasted."

"That's good, because that's exactly what I'm in the mood for. Bristol?"

Skylar's attention swung back to me. I hadn't looked at the menu and hated the idea of a date ordering for me, but when it came to food, my trust in Dawson knew no limits. "I'll have the same."

She turned back to Dawson. "You need to save room for dessert. Shepp's mastered his tiramisu." Skylar rolled her eyes and grinned, but I could've been a ghost for all the attention that was paid to me. "The kids were his happy taste testers."

Dawson's good-natured laugh spurred a smile from me but Skylar didn't spare me a glance. "If the kids say it's good, then we'd better try it."

Skylar scurried away. Dawson took a drink of his ice water and glanced around. Silverware tinkled on plates and murmurs of conversation carried through the restaurant. "Do you know Sky and Shepp?" he asked.

"Not personally, no." He could ask that of anyone in this place and that'd be my answer.

"They always feed me when we talk business." His grin was sly. "They think it'll help with negotiations. That I'll sell the meat cheaper because I'm a bachelor and can't cook."

My lips twitched. "And you don't bother to tell them otherwise?"

"Dad taught me better than that."

My smile dissolved at the mention of his dad. Gentry King didn't glare at me. He didn't say mean things. He just didn't talk to me, and he'd rarely talked to Pop, since any discussion would have dissolved beyond "hi." No, when Gentry looked at me, there was nothing but disappointment. Like any hopes he'd had for me had been dashed the day of his wife's funeral.

Grief tugged at my heart. Old and

familiar, I stuffed it away and took a drink of ice water to calm my nerves.

Dawson tracked the move. "I didn't ask if you wanted wine."

He'd offered at his place, but I always said no, thanks. He hadn't inquired beyond that. "I don't drink." When his eyes turned knowing, I amended my answer. "I mean, it's not like a personal crusade against all things alcoholic, or that I'm afraid one drink and I'll end up like Pop. I never liked what it did to Pop, so I was never interested. I'd rather drink a root beer than a Bud Light, and I don't know wine from bad fruit juice."

"Dawson," a male voice boomed and I cringed. At least the jovial quality to it kept the sound from being nails on a chalkboard. The local bank president, Richard Lang, swaggered to the table, his grin wide and his suit coat hanging open. "I'd ask what you're doing on a Saturday night, but I can see you're—" He looked at me and stopped like someone had stuffed a sock in his mouth. I could do it. His mouth hung open wide enough.

Big Dick Lang. I happened to agree with Pop on that opinion. Richard Lang had taken a lot of pleasure in humiliating Pop when we'd gone in to inquire about loans, credit, and even savings. Big Dick wouldn't let us open a checking account with money we held in our hands.

Big Dick blinked and swiveled his gaze back at Dawson. "Everything okay?"

"Just fine, Richard," Dawson answered calmly. "Did you get the special?"

"Of course. King beef is the only palatable meat in this town."

I bristled at the pointed jab, but Dawson just cocked his head. "There are a lot of fine ranchers in town."

Big Dick slapped him on the back. "And they work for you, am I right?" He guffawed and wandered away.

Dawson's apologetic gaze landed on me but I waved it off. "That was tame compared to his last conversation with Pop."

"It wasn't right." His brow furrowed but I only wanted this conversation to be done.

"Look, I get it. I know the price I get per head is half what you get. For good reason. But I have plans. It's going to take time, but I know what I'm doing."

"That's what pisses me off."

"What?"

Dawson shot a glare toward the exit but Big Dick was gone. "They can't see that you know as much about the business as I do."

I knew as much about ranching. Thanks to Pop, I didn't know as much about the business. "Didn't you go to college for it?"

"Farm and ranch management, yeah."

"Then I don't know as much as you. It's okay, Dawson. I don't need Big Dick to tell me I can do a good job. His validation is shit."

Dawson's mouth quirked. "Part of his issue might be your dad's unfortunate, but completely predictable twist on his name."

Skylar's arrival with plates of food ended the discussion. She set my plate down without a word but aimed her proud smile at Dawson. "Shepp said he'll dish out the biggest piece of tiramisu for you."

Dawson glanced at me, then to her. "For us."

Skylar still didn't look at me. "Absolutely. Can I get you anything else?"

He was the one to check with me, but I shook my head and cut into the meat. If Skylar wanted to chitchat with him, that was fine. I was hungry.

She left and Dawson watched me a moment before picking up his utensils. "How's the food?"

"Delicious," I said around a savory garlic explosion in my mouth. The butterhorn roll was as big as my head and I debated the minimum number of bites considered civilized.

He finally dug in and we didn't talk until the meal was finished. Skylar checked in with Dawson once and returned with dishes of tiramisu. True to her word, Dawson's piece was twice the size of mine.

His fork thumped the tabletop and he muttered, "Seriously?"

I swiped an edge of my dessert with my spoon and tasted it. "I'm not really a coffee-flavor person. Don't worry about it."

"Dammit, I forgot you didn't drink it." He made a cup of coffee every morning. I'd turned that down too, but if I was up early enough, I started the coffee maker for him.

"I like the smell but never got a taste for it." I tapped the top of the dessert with my fork. "The flavor's not too strong. It's fine." I'd eat the whole thing because that was what I'd been raised to do.

Dawson had one bite left when Skylar came back with the tab. My heart stuttered when she set a slip by me and one by Dawson.

Crap. I was always ready to pay my way. I didn't take for granted that my date would one, pay, and two, not expect favors if he did. I'd been complacent with Dawson.

Filet might be the special, but chicken or pasta was always cheaper.

"Skylar, seriously?" Dawson snapped. Skylar's hand went to her chest. I think she was more shocked than I was at his tone. "I'm trying to have a nice night out with Bristol, but between you and *Big Dick* Lang, she's been nothing but ignored and insulted, and honestly, I expected better when I thought of coming here."

Skylar blinked. "I-I . . ." She stiffened. "I can't take responsibility for what Mr. Lang might've said or done, but I . . ." Her gaze flitted to me, then over my shoulder. Repressed anger and embarrassment mingled in her blue irises. I bit the inside of my lip. Should I laugh or slide under the table? "I apologize. Your meal's on the house." She said the words like it pained her.

I was not getting a pity meal. "No—"

"No, absolutely not," Dawson said. "I'm paying. Please don't comp us anything."

"Dawson." Skylar's shoulders sagged and

she finally met my gaze fully. Had she figured out I was a real person instead of an apparition she hoped would go away? "I'm sorry, Bristol. It's just that the last time you were in here, you were—"

"Treated like shit and gave you attitude right back?" I said flatly.

"I didn't treat you like"—she lowered her voice—"*shit*. But you can't expect exemplary service when you insult the food and don't tip."

A flush wicked up my neck and heated my cheeks. "If I paid, I tipped."

"Your dates never did."

"So you're holding that against her?" Dawson cut in.

I talked over him. "And I never insulted your food."

"Bland and tasteless. When you were here with Foreman—"

"That was years ago." The calculation flew through my brain. It'd been summer and I'd still been dabbling in the dating pool in town. Foreman was the reason I now drove to meet a lot of my dates. "Six, to be specific." I didn't know why I kept talking. I didn't like defending my actions. "But hey, when it looked like my chicken had walked across the floor by itself to get on my plate, I should've just smiled?"

I wedged my crutches out and scooted to the edge of the seat.

Dawson slid the keys across to me. "I'll be right out, Bristol."

"Take your time," I said and thumped away as quickly as possible. The diners around us watched me the entire way.

Dawson

THE RIDE HOME WAS QUIET. I'd been half afraid Skylar had pissed Bristol off so much that she'd drive home without me.

I pulled up in front of my house. The porch lights lit up the yard, welcoming us home, along with Daisy and her wagging tail as she rushed to the front door, waiting to be let in. I parked in front of the porch and killed the engine. "I can make some popcorn and we can find a movie."

Bristol paused with her hand on the handle, confusion screwing up her face. "Aren't you mad?"

"About what happened? Hell, yeah." Her expression turned stricken and I grabbed her hand. "Do you know how much I wish I could rewind the night and take you to Billings instead?"

She shook her head. "You're not upset with me?"

"With you? No, Bristol." How could she think that? Because I'd come out of the restaurant after paying for my meal and listening to Skylar's profuse apologies. I reached into my wallet. "Sorry I didn't give this to you right away."

She stayed close to the door, watching me hand over the gift card, her gaze wary, like I held a live viper. "What's this?"

"Skylar feels horrible about everything that happened and how she misunderstood it all." I held it out but she didn't accept it. "It's a fifty-dollar gift card."

"I don't feel like—"

"It's not pity, Bristol. It's good business. At least three other tables heard you tell her that they ignored you when it looked like your chicken mopped the floor before it got on your plate."

Her lips twitched before anger pursed them again. "It was like they dropped it by the door to get the most dust bunnies."

I believed it. Fuck, after the last two hours, I believed everything Bristol said about how the town treated her. She didn't put up with it or the bullshit flung her way, and that made it worse for her.

"I promise to serve only popcorn that's fallen no farther than the counter. Do you like extra butter?"

"A little cayenne pepper."

I grinned. "I'll keep your batch separate. I don't like my food to fight back."

She chuckled as she got out and I could've pumped my fist in the air. She'd had an epically shitty day, followed by a night that was supposed to have cheered her up but had demeaned her instead. But I could still make her laugh and end tonight on a good note.

My smile died when I realized I still held on to the gift card. Stubborn, proud woman.

I jogged after her. The stairs hardly slowed her down. Inside, she sat on the couch and clicked through the movies.

As I made popcorn, she asked, "What do you feel like?"

"Comedy." Hands down. We both needed a laugh after today.

By the time I had made the popcorn and buttered and seasoned it while she peppered me with questions on what I'd already watched, we'd settled on *Deadpool*. I insisted she needed to see it even if I had three times already—once with each brother.

I took my post at the end of the couch. Daisy sprawled between us, alongside Bristol's cast-encased leg, which was propped on pillows. I kicked my boots off, tossed my feet over the coffee table, and watched the show.

Movies used to be a way to pass the time. I enjoyed them, but whenever I watched them, I wished for more.

I wasn't wishing tonight. I wanted Bristol to laugh and she did in all the right spots. But when the show was done, her eyes were closed. Her lashes, a shade or two darker than her hair, swept over her cheeks.

I eased up and collected our popcorn and cans of mineral water, hoping she'd wake up. No luck. Daisy did though and wandered to the giant doggie bed I'd bought the day after I'd let her in the house.

My next decision tore at me. Move her? Wake her up? Or cover her and let her sleep there?

I could take one of the bedrooms

upstairs. I could sleep in my own bed again for the first time in five weeks.

I didn't want to do either of those. But picking up a sleeping Bristol was like poking a hibernating bear. She could go from REM to slapping me in two seconds.

She blinked her eyes open and caught me standing by the coffee table, watching her. The corner of her mouth pulled down and she half sat up.

"You fell asleep during the credits." As if that explained why I was looming over her while she slept. Like a creeper.

"Damn. That was a good movie too." She grabbed her crutches and rose. When she headed to her room, I followed.

"I'll get the door." Another lame reason for my actions.

She hopped to the bed without turning the light on. Residual light from the living room spilled in, highlighting the neatly made bed and the old T-shirt of mine she slept in that was folded on the nightstand.

I leaned against the doorjamb. When

she looked over her shoulder, I said, "I don't want to leave."

It was the God's honest truth. I'd spent a lot of the day with her and leaving her side right now was too soon.

"I don't want you to."

Her words propelled me across the room before they'd registered in my brain. I slid my hands around her waist and kissed just below her ear. She tilted her head to make room for more. I kissed along the length of her graceful neck and she turned her face until our lips met. An awkward angle for our first kiss, but I wouldn't have it any other way.

A soft touch of the lips wasn't enough. I spun her in my grasp, supporting her on her good foot, and deepened our kiss. My tongue licked along hers, tasting the spicy popcorn she'd had, and a soft whimper escaped her. Another sound I was motivated to get out of her as often as I could.

I untucked her shirt and swept my

hands up her back. Her soft skin under my touch was more than I could've asked for. She wasn't giving me this chance lightly and I'd make sure she didn't regret it.

Without breaking us apart, I hugged her to me and lifted her to the bed. Swallowing her startled squeak, I laid her back and spread myself over her, taking the kiss slow.

She dug her hands through my hair and adjusted under me until we were perfectly aligned. Her body cradled mine. I didn't mean to, but I rocked my hips into her, seeking some relief for the hard throbbing against the fly of my pants.

There were so many things I wanted to do to this woman. So many ways I wanted to make her feel good. Did I kiss my way down her body and lick her until her thighs clamped around my head and her cries echoed off the walls? Did I strip off her pants and pray the condom in my wallet wasn't expired? Did I do both?

What I really wanted was to hold her

while she came. I wanted to keep tasting her. I wanted to be the reason for her pleasure.

I shifted to the side to make room for the hand that wasn't propping me up to roam along her satiny torso and cup a round breast. She was lean, but her tits were a fucking perfect handful. She arched into me as I thumbed her nipple.

I'd taste those later. I'd taste every part of her. But tonight, I just wanted to hold her.

Our clothing would stay in place, but that didn't mean she couldn't come. Hard.

I feathered my fingertips down her belly, loving the shiver that shook her body. I'd told her she'd want me to tickle her.

At her waist, I flicked open the jeans she'd managed to get over her cast. They made her legs look impossibly long. A fantasy I hadn't known I had. When it came to Bristol, I seemed to be a *whatever body part she'll share with me* guy.

One of her hands was still in my hair

and the other fisted on my shoulder as I worked my fingers under her pants and underwear. She widened her legs to give me more access and I took it, stroking a fingertip over her clit.

She bucked against me, her wet heat coating my hand.

This woman.

Just like the kiss, I took my time, but I made it count. I matched the stroke of my finger with my tongue, my body blanketing hers.

She had to break the kiss as she gasped. Perfect. I wicked my finger through her folds and entered her with one smooth move. Her needy groan was pure heaven. That was all I needed. Between the rocking of her body and the rhythmic thrust of my hand, she flew toward the precipice.

"That's it," I whispered. "I want to hold you while you fall apart." *You're safe with me.* Instinctively, I knew saying that would stop everything and she might shut me out. But I could show her.

She clung to me as she broke apart. Her cry rang off the walls and was so damn satisfying. I kept my hand in place until she drifted down from her peak, then removed it and kissed the corner of her mouth down to the crook of her neck. I nuzzled into her hair while she caught her breath.

"Of course you're good at that too," she whispered, her voice dreamy.

I chuckled, my breath wafting over her neck, earning me another shiver. I held her tighter. "You thought I wouldn't be?"

"No. You've been good at everything."

"You are too."

"How do you mean?"

"You ride like you were born on a horse. And don't think I haven't seen you ripping around in that old pickup of your dad's down by the river."

She laughed. "I might've gone muddin' for fun once or twice."

"Knew it. But you didn't get stuck."

She rolled to her side, her grin still in place. "I didn't. Not once. It's all in how you handle it." Heat filled her gaze and her hand slid from my shoulder down to my chest.

I curled my hand around hers. "I got what I wanted tonight." I soothed the flash of hurt in her eyes with a kiss. "This isn't quid pro quo. I've been wanting to hold you for so long. I'm fine. Just like this."

"You're fine?" She couldn't sound like she believed me less.

"I have a lot of plans for us, Bristol. Don't get me wrong. I'm a guy and you're my sexy neighbor."

"I didn't see a King calling me that."

"You're hot as fuck. I'll prove it as often as you want me to. But tonight, I'd like to stay here, like this."

"We're still dressed."

I leaned up and pulled back the covers. She wiggled around until she was under them. I stood and waited. She had to be sure.

She pulled back the other side and my smile grew wide. *Yes*.

By the time I shut the light off in the

living room and got back to the side of the bed, she'd tugged off her shirt and put my old one on and wriggled out of her pants. "There. That's better." She eyed my chest. "Feel free to do the same."

"Aw, honey, if I start taking stuff off, I don't know if I'll quit." I dropped my pants. My shirt hung over the worst of my obnoxious erection.

I slid between the cool sheets until I was close enough to wrap her in my arms. "Night, Bristol."

"Night, Dawson."

Her warm body, combined with my soft bed, was the perfect sleep aid. I wasn't sure which one of us fell asleep first, but I knew that sleeping alone after this was going to suck.

CHAPTER 6

ristol

THE ROLL of the walking boot wasn't as bad with my boots on. I left the exam room and found Dawson where I'd left him in the waiting room. He'd refused to leave me at the clinic, but I hadn't let him into the room with me. I'd done enough research to know what my casted leg would be like.

I needed a bath and a razor.

Dawson grinned when he saw the black

walking boot and took my crutches from me like the gentleman he was. The retired rancher he'd been talking to stared at us. Denny Yellow Bird had known my grandparents but had given Pop a wide berth. I'd never talked to him, but I'd seen him around.

"You must be Bristol," Denny said, his face wrinkling with his grin. "You look just like your grandmother." He winked. "But a little taller."

My laugh surprised me. "Just a bit." Grandma had needed to sit on a pillow to drive her Cadillac.

"Glad to see the younger generation has more sense than their parents and grandparents." A nurse came out and called his name. He shuffled away with a little wave.

I kept my head down as I limped out. Dawson chattered about how Denny's ranch was doing under his son and that his granddaughter might take over but that she had to finish school first.

Denny had seemed happy to see me and Dawson together. Would that be the case with the rest of the town?

Was I really dating Dawson? He'd been sleeping with me since the first night we'd messed around together, but he only held me.

I want to wait until your cast is off and you can wrap those long legs around me.

Well. When he put it that way, yeah, I couldn't wait. I'd been having a hard time waiting. I had the worst case of lady blue balls and Dawson had to be suffering. But other than feeling the massive erection pressed behind me when we lay together, I hadn't gotten my fill of his body.

It was frustrating. And exciting.

I was a cow in heat, pushing at the gate to get in the same pen with the bull. Only the bull wanted to spoon.

For fuck's sake. Dawson King liked to cuddle.

No wonder women flung themselves at him, hoping to one day land in the same spot I'd been for six weeks. He was a dream. A fantasy. A goddamn unicorn.

And he was with me. That was between us. But our family feud was town history, murmured about among old and young alike. What would they think if the feud was over?

I got into the front seat of his pickup. I had a lot of questions about what my life would be like as I finished recovering from this injury. Dawson had said he and the guys would continue to help. I might be able to modify the rest of the job. I'd only be in this walking boot for a couple of weeks.

Dawson pulled out of the parking lot. "Everything go okay in there?"

"Yeah, why?"

"You got quiet."

Should I tell him what was bothering me? "If we're doing this—us—how do you think the rest of the town will react? Do you think Denny's reaction is going to be one of a kind?" I couldn't take more hate because I'd corrupted the most eligible bachelor of the county.

Dawson didn't brush off my question. He read my underlying anxiety. "I don't know. I only care because you seem to."

I shrugged. "I don't know if I care yet or not." That wasn't true. I cared. What if this didn't work out between Dawson and me? We'd go back to curt messages regarding cattle and fences. He'd come out of the relationship looking like a hero no matter what happened and I'd still be sour Bristol Cartwright. They'd feel sorry for him—and they'd probably have a right to.

He was the unicorn. I was me. If this relationship, or whatever we were doing, ended, it'd be my fault. I couldn't see any other reason why.

"I think we should celebrate," he said suddenly.

I cocked a brow. "That went so well last time."

He flashed a grin. "In Billings. We aren't

going to let the good townsfolk of King's Creek fuck this up."

"Billings?"

"We could go to Miles City."

Marshall lived in Miles City. My luck was too poor. He'd be wherever we chose to eat. "Billings is fine. When?"

"You go do your thing, and I'll talk to the guys, make sure they don't need me around today."

The guys. Kiernan and Tucker rarely came into the house. Dawson assured me they didn't mind helping out with my place, but it was another thing for them to realize I was with Dawson.

"You've been feeding me and doing my work for a month and a half." I was grumbling. It was easier to accept his charity when I had a cast and almost no choice. My cast had been off less than an hour and he was still providing food and shelter.

"It's only another half day. The ranch could go bust tomorrow and I'd be fine.

Like I said when you first came to stay with me—you're doing me a favor. Sucks being by yourself all the time."

"If you're a charming extrovert, maybe."

His grin was unrepentant. "You think I'm charming?"

"I've always thought so. It's one reason why I hated you so much."

"What are the others?" he asked, as if my answers wouldn't bother him.

"Other than how everything came easy to you, how you had all the money, and how the whole town thinks you and your family hung the moon, the stars, and make the earth spin? Hmmm . . ." A smile played over my lips. "Maybe how you won over Daisy so easily. Or how you snuck my horse treats but you knew I wouldn't get mad because I love the shit out of Bucket."

"You know what pissed me off about you?"

"My stunning personality?"

There was that grin again. "Actually, yes. You acted like you didn't care and everyone bought it. Everyone. But you do care, and that's why I kept telling you about downed fences and lost cows. You were so focused on your work and you didn't need anybody."

Until I had. I had needed him. Now, I wanted him. But I also needed him.

He turned down the long drive to his house. "There's Tucker. I'll park by the door. Take your time. We'll go when you're ready."

"I'm going to take you out sometime," I blurted. "I'm going to pay and I'm going to drive." Hopefully, Pop's old pickup would start after sitting for so long.

"I've never been taken out before." He parked by the porch and grabbed his cowboy hat from the back seat. "I look forward to it."

We both got out, but instead of going to the house, I went for the barn.

"I don't have a tub in the shop," Dawson said as he caught up with me.

"I gotta say hi to Bucket." I wouldn't

have to lean over the fence while he ignored me as he munched on the new growth on the ground.

Bucket's tail swooshed. Breaking my leg had been a giant pain in the ass, but I was glad it had been me and not him. I'd get my business to a place where I didn't have to take him out when he should stay safe in the corral.

Dawson opened the gate for me. Bucket swung his shaggy head toward me and bumped me on the shoulder. I laughed and wrapped my arms around him. It wasn't muddy, but I'd have to wipe off this walking boot before I clomped through the house.

Worth it.

Dawson went to the other side. Bucket nuzzled him like he was doing a pat down for treats.

"Not today, big guy. If I keep giving you apples, you're not going to be able to work cattle in a month."

My body tensed. The daily operation of

the ranch had been on my mind for weeks but I'd purposely kept myself from thinking about working cattle. It was impossible to do alone. Pop hadn't been much use in the last few years, but he could still update records while I did the work and while the noobs he hired waved their arms to get the cows to go where I wanted.

"He missed you," Dawson said.

"Right." I patted Bucket's neck and swept my hand into his coarse mane. "He's going to follow me right out and want to go home right now."

My horse looked healthier than ever. He was getting the best feed, had a nice pasture with a barn, and was enjoying the other horses' company. Bucket didn't have to whinny from a half mile away to chat with his buddies.

I petted Bucket along his firm cheek. I could commiserate.

I was getting the best food, I had a sturdy roof over my head with a bathroom no farther than the next room, and I got to talk to Dawson every day. I didn't want to go home either.

~

Dawson

"An Irish pub in Billings, huh?" Bristol studied the place as we approached the entrance. A cute line formed between her brows. She was dressed more casually than when we'd gone to Hogan's. Faded jeans and a lilac long-sleeved shirt that looked like it could've doubled as long johns.

Sexy as hell. Add in the exaggerated roll to her hips the walking boot gave her and I was tempted to walk around the block just staring at her ass. If she weren't recovering, it'd be a nice night for it. A cool, late-April night. Partially cloudy and the sun was still out at dinnertime.

I had tossed on a blue Yellowstone hoodie and picked a place she'd be comfortable in. The pub in downtown Billings was full for a Thursday night.

"Kate told me about this place," I said. "She takes me here every time I come to town."

Inside, I pulled out the chair for her and sat. She ordered nothing but water like usual, and while it was a pub, I didn't want her to drive back on a freshly freed foot, so I ordered a Coke.

We ordered and talked about Billings and how she'd come here a few times a year but didn't usually go anywhere but McDonald's for food. I told her where Dad's office was, his house, and Aiden's.

Bristol played with the tab that had secured the napkin around the silverware and her gaze glanced off every table. But her posture tonight was the opposite of how it'd been at Hogan's. Billings was big enough for anonymity. If we lived here, maybe we'd run across someone we knew once in a while. But Bristol and I weren't from here and we didn't know anyone.

The meal arrived. I sampled her burger and she stole a few of my waffle fries. My mind was working over what we could do before we went back to King's Creek when a familiar voice broke into our conversation.

"Dawson?" Kate broke away from a group of women all dressed in business-casual wear. She shoved a lock of light brown hair behind her ear and smiled at me.

I grinned and rose, wrapping my arms around her. "Kate, my favorite sister, how ya doing?"

She laughed and patted my back. "I've heard you say that to Eva and I'd bet my paycheck you're going to say it to Savvy the next time you see her."

Of course. They werc all my favorite, but I considered Kate my oldest sister since she'd married into the family first.

Kate's gaze landed on Bristol and I tensed as much as my date. But leave it to Kate and her calm manner and warm heart.

"Bristol, so nice to see you. Emilia said you broke your leg. Are you doing okay?"

The corner of Bristol's mouth lifted. "I had a good nurse."

Her joking with Kate surprised me as much as Kate's hearty laugh. "I imagine. Rancher. Chef. Nurse."

"You wanna join us, or do you have plans?" I'd love to have Kate around anyway, but Bristol had had a whole lot of me and she seemed to be enjoying Kate's company.

Kate peeked over her shoulder. The group she was with had found a table on the other side of the restaurant. "I'd hate to intrude." She worried her lip. "But it would be fun if I could peel Aiden away from the office."

I hadn't thought of my brother. The guy worked a minimum twelve-hour day. When he was at my place, unless his ass was in a saddle, he was always on his phone or computer. "Call him up. Tell him I said to get his lazy ass over here."

I'd messaged Dad, given him a quick rundown of what had happened with Bristol and how she was staying with me while she mended and that Grams was on the rampage. His reply had been the quintessential father washing his hands of the whole deal: *Do what you think is best.*

Kate bit her lip again and glanced between me and Bristol. "Are you sure? You two were probably loving not having everyone all up in your business."

That was Kate. Quiet. Shy. Sharp as hell. I asked Bristol, "You mind?"

"Actually, I don't." Shock resonated in her voice, earning a beaming smile from Kate.

"Let me go talk to them and I'll call Aiden." Kate rushed off.

I sat back down and lifted a brow. "She's awesome, right?"

"She knows I've been at your place."

I dipped my head. "I texted Dad, but all I said was that you'd broken your leg and I'm helping you out and Grams can mind her own business." I had expected Dad and my brothers to double down and bug me every day. Every week at the minimum. But they hadn't. I'd been left alone.

Were they phoning each other like nosy church ladies?

Hell, I was surprised the *actual* nosy church ladies hadn't phoned me. If I'd broken my leg, I'd have been stocked with more casseroles than one man could eat in a lifetime.

I looked to where Kate had ducked between the two sets of doors that made up the entrance to call my brother. "I wonder if she'll get Aiden to leave the office."

"Is he really . . ." Bristol shook her head. "Never mind. None of my business."

"Is he what? Really working? What else would he be—oh. No, I don't think he's like that." I shouldn't continue but it was nice to talk to someone honestly about my family. "But if he's not careful, he's going to fuck it up anyway."

"How can he work that much?"

"Grams. She has this rule about who can be in the inner office. She waived it for Kendall obviously, but she doesn't think Dad and Aiden should have much else going on in their lives. She wants to micromanage everything, and to do that, she won't approve more positions to lighten the load on Dad and Aiden."

"Wow. She'll even burn her own family for money."

I should defend Grams, but Grams was who she was. "Yeah. Basically. But Kate's a librarian. She doesn't work in the oil industry and therefore doesn't see Aiden all that much from what I hear."

Kate bounced our way, her smile tight. "He's going to try to get away."

"Is this a busy time of year?" Bristol asked.

Kate sat next to her, braver than anyone in King's Creek would've been to sit that close to Bristol. "Every season is busy for the inner office. Even when production is down, there's just as much or more to do."

She forced a brighter smile. "So, what brings you two to town?"

Kate peppered Bristol with tentative questions about what had happened and got Bristol to talk when she asked if Bucket was okay. Kate even asked about Daisy. And when Bristol talked, Kate rested her elbow on the table with her chin on her palm and listened. Like, really listened.

I tried to interject with details, but the bond between the girls was growing so strong so fast, I just sat back and watched.

"What'd I miss?" Aiden bypassed me to go behind Kate and drop a kiss on her head.

Kate's expression lit up and she raised her face to his, but he'd already rounded the table to sit by me. He nodded to Bristol as he picked up the menu. "How's it going?"

"Fine." The tension was back across her shoulders. She sat straight in her chair instead of being half turned to chat with Kate.

"Bristol was telling me about her injury,"

Kate said. "I'm so glad Dawson was around to meet Daisy when she went for help."

Aiden's brows rose. "Your dog?"

I told the story of finding Daisy at my door. Aiden didn't bat an eye at the conditions Bristol had taken Bucket out in.

"That's a good dog," Aiden said as he got out of his chair and walked away without explanation.

Typical Aiden. Spared his admiration for animals, not for people. At least it was a sign he wasn't one hundred percent robot.

Kate didn't take her eyes off her husband, her hazel eyes liquid. "Want to come over to the house? It'll be easier to chat."

"Sure. Let me get the check—"

"Oh, that's what Aiden's doing. He just never tells anyone. Hates the back-and-forth."

"Too much human interaction for him?"

Kate ignored the jab, used to me bitching about how uptight my brother was. She put her hand on Bristol's arm.

"Their mom's pictures inspired me to fill the house with local photographers' photos. I love showing them off."

The sun was sinking by the time we left the pub. I drove Bristol, and Kate and Aiden each had separate vehicles. I parked on the road in front of their secluded property. Bristol stared at the house. An entire trailer court could fit on the acreage Aiden had purchased by the river. The place was big and there was a lot of land, but the place was like Aiden. Straitlaced and not flashy.

The sprawling two-story home was beautiful, but simple, a plain design with clean lines. A modern take on the old farmhouse. Steel siding and rock that carried across to the three-car garage that both Kate and Aiden were pulling into. Timber beams decorated the porch and framed the door, but Aiden left his garage door open for us to enter through.

"This place is nice," Bristol murmured.

"Yeah." But when Aiden put in long

hours, I bet it was just as empty for Kate as my house was for me.

Kate grinned and beckoned Bristol to follow her. I'd never seen Kate so bubbly, but she probably didn't come across someone as socially ambivalent as Bristol often.

Aiden hung back and hit the control for the garage door, closing us inside. The door to the house closed and I was alone with my brother.

I shoved my hands in my pockets, sensing big-brother interference. "Go ahead."

His intense gaze bored into me. "Does she know about the trust?"

I hated that fucking trust. No wonder my brothers had all been pissy as hell six months before they turned twenty-nine. "No."

"Grams will make sure of it. She'll see Bristol as nothing but one giant cockblock."

"Grams can butt out."

"But she won't, Dawson." Aiden scowled

toward the door. He either trusted Bristol alone with his wife, or thought Kate could handle herself. At first glance, Kate didn't look like she could deal with a mouse running through the house. But I'd seen her kneeling in the straw to tame some half-feral kittens. "Look, I'm man enough to admit that I don't know her. I have an idea of what she went through in life and I could've been less of a dick. But if you helped her, and she let you, then I was wrong. About her, not Danny."

"I think we might've been wrong about Danny too," I said quietly. "No, not wrong. But we could've understood him better. Helped him out."

"Don't you think Mama tried?"

"Then she died, and Danny refused to let Bristol come to the funeral."

We both fell quiet. Mama dying had been a turning point for both families. She didn't have to marry Danny for him to want to be better for her. The fact that she'd given a shit had been enough for him. And then she'd been gone and we had regularly proved we didn't give a shit about him or Bristol.

"Fuck," I said.

"Yep. So how do you think Bristol's going to take it when she finds out that all of us happened to get married before we turned twenty-nine, which coincidentally meant she wouldn't get a dime of the money Mama seemed to think she had some claim to?"

"I'm not married yet," I said tightly. I liked being with Bristol. She was opening up to me and I wanted more. The trust didn't need to fuck it up.

"So how are you going to phrase it?" Aiden kept his voice low. " 'Hey, do you mind getting married before July so I can get a lot of money and you don't get any? But on the plus side, if you stick with me for a year, then you'll get half?' "

Bristol would walk away from me and pretend I didn't exist, that I never had. She had let me help her because she'd had no other option. I liked to think she was still with me because she felt the connection between us and it was too valuable not to explore. She might be willing to forgive the past, but her pride wouldn't forgive what my family had continued to do to hers. She lived in poverty. If it hadn't been for Daisy, that poverty would've cost her her life.

"And if you don't get married by your birthday," Aiden continued as if I couldn't see the rock and the hard place I was stuck in, "then you get to ask her to keep dating you after she's richer than shit. After you explain that even a hundred million dollars wasn't enough to make the prospect of marrying her palatable."

All the scenarios sucked. Bristol and I had just started dating and Aiden was lobbing marriage scenarios at me—all of which ended with me losing Bristol—and ruining a perfectly good night.

"I dunno," I said, knowing I should shut my mouth. I'd been around Bristol and learned that a laugh and a smile weren't always necessary in conversation. "Want to tell me how your talk with Kate will go when you tell her you married her for the trust money?"

His jaw ground down so hard he could've turned all the rock on his land to dust. "Why I married Kate is no one's business, and we're not talking about me. We're talking about you and that woman in there. It's your turn to figure out what you're going to do about the trust, and like me, someone else's feelings are involved."

Like me. He hadn't said "like the rest of us." Beck had told Eva the terms and recruited her to help him get the money. Then they'd fallen in love. Xander had agreed to a sudden Vegas wedding and used the trust to convince Savvy to stay married afterward. But Kate and Bristol were blissfully ignorant, and if the terms got out, they'd both be hurt.

I'd ignored the subject for a month and a half. My birthday was in a little over two months and I didn't want the money. I hadn't cared much for it before, and then I'd seen how Bristol lived. How she'd loved her father despite the cards he'd been dealt and how he'd played them.

Yet I couldn't just turn it over to Bristol and expect to be her hero. Learning the details would hurt her and leave her with questions about why the woman she'd adored like her own mama would do something like this to her.

ristol

MY BODY ACHED in the best way. I'd worked
all day. If I kept this up, I'd need a
replacement walking boot.

I sat on the porch steps in front of
Dawson's house, a bucket of water next to
me, and scrubbed the boot clean. I was
covered in dust and grit. Bucket was back
in my pasture, but he'd been whinnying all
day, missing his friends. As if I didn't feel

guilty enough when it came to that horse. I was heading inside to soak my aching leg. If I hadn't canceled the physical therapy appointments the clinic had made, I was sure I'd be told that I'd overdone it today.

I'd overdo it again tomorrow too. Because I had to.

Dawson's truck had been parked by my barn off and on throughout the day, but we'd crossed paths. I had split my time between working in the shop or roaming my land and making a to-do list about what I could get done this summer or save for next. There were some fence sections I could reinforce. I'd checked on the cabin. And being in my pickup had given me an excuse to swing by Dawson's when I'd had to use the bathroom.

I set one boot aside and cleaned the other one. Tucker rumbled from the pasture down the drive in the big John Deere. They'd been using the tractor to do chores at my place. He parked it by the barn and swung out in a move all the single women in town would've loved to witness. His cowboy hat was pulled low and he walked like he'd been on a horse for the last twenty years, which was probably the truth.

"I think that's all for today, Bristol. You need anything else?" I'd talked more to Tucker today than I ever had. He was in his thirties and had a more *aw shucks* appeal than the King brothers.

"No, that's more than enough. After we work cattle, you won't have to worry about me anymore."

I'd sucked down enough of my ego for the cows and calves I raised. I couldn't wait to be on my own again.

My heart sagged like I'd hung a sandbag off it. So maybe I'd miss the company. And the help.

I'd really miss the help. But I wouldn't miss not being able to afford it.

Thanks to Tucker and Kiernan's TLC, my cows were fat and the calves were thriving. If I could keep it going, sales this fall would be the best I'd ever seen.

I'd love to reinvest the profits, but I'd have to reimburse the guys for all they'd done.

"Ain't no worry," Tucker said. "It's not much extra work with the right equipment."

And there was the rub. I'd be offended, but he'd just stated a fact. His tone didn't make it sound like I was at fault for what Pop had left me. "I'll get there."

"I know you will."

I wasn't sure what "there" would look like yet. Today was the first day I'd comprehended that I could do anything with Cartwright Cattle. My means were meager, but my ambition wasn't. Could I build my cow-calf operation to the point where I could hire help?

Would I be picky about the people I hired, or would I try to find someone who needed the work mentally as much as they did economically, like Pop?

I'd be smarter about it.

Right. Time to rein in my fantasies. I

should arrange a real roof over my head first.

Tucker tipped his hat and shot me a knowing look. "You'll get there faster if you don't kick us out as soon as the cattle are moved."

Before I could tell him that I couldn't afford his help—and I wasn't going to take his charity if I could keep the cattle healthy by myself—he climbed into his pickup and fired up the engine. He gave me a wave as he rolled away.

I wiped off my boot and slid it on. My leg both welcomed and hated the intrusion. I tossed the water on the grass and put the bucket by the door. Other than to get a nice bath, I wouldn't delay any longer. It was my personal bargaining chip. I'd take a bath, then go to the RV. In the morning, I'd clean the entire trailer so I wouldn't dread using the bathroom. Maybe I could clean it well enough that I wouldn't have to live at the cabin all summer. But I wasn't going to worry about it tonight. If that was possible.

I went inside. Dawson's place was quiet. I would miss this quiet. My RV didn't block a single moo, and the wind made everything creak until I fell asleep afraid I'd wake up in another county. Did Dawson want his place back to himself? Would he ask me to stay longer? The invitation had been extended but we hadn't discussed it.

We hadn't had sex yet either.

I thought he'd want to go beyond spooning after our date in Billings. But he'd been quieter than normal all the way home. Had Aiden said something to scare him off? I'd never had much to do with the oldest King brother. Growing up, he'd been even more untouchable than his brothers as far as I was concerned. He still acted as lofty, but like he functioned on his own plane, one that no one else could reach. Not even his wife.

Kate had chattered the entire time she'd taken me through their gigantic house. The pictures were beautiful. All local artists, all Montana scenery. I'd managed to hold back my heartache when she'd stopped in front of Sarah's framed photos. The first King matriarch had used nothing but the intrinsic beauty of the land and natural lighting. And her pictures included my land. She'd never separated the two.

Once, she'd even told me that our families weren't meant to be separated and that I'd always be welcome in her home. I had believed her.

Then I'd been hurt for years because I thought she'd lied.

I believed her again. But being welcomed on King land was different than living there. Was that the divide Dawson had a hard time spanning?

I needed to move back home. I didn't mind moving slow, but it was starting to feel like I was the only one who knew the terms.

I took my bath, groaning as I sank into the warm water, bubbles covering my chest and giving me teeny-tiny massages as they burst. The whole time I was in there, I searched my phone for the type of physical therapy exercises I should be doing. Whenever I found one, I took a screen shot. I couldn't afford PT, but I also couldn't afford to hobble around and possibly hurt myself again. I kept thinking I heard doors opening or footsteps, but the house remained quiet.

It stayed that way as I dressed and loaded my clothing into the grocery bags I'd packed them in. I stopped in the kitchen and made a peanut butter and jelly sandwich. I'd have to get groceries for the RV tomorrow. After I threw out everything in my little dorm fridge and wiped it out.

I took a bite of my sandwich and went out to the pickup. The bath had helped ease the ache in my leg. My sandwich was gone before I reached home. Dawson's pickup was no longer by the barn.

I looked at the rust-stained trailer. Then at the barn that needed a new paint job twenty years ago. The shop with the door that'd been stuck open for five years and the fences that had been cobbled together out of scraps. Some posts were wood, some were metal. Some were round, some square, and some probably stolen from someone's garden in the middle of the night.

Pop wasn't a thief unless he took something that wasn't worth pursuing.

Daisy romped into the RV, happier than I was about being back but not as excited as she was when she darted into Dawson's place.

"Home sweet home." The words died in the silence. It wasn't like I'd meant them.

I put my stuff away and started cleaning. The place was dusty and I changed my bedding, grunting to get between the full mattress and wall of drawers on each side without wrenching my leg.

There. Done.

I looked out the window toward the trailer house. Could I make it all night without using the bathroom?

Probably. But I'd forgotten to bring a water jug.

Damn.

I sighed and flopped onto my back. The sun had set. My phone stayed silent.

Had Dawson been that content to get rid of me? Had I misread everything between us? It wasn't like I had any experience in relationships that didn't revolve around sex. As long as I was putting out and the guy wasn't an abusive asshole, the relationship was fine.

The wood-paneled ceiling wasn't going to answer me. I changed into a nightshirt that I'd shamelessly stolen from Dawson.

I wasn't that far removed from Pop.

As I was pulling back the covers, a knock startled me. Daisy popped her head up.

"Way to be on guard."

"Bristol!" Dawson called. "Open up."

My heart flipped and I didn't realize I was grinning until I reached the door. A guy yelling outside my door should hit all the wrong buttons, but Dawson's voice was a balm to my healing nerves. I whipped it open.

He entered, stooping to keep from hitting his head on the frame. "What the hell are you doing?" His scowl was somehow sexy as hell. A lock of damp hair fell over his forehead and the scent of fresh soap surrounded him.

"I was going to bed." I put a hand on my hip, which only hitched his T-shirt higher and drew his attention to my bare legs. My healing leg was half bent and I hoped it appeared sexy and not withered, so much smaller than my left leg.

"Without saying good night to me?" he growled and crowded me backward toward the bedroom. The mattress hit the backs of my legs and I dropped.

He closed the pocket door.

My tiny bedroom became minuscule with the tall cowboy towering over me.

"You hadn't gotten back by the time I

left. I didn't know if you wanted me to wait."

He yanked his shirt over his head. "I didn't want you to go."

I loved hearing those words. But how could I stay? How could I live off Dawson when I was able-bodied enough to take care of myself? How could I go from one man with all the authority to another within a span of months?

But I stuck with, "I didn't want to go." The ripples of his abs made my mouth water. Bronzed skin. His forearms and biceps were more tanned than his torso. I never gave farmer tans a second thought, but on Dawson, it worked.

He flicked open the button of his jeans. As much as I wanted this to keep going and advance beyond spooning, my logical brain wouldn't shut up.

"There's no convenient bathroom." He'd have to clean up when we were done, and if I couldn't afford physical therapy, I definitely couldn't afford a walk-in visit for a bladder infection either. I'd have to wander across the yard to use the bathroom too. As much as I wanted to ride Dawson like he was a prized horse, he had to know what he was getting into with me.

"The trailer's bathroom is clean." He stepped out of his boots.

"What?" I dragged my gaze from the V above his waistband to his eyes.

"I cleaned the trailer all day. Hauled garbage out. Scrubbed. Any belongings are packed into garbage bags with fabric softener sheets. I put them into the shop to air out so you can go through them later."

The fabric softener sheets were supposed to keep mice away. I'd squirreled them all over the trailer and RV. "How did you—I didn't see you at all today."

"I told Tucker to tell you what I was doing if you asked." His lopsided grin was adorable and drop-dead sexy when he reached into his pocket and withdrew a string of three condoms. He tossed them onto the shelf my drawers made along the wall, then shoved his pants down.

"You cleaned the trailer? All of it?"

"Most of it. Febreze has been sprayed over all the cushions and carpet and I added a plug-in air freshener, so you should be able to use the bathroom without getting nauseous."

I sat up, trying—and failing—to keep my gaze off his proud erection. He was a large man. "Dawson. Why?"

He stepped out of his pants. "Because I knew you'd insist on coming back here once you could move around freely. And I knew how stressful facing the trailer was for you."

It must have been a filthy job. Yet I couldn't deny the surge of relief inside of me at the thought of using the bathroom in a trailer that wasn't festering and smelly. "That was sweet. Really, really sweet." My throat tightened. No one else had ever done that much work for me. It'd been easy to tell myself that Dawson and his employees helped me because they didn't want to see the cattle suffer, or Bucket, or Daisy. But none of the animals used the trailer. Just me.

"I don't plan on being sweet right now."

Again, my logical brain wouldn't shut off. Too many years of protecting myself. "Why now?"

He was gloriously naked. I couldn't believe I was still talking. But as much as I wanted to sleep with him—and do more than sleep this time—I had to know why we hadn't done more than cuddle. I couldn't figure out a reason why, but no one did anything for nothing.

He propped his hands on his hips. His erection bobbed with the movement, but he didn't advance, like he was waiting for me to open the gate and let him in. "Are you telling me you wouldn't have beaten yourself up about sleeping with me when you were only staying at my place because you had no choice?"

"I . . ." Totally would've done that.

Maybe not obviously. But a small voice in my mind that sounded a lot like Pop would have pointed it out during my low points.

"You're not in a cast anymore. You worked all day on your own ranch. And you're staying in your own place. I think it's time, and I'd like to unwrap you and find out how ready you are."

So ready. I'd been ready for weeks. He'd gotten to me. He not only wanted to understand me, he already did. The work he'd done today, and that he was standing in my tiny bedroom, proved it. "Then what are you waiting for?"

Dawson

THIS WAS GOING TO HAPPEN. A week of excruciatingly blissful sleep. I couldn't get enough of holding her, but I'd been painfully hard until she'd fallen asleep and

I'd become too tired to maintain that much blood flow to my dick.

I prowled over her. First, I had to taste her. I dropped my mouth onto hers and she opened for me. I swept my tongue inside and grinned against her lips. "Mmm. Peanut butter."

"I don't have groceries."

Yet I had a whole damn fridge full of food. But the cast was off and she was done being reliant.

I caught her mouth again but didn't settle my weight on her. We'd waited long enough. I hadn't ever held out this long before sleeping with someone. Either my date and I had already moved forward or I'd broken it off. It was probably the same for Bristol. She didn't waste her time. That we'd both waited—even after we'd known each other as long as we had—told me that the chemistry between us wasn't ordinary.

Her past influenced how much she was willing to give of herself. And I had that damn trust. But this thing between us was strong enough to get over both of those hurdles.

It had to be.

As I kissed her, I worked her shirt up, the backs of my fingers grazing against the undersides of her breast. I broke away from her and slid the shirt over her head.

My breath whooshed out. Creamy skin greeted me. Perky tits. A slender torso with gently sloping hips that slid into mile-long legs. Her red hair was rumpled around her shoulders and desire filled her crystalline-green eyes.

"You're so beautiful," I murmured.

A faint blush brushed her cheeks. She hadn't been told that enough.

I worked my way down her body until I could lick a circle around a peaked nipple. She arched into me. Her underwear was still on. I had plans for her spectacular boobs, but those would have to wait.

I hooked my fingers over the waistband of her plain, pale blue underwear and dragged them down.

A naked Bristol. My chest got tight.

I'd never thought this would happen.

After it had become clear there was more between us than animosity or friendship, I still hadn't been sure it'd happen.

I caught her gaze and settled between her legs. She spread them to make room for me. And here I'd thought I couldn't get harder. There were no pants blocking my erection, but it throbbed like it was trapped behind a zipper.

A sound ripped out of me that I was afraid would bring a growling Daisy to the door. I'd turned into an animal. Only one thought in my head.

Pleasure my woman.

I spread my hands along her thighs and stroked closer to her center, to where she was wet for me.

I tried to be gentle. I started slow, but the way she swiveled her hips against my tongue broke my restraint. I devoured her.

She fisted the plain brown comforter we lay on. "Dawson."

She wasn't going to last long. I wanted to feel her clenched around me again. I threaded one finger inside of her and she shattered, coming against my face. I strung her orgasm out, easing my tongue and stilling my finger inside of her until she sagged on the mattress.

"Oh my god, that was fast," she gasped. "I should be ashamed."

I rose, grinning. She rolled her head to the side and her hair spread out like a fiery halo. Her lips curved up. My siren didn't have to do anything to beckon me closer.

"I'm pretty damn proud." I grabbed a condom and got it on in record time. "But speaking of being fast, I'm going to need one round with no expectations." I gestured to my dick. "It's been waiting too long."

"That's your fault," she purred as she reached for me.

I draped myself over her and positioned

myself at her entrance. Wet heat radiated from her. I wasn't going to last long.

I didn't slam in. I didn't enter in one smooth thrust. I took my damn time even though it killed me. One inch at a time, her tight heat swallowing me.

"You're killing me." Her fingers curled over my shoulders.

I was shaking before I'd fully seated myself. "You feel too good to go fast right now." I backed out and thrust in. Her breath hitched and her breasts ground into my chest. We were as close as we could possibly be. She couldn't rock up unless I gave her room to.

This woman made me selfish. I wanted to savor her. Relish her. Take my time, but consume her before I missed my shot.

I managed a steady pace, somehow keeping myself from hurtling toward my peak. Her body told me what she needed and how hard. I hitched her leg higher and rested a finger on the sensitive bundle of nerves I'd savored earlier.

She barked out a cry, her body fisting me so exquisitely I probably couldn't repeat my own name.

"You feel so fucking good," I groaned. I was sure there were more romantic things I could say, but it was the truth.

Energy coiled at the base of my spine and exploded. I buried myself in her until I didn't know where I ended and she began, and I came. Hard.

"Bristol!" My release jetted out of me. My hips swung like they were on a hinge and I emptied myself while she wrapped her arms around me, her tongue licking across my chest.

A ragged groan left me and I sagged over her. She caught me.

I didn't have to worry about smothering her. She was strong. My face was buried in her hair and her legs were still wrapped around me. Neither of us moved. We enjoyed our postcoital bliss together.

The relief cascading through me shouldn't be a surprise. Half the day, I'd been afraid the last month and a half would dissolve and we'd return to being acrimonious neighbors. Tucker had said she hadn't asked about me, and yeah, I might've been a little insecure about it.

Until I'd thought about who Tucker was referring to. Bristol wasn't going to sit around and wait for some guy. She'd only let me take care of her because her cattle had needed as much help as she had. She wasn't waiting around for me to get done with work; she had her own shit to do.

And when I'd returned to my house, half frantic that I'd kept her waiting too long and expecting a lecture like what I'd gotten from my college girlfriend, I'd found the place empty. Because she had her own shit to do.

Then I'd scrubbed the grit and stench of the trailer off me and rushed over here, half frantic again that she'd be mad as hell that I'd stood her up and hadn't talked to her all day.

Instead, I'd found Bristol getting ready

for bed. Because she knew what being a rancher entailed. Long hours, and we couldn't be around to babysit people when we had hundreds of cows to keep alive.

I pulled out of her but kept her curled into my side, much like we'd done every night for the last week. Goose bumps rippled over her body.

Right. She didn't have heat unless she ran the generator. The nights still got cool.

"Get under the blankets. I'll be right back." I opened the pocket door. Daisy rushed past me like she had to check on Bristol. One more step and I was in the impossibly small bathroom.

There was a little trash can I used for the condom. She'd put a piece of plywood over the toilet so it made a little shelf. I grabbed a tissue and wiped my hands off. That was about all I could do.

I wished I could be with her in my house, but being in the RV with her was more important. She'd hidden this part of her life from everyone. I refused to be just another person to her.

I went back in and shooed Daisy out. I swear the dog slapped me with her tail as she passed.

"I'm not going to score any points with that dog, kicking her out."

"She'll get over it." As I closed the door, she looked past me into the shadowed RV. The yard light cast enough of a glow to see the interior. "Or maybe not. We usually share body heat."

"I'm sharing your heat tonight," I said as I crawled in beside her naked body. Good. She hadn't put her shirt and underwear back on.

"You're staying the night? Our feet hang off the end."

"Yep. But I have two more condoms, so . . ."

She chuckled and snuggled into me. "I've never had anyone over."

"Believe it or not, me neither." She looked back at me and I shrugged. "If I wasn't feeling it, it seemed, I dunno, douchey to have sex in the house I never plan to leave." I let out a sigh. "Never mind. There was my college girlfriend, but she and I slept in my old bedroom upstairs."

"I'd heard you two were serious."

"Yeah. I guess." I thought back to those days. How hopeful I'd been to have someone to share my passion and my life with. Only to defend it every time we'd talked about the future. "I think I was more serious about the idea of her than her." That sounded worse than I'd thought it would.

"It's easy to do. How do you think I put up with Marshall for so long?"

"I want to drive to Miles City and key his flashy car. But, yeah. If someone doesn't understand our life, it's not like there's a future." I hugged her to me. I'd come home late most nights the last six weeks and she'd been watching Netflix or reheating leftovers. "I'm to blame too."

"How so?"

"I assumed we'd marry and she'd move

here and we'd be happy forever. But she was going to school for architecture. It wasn't like she could move to King's Creek and get a good job. It'd pretty much be career suicide before she even started. When she finally got that through to me, I realized we were done. She didn't take it well."

"Thought she should be enough to leave the ranch for?"

"Yep."

She went quiet and I was regretting telling her about my past. I hadn't been as serious about McKenzie as I'd been about settling down, but it wasn't cool to talk about another woman right after your first time with someone special.

I was about to apologize when Bristol said, "I like to pretend that was why it didn't work out between my mom and Pop."

Whoa. That was heavier than my youthful ignorance.

"I know everyone says that she left

because she couldn't stand Pop, but I think it was being miles from everyone. Pop wooed her to the trailer and knocked her up. She stayed long enough to realize that I was the chain and Pop was the ball, and she couldn't be just a rancher's wife or a mom. So she left."

And left Bristol too. "I know this life isn't for everyone, but I don't agree with what she did."

"She went to LA. Wanted to model or something, Pop said. I don't think he was lying since that's where she died."

I jerked and rolled to my elbow, staring down at Bristol. "She died?"

Bristol nodded like it was old news, and fuck, it probably was. "When I was fourteen. Car accident. Her parents had already passed sometime before that. I don't know. I never met them."

"Damn, Bristol. I'm sorry."

"It . . ." She blew out a gusty sigh. "It helped when I heard, actually. I'd been left behind, but I was still alive. That must mean I was supposed to be where I was. It doesn't make any sense. It sounds bad when I say it out loud."

"It makes perfect sense." It didn't, but I wasn't the daughter some woman had abandoned.

"There's an extra blanket in one of the drawers behind you. I can always turn on the generator and get some heat going."

"I plan to keep you plenty warm tonight."

She blinked up at me. "Oh? How do you plan to do that?"

I flipped the blanket over my head and worked my way down her body. "Let me show you."

ristol

I DROVE down Dawson's drive. We'd made plans to have breakfast before we worked my cattle today. Other than the first night I'd been back in the RV, Dawson hadn't slept over. But we'd still had sex. Every night.

Yesterday morning, he'd caught me as I was coming out of the trailer and we'd had sex in his pickup. I'd been half terrified

Tucker would drive up on us, but Dawson had assured me Tucker and Kiernan were on the opposite side of his land.

It wasn't bad being back home. As long as I wedged a window open in the trailer most of the day, it was tolerable. I wouldn't say pleasant. The carpet would have to be ripped out and the furniture hauled to the dump, but between the air freshener and real fresh air, my stomach didn't twist at the thought of using the bathroom.

I parked where I usually did in front of the house, but Dawson was perched on an overturned five-gallon pail next to the barn door. He had a fluffy kitten tucked into his chest.

My grin spread wide as I got out and crossed the drive toward him. My boots crunched in the dirt and he looked up. Two more fluffy bundles bounded at his feet.

"Do all the Kings cuddle kittens, or just you?"

"My brothers will say they don't." Dawson scratched the tiny kitten's head. "I try to limit how many are running around so they stay healthy, but Magnolia got pregnant before I could get her in to the vet."

I squatted and picked up a long-hair tabby kitten. The little thing practically jumped into my hands and was madly purring before I got her tucked into my arm. "I don't think you have to worry about them being feral."

"Nope. I make sure of it. Between me and Kiernan's daughter, we tame them. Magnolia's a wicked hunter, so I'm hoping to move this litter to the old chicken coop by the far shop."

I didn't have an official farm cat. A couple of strays had called dibs on my shop and one of the toms had a spraying problem. If I were friendlier with the rescue organization in town, I'd ask for their help to catch and fix them. But I wasn't, so saving up for a couple of neuterings was on my list. Until then, they'd probably knock up the females that Dawson didn't get to in time.

But we had plenty of land and a ton of rodents. The gophers had been downright obnoxious until one of Dawson's female cats had swung by to hunt the yard.

I put my knees on the cool grass and scratched the little one's ears. Daisy would have been jealous but she'd stayed behind. Dawson and I were heading right back after we ate. Tucker and Kiernan were meeting us.

I'd woken up excited about today. I'd get to work cattle with experts. Guys I could glean tidbits of information from. Ranchers. Actual ranchers. Not someone off the street who'd done nothing more with a cow than buy a steak at the supermarket.

A day like today would usually have made me cranky, but the three of them were really good to me. And thinking about today helped distract me from tomorrow and the weekend. Dawson was working his own cattle tomorrow, and I was helping. I had to, after all they'd done for me. It wasn't like they needed me, but I could also accumulate more helpful tips. That wasn't the problem.

The problem was his dad was coming tonight, along with Beck and Eva. Aiden and Kate were coming after they were done with work tomorrow. Even Xander and Savvy were flying back from whatever country they were in. Dawson had said they'd only just started building their new house near Billings, so they would be staying at Dawson's too.

Working cattle was *a thing* for the family. A weekend of hard work, family gathering, and downright fun.

I wanted to have fun working cattle, doing hardcore cowgirl work, like rounding them up with Bucket. But it was harder when *all* I had was Bucket. I didn't have many head, and they were used to me, but funneling them to a smaller pasture, into a smaller corral, and then into pens was a shit ton easier when I had others who knew what they were doing.

Working the cattle was a different story. I could castrate a calf in seconds, but last year one of the guys Pop had hired had passed out at the sight and damn near got trampled. Then Pop had nearly collapsed from the exertion of helping the hired man.

I wanted to see how the Kings did it. But I'd have to hang out with the Kings—with all of them—to do it.

Would they be as chill as Aiden?

Chill wasn't the right word. Nonhostile?

But then there was the attitude change in Dawson after our night out with Aiden and Kate.

As if he sensed my nerves, Dawson gazed up at me. "I have some news."

I looked up from the fuzzy head of my kitten.

"Dad and Kendall are going to be here soon."

I clutched the kitten to my body. It squirmed and its tiny claws scraped my skin. "Sorry." I set it down and it toddled away with its tail pointing to the sky. "How soon?"

His gaze drifted toward the drive. The purr of an engine approached and I didn't bother to look.

Despite the warm sun, ice washed through my veins.

Dawson could ignore his family when they weren't in King's Creek and he just had to send a terse reply to butt out. But they wouldn't butt out when they were staying under the same roof.

"I'm sorry," Dawson rushed out. "He called as he was getting to town. I swear I didn't mean to spring it on you."

"No. It's your dad. I shouldn't be the deciding factor for whether he comes over or not."

"I know, but"—Dawson put his kitten down and it bounced in the same direction as its littermate—"I'm sure he'll be fine."

Gentry was usually fine. If we crossed paths in town, he'd give me a terse nod and

I'd lock up and not know what to do. I'm sure I came off as a cold bitch. Usually, that was my goal, but with Gentry King, it was different. I didn't want him to think I was all ice when it came to losing Sarah. But I wasn't sure how else to act. I couldn't bring myself to say hi and risk a *fuck off*. It would've been like coming from Sarah herself.

I followed Dawson to the house.

Kendall shot out of Gentry's pickup and ran for Dawson. She gave him a bear hug, pounding his back. "It feels like it's been forever." She broke away and came toward me. I stopped like a deer caught in the beam of her brights. "It was a long winter, wasn't it?" She stopped short as if she knew a hug was as far out of my comfort zone as the moon. "Hey, Bristol. Nice to see you more than in passing. How's your leg?"

My leg had been the icebreaker with Kate too. It was like the powers that be had pushed me off Bucket just so Dawson's family would have something to say to me. "It's healing well."

Three nights ago, I'd had to soak in Dawson's tub. He'd been in there too, but he'd given my leg time to quit throbbing before he'd climbed in and made the rest of my body forget to ache.

"Good." Kendall glanced back at Gentry. He was walking toward us with Dawson.

Gentry was dressed like I'd grown up seeing him—boots, hat, worn jeans, and a long-sleeved, solid-colored shirt. So different than the pictures of him that were splashed all over town. And across Miles City, and of course Billings, where the head office had moved to years ago. Seeing him with slicked-back hair and dressed in a suit had been odd. Usually, I tried to avoid looking at him at all. Whenever I did, I thought of Sarah.

"Bristol," Gentry said carefully, like he was testing my volatility. "Nice to see you."

I dipped my head. Dawson stepped next to me and put his arm around my waist. My eyes flared. I didn't mean to aim my astonished gaze at him, but I wasn't the only one. He'd said he'd messaged them about me, but it seemed like no one had believed him, including me.

Dawson lifted his chin toward the house. "I have an egg bake in the oven. Head on in."

Kendall broke the tension and clapped her hands. "I was hoping you'd feed us. I was just asking Gent if I should run to town for egg bake ingredients or if that was too bold."

Since I'd had his egg bake before, I didn't blame Kendall. I, too, had been thinking about buying the groceries and hoping he'd get the hint.

Dawson chuckled. "You know I take orders. I have a French toast bake I want to test on you all this weekend." He started for the house and I walked next to him, my legs wooden and my mind spinning.

Inside, Dawson and I washed our hands

in the mudroom while Gentry and Kendall set the table.

This morning had gone from pleasant excitement to coiled dread. I was going to have a meal with the villain of Pop's life story. Anxiety wound around my gut, squeezing off the appetite I'd come here with.

"Hey," Dawson said quietly. "It'll be all right."

"I know," I replied automatically. This was Dawson's house. His family. I would be civil. I doubt Gentry would give me a reason not to be.

But Gentry was going to help work my cattle? Did he have some morbid fascination with how bad it really had been for Pop? How broke I really was? Gentry and his kids had the best view of my shit show of a life. Pop and I had seemed reclusive and secretive, and I'd never shared the specifics, but I hadn't needed to. Our life had been on display. Anyone could have extrapolated and figured out how we lived.

There was a knock on the mudroom door. Gentry leaned against the frame. He gave Dawson a little smile. "Mind if I have a word with Bristol?"

I tried to avoid confrontations, but when I found myself in one, I stood my ground. Yet right now, I wanted to run. Why did Gentry want to talk to me alone? To warn me off his son? To tell me I wasn't worthy of any of his family? I couldn't think of any other reason.

Dawson glanced at me first before he answered.

"It's not a problem." My voice came out raspy. Way to stand strong. It was easier to look like an uncaring bitch in the grocery store, where there were five aisles to disappear down and an exit.

Dawson gave my hand a squeeze and left.

I leaned against the sink and tried not to groan as water seeped into my backside. Because of course it did. "What's up?"

"If being here is going to be a problem, I

can go." His voice was gentle, his small smile still in place. "Kendall and I can get a room in town."

My mouth opened but nothing came out. I clenched it shut. Was he really offering to leave if I wanted him to? "I'm not staying here. You don't have to go on account of me."

Gentry's eyes crinkled at the corners. "It seems as if Dawson would rather have you around than his dad stepping all over his business."

Confusion swirled in my brain. The Kings had been the bane of our existence for so long. I was sleeping with Dawson. We'd practically double-dated with Aiden and Kate. And now Gentry was being nice. "What's this all about? Why are you even offering? Why do you care?" The questions poured out and I couldn't stop them. "And why do you want to help me work cattle? Nothing's going to be a surprise. I'm dirt poor. The ranch is on the brink of collapsing. Pop drank every spare cent we had. What do you want to prove?"

I pressed shaky fingers to my forehead. God, had I just snapped at Gentry King? I hadn't said more than a sentence to him in almost twenty years.

"Bristol, I don't want to prove anything." There was that gentle tone again. Like I was a green horse ready to buck. "I'm offering because it's the neighborly thing to do, and I thought maybe you'd take me up on it when your dad never did."

Pop never what? "You offered to help Pop? Was that before or after you called the police on him when he left The Tap after a bender?"

"To clarify, I called a friend of mine that was a deputy and asked him to make sure no one got hurt. My kids were out on those roads." He shoved a hand into his jeans like he'd been busted stealing candy. "And also to be clear, Sarah made me offer—to help with the cattle, the fences, equipment repair. And I extended the offer most years because of her." He blew out a breath. "And . . . because the more I got to know Sarah's parents, the more I could see that your dad and I were dealing with the decisions of our parents. Your grandparents got the land your house is on based on a gamble. Your dad didn't deserve any hard feelings about that. As for the rest of your land . . ." His dark brows knit together. "I think that a lot of the animosity might have been deserved on the part of the Boyds."

"You mean how Emilia and DB sold that land to get the money to start their company and made sure to keep the mineral rights so they could then drill on it?"

His mouth tightened. I wasn't going to apologize for the way I was, and I had no wish to rehash the history between us, but I refused to pretend that my family had been anything less than swindled and that it'd cost us. After the oil booms of the last couple of generations, keeping mineral rights on land sold was becoming standard practice. But selling that land in order to get the money to start a business that would later use those mineral rights to drill on it? Then using that revenue to grow a lucrative empire while inhibiting how much cattle could graze on that land, thereby decimating its value? That was dirty.

He let out a long exhale. "I never heard that part of the story, but after what I've seen of Emilia and DB's business ethos, I can't *not* believe it."

My anger ebbed. He believed me?

Then he went one step further and said, "I also think land shouldn't have been used in a poker game." He spread his hands. "But here we are. I enjoy working cattle. I love how it's become a tradition that brings all my kids together. I came to King's Creek a day early because it's too beautiful out to sit in an office. And when I learned Dawson was helping you today, I thought it'd be rude as hell to sit it out. But the truth is, I don't want to sit it out. I'd like to see the cowgirl you've become. Sarah thought the world of you."

I would not cry. But my chin did an unfortunate tremble. "I thought the world of her."

"She'd be proud of you."

My watery gaze shot to his.

He nodded. "You held that place together. I know it was hard on Danny after Sarah died. I know he loved her and thought she was just more proof that the world was out to get him. And I admit, I wasn't sure what kind of person you'd grow up to be. But Aiden told me how you broke your leg. That wasn't just about the money you'd have lost if the cow had died. You care about those creatures, just like you've been caring for them since you could ride."

My body was rigid, but I held the tears at bay. My eyes burned.

He tilted his head. "I'm not wrong, am I?"

I sniffed. "You don't strike me as a guy who's wrong very often."

"In business? No. But people are harder to figure out." He took a step back, giving me space. I'd need a moment before I went into the dining room and pretended I hadn't just had the most poignant conversation of my life. "People make decisions that can hurt another person when they're only trying to protect themselves."

That statement sounded like I'd missed something. I pushed off the sink to give the back of my pants a few minutes to dry. Was he talking about my family, or his?

Dawson

I MANNED THE GRILL. Beck had stocked the beer fridge I mainly used when my family was around. Beck and Xander stood behind me, chatting about Xander and Savvy's recent trip to Kosovo to visit friends. Aiden and Kate hadn't arrived yet, but they'd eat when they got here.

During a break in conversation, Beck peered over my shoulder. "You burning my ribeye?"

I snorted. "Do I ever?" He loved giving me shit while I cooked, but he was always the first in line to eat my food. The guy had eaten in some of the best restaurants around the world, but he loved my cooking. I'd never tell him how proud that made me.

He peered down the driveway. "Bristol's coming, right?"

"Yes." I kept the hesitation out of my voice. She'd been quiet while we'd worked side by side today. She'd followed my directions, stayed out of my brothers' way, and kept her hat low and her head down. "She probably saw how whipped you all are and realized you're not as badass as the town thinks you are."

Xander chuckled but Beck frowned. "Do I need to rip through town in my old pickup and show them I've still got it?"

Beck's old pickup was loud, obnoxious, and every teenaged country boy's wet dream. He drove it whenever he came to town. When he wasn't around, Xander drove it. I doubt I'd ever see Aiden behind the wheel, but the envy was apparent in his gaze when the pickup's pipes rumbled the beams of the house. He was here more often than the others; I didn't know why he never took it for a spin.

He might putter around as slow as a brand-new driver if he did, unwilling to give up control.

"You can try to rip through town," I said, "but we both know that Eva's going to take the wheel after five minutes."

"True." Beck took a drink off his longneck. "So . . ."

I rolled my eyes. Here it came. Beck and Eva had arrived earlier with only enough time to drop their luggage and run out to the barn. Xander and Savvy had arrived a little later. Xander had jumped in and Savvy had used her husband's camera to snap pictures of all of us all day, muttering something about how our denim-clad asses would get a lot of traffic.

Savvy had taken Bristol by surprise when she'd asked to get her in the pictures. *A redhead, with your body? We'll get so much dude traffic on the site.*

I'd expected a scowl and a curt refusal to have her pictures plastered all over Savvy Energy's blog and Instagram, but she'd lifted a shoulder and said, "Happy to help." She might not be intimidated, since I was sure she didn't have a social media account of any kind.

But I'd have to get those pictures. Her tight ass in those Wranglers did me in. Could I get away with sneaking over to her place tonight? Or should I get some restless sleep dreaming of her strong body in my own bed?

"This thing between you and Bristol," Beck continued. "How serious?"

I delayed my response with a long drink

of my ice-cold beer. "As serious as she'll let it be."

Xander had closed in on us until the three of us stared at the sizzling meat.

"You know my next question," Beck said.

"Yep." A subject I'd been actively avoiding.

"Are you going to wait to tell her until you know she's not going to strangle you in your sleep with her legs?"

I loved her legs wrapped around my head, and I wouldn't be suffering. "How do you tell someone that? I mean, really? It's not just me that'd sound like a grade A asshole. You all deliberately kept her from getting the money."

"We're all happily married," Xander said. "And outside of the year window. We married for real."

"Yeah, but the three of you made sure to do it before you turned twenty-nine. Days or hours before," I stressed. I looked around to make sure I hadn't missed Bristol pulling up. She wasn't around, but I lowered my voice anyway. "Do you know how awful she's been living? How fucking poor she is? We *actively* kept her that way."

Beck didn't flinch. "To be fair, that money was our family's."

"To be fair," I echoed, "Grams screwed her family out of it. Did you know Grams and DB sold the land in order to start the oil company? They *planned* to drill on it after it was sold."

Xander whistled low. "Selling the land intentionally like that—are you sure?" He shook his head. "Never mind. I should've figured it out. Do you think that's why Mama did what she did with the money?"

I was too young to remember a lot about Mama and her relationship with Grams. But I remembered Mama and her big heart and, as a kid, wondering how she could be so warm and happy when Grams was so cool and aloof. DB had died a few years after Mama, but I recalled him being brash and boastful.

Beck shook his head. "What if we'd all married earlier and hadn't realized the trust existed until Aiden turned thirty and got the first windfall? We wouldn't be having this conversation."

"I would've been divorced by now." If I'd married McKenzie after college, would she have gotten half and then gotten sick of the ranch life and left me five years later?

Beck nodded. "We all would've been. Like it or not, that trust forced us to find the person we wanted to spend our life with."

I wish I could be as happy about it. "But Bristol's not going to spew joy-filled rainbows when she hears the good news. After what our grandparents did, it's going to feel like four more slaps in the face." It would hurt even more that Mama had planned it all.

Xander toed the concrete of the parking pad. "You're kinda screwed either way, then. You either have to tell her that you need to get married in the next two months so she doesn't get the money. Or you wait, and it's like telling her that not even a hundred mill is enough to *make* you marry her. How would that go over with her? Or with the rest of the town when the news gets out and spreads like a forest fire?" He gave me a wince like I had one lifeline and it had just snapped. "Sucks, man."

I blew out a breath. "You could say that. I mean, it shouldn't be hard to ask for time to date her without worrying about the damn trust. I wish I could just forget it, but as soon as July fifth hits, she's going to get a windfall and have a few questions."

"Then hate all of us," Beck added.

I shot him a disgruntled glare. Sometimes, brothers were just good for pointing out obvious shitty details. "I really like her." I flipped the steaks, half muttering, half gushing. "Her eyes don't glaze over when I talk about why I think the Black Angus breed is the best for Montana winters. I even told her about the genetics deal we were offered and that I passed because Tucker and I are working out a plan to do our own Black Angus seed bulls. I didn't have to explain a thing; she knew what I meant. I can talk shop without one single eye roll. Not only doesn't she feign interest, but she actually contributes to the conversation."

"Do you two talk about more than work though?" Xander asked. "Just because she lives the life doesn't mean you're, like, fated or something. You two need more in common."

"You mean other than being rich and wanting to travel?" That might've been a shallow dig, but they didn't understand Bristol. She wasn't one-dimensional. She had a million facets that shone even in the dismal light of her life. "She loves my cooking, and I like cooking for her. Even more than for you fuckers. And we both have a weakness for formulaic romance movies."

"Dawson," Beck said carefully and my hackles rose. He was speaking slowly, cautiously. Like I wasn't going to like what he had to say. "You two need more than liking a few of the same things and ranching together. She's lived a different life than you."

"And you and Eva came from the same backgrounds?"

"You know what I mean."

"No, I don't think *you* know what you mean. I had less in common with McKenzie. We were both from Montana and went to the same college, and you all thought she was great." I flipped the hood of the grill down before I hurt my eyes glaring at the flames. "Bristol sees the world like none of us ever will. She saw her dad as a person. Same with all the help he hired."

"No." Beck's jaw clenched. "No. It's because of that help—"

"What's going on out here?" Dad walked out of the garage, Aiden on his heels. His eyes were narrowed, no doubt because I had rounded on Beck, and Xander was shaking his head.

A muscle jumped in Beck's jaw. "Dawson here was saying that Bristol has compassion for people like the guy that beat Mama to death."

Dad winced at Beck's blunt words. Hell, we all did.

"Shh." I looked around. "Is she here?"

Dad looked between us. "Yes, but don't worry. I think Kendall waylaid her, assuming she wouldn't want to walk out here with all of us. So. What's going on?"

"She said Danny was sick." I gave Beck a pointed look. "And the meth head too. And that she thinks Danny kept hiring those guys because a part of him wanted to give someone a second chance. Since for whatever reason, they wouldn't seek help on their own."

My brothers stayed quiet, but some of the heat drained from Beck's gaze.

"Danny was really sick. You guys don't know—"

"Then why don't you tell us?" Aiden's

hard tone surprised all of us. "Tell us how he was so sick that he got Mama killed."

"He lived in squalor. It was so bad, Bristol lives in the RV during the winter and the hunting cabin during the summer."

"That's not possible," Beck said.

"She managed to clean the bathroom. It was about all he'd let her do. I cleaned it so she wouldn't have to . . ." I sucked in a breath. "So she wouldn't have to once again deal with how he'd lived when she's still mourning his death."

My brothers were quiet. Dad's gaze was aimed across the pastures like he could see it.

"He was sick," I stressed. "The guy that killed Mama was sick. I think he needed to be punished, and he was, but come on. No one wakes up one day and decides to be addicted to drugs."

"There were obviously a lot of bad decisions made, by both Danny and . . ." Dad pinched the bridge of his nose. We were all trying not to get lost in that night. Coming home. Finding Mama. The terror.

The way panic had paralyzed me. How my kid brain was stuck on how I hadn't told her that I'd gotten all my spelling words correct for the first time that year, and she couldn't be gone because I had to tell her. She would've been thrilled. She'd helped me study the night before.

Tears burned the backs of my eyes. Fuck. Nineteen years could seem like two days at the oddest moments.

Dad cleared his throat. "But none of it was Bristol's fault."

"Why didn't she come to the funeral?" Beck asked, but less hostility coated his words than earlier.

"Think about it," I hissed, my gaze darting around. "She was eight. Danny fucked up and he knew it. What was she going to do? Walk out on her dad and go anyway?"

"And after?" Xander sounded more curious than resentful.

"He had nothing left but her and his pride."

Beck stuffed his hands into his jeans. "And I'm guessing how we treated her didn't help."

Aiden folded his arms, but he was staring at the concrete.

Xander bobbed his head, his expression resigned. "It hurts to say it, but Mama would've been ashamed of us."

"She brought on a lot herself," Beck said, then sighed. "But I can see why. The town turned against Danny after the funeral. And against her."

"We didn't give them any other lead to follow," Dad agreed.

I shoved my hand through my hair. It was long dried after my shower and probably sticking up in a million directions, but Bristol seemed to like me rumpled as much as clean. "Can you see why this trust is fucking things up? What the hell do I do?"

Aiden's brows pulled together like we

were in a boardroom and he was mentally running the numbers. "You're going to have to prove that your feelings for her are real enough so that when you tell her, she'll understand the dilemma you're in, even if she's hurt." He looked me in the eye, his gaze the most serious I'd seen since the night Mama died. "But whatever you do, don't marry her without telling her about the trust."

Aiden might not have told Kate, but she was so head over heels with him, she wouldn't leave him. Not in a million years. They were *married*. I wasn't my brother, and Bristol wasn't some smitten librarian. If I told her about the trust, she'd see right through all the excuses we'd used over the last few years to justify our actions, and I'd be back to being just another guy who'd treated her like crap.

CHAPTER 9

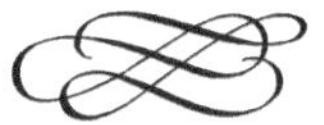

ristol

I WAS USED to feeling like a rusted nail in a jewelry display, but being around the King women was next level.

Kate was dressed similar to the night we'd met up at the pub. Kendall wore a gauzy burgundy top and cute jean shorts that probably had a brand name I'd never heard of. Her hair was gathered in a top bun that must really be a thing since that was how Savvy wore hers too. Savvy's impossibly long legs were in leggings, or tight jeans, I couldn't tell without staring. Then there was Eva with her pixie cut and pink-tipped hair. She might be wearing leggings and a baggy T-shirt full of gamer controls tied at her waist, but she and the others exuded a polished air that I would never attain.

My drying hair was pulled back into a ponytail. I pulled at my plain red Hanes T-shirt. It was clean with no frays. It didn't seem like enough.

Kendall must've sensed my nerves. As soon as I'd walked in, she'd pulled me to the counter and given me strawberries to cut for a fruit salad. We were getting the side dishes ready since Kendall claimed the guys had flocked to the grill like flies to a yard light.

"You're coming tomorrow, right?" Savvy asked. She'd been tasked with mixing the chopped vegetables into the cooled pasta and dousing the mixture with Italian dressing. My stomach growled. This wasn't typical Dawson fare, but I was surrounded by good food and I wasn't going to ignore it.

"Yes." I owed Dawson. He had plenty of bodies, but I couldn't stay home when he was working cattle all weekend. I had plenty to do, but so had he when my leg had been in a cast.

Eva took a drink of her beer. "You're coming back to hang out tomorrow night too, right?"

All the women looked at me, waiting for my answer.

Anxiety tightened my body. The tip of my knife hadn't moved from where it had sliced through a strawberry. "Sure?"

Eva grinned. "Good. It'll be fun to actually talk to you instead of running into you here and there."

I readjusted the paring knife and cut another hunk. My mouth was watering. Fresh strawberries. As fresh as Montana could get, and they were the best in the spring. I could eat a bushel. I loved a good grilled steak—I was a rancher—but all the fruit littering the counter was a luxury. By the time they were marked for sale at the store, mold had usually started to grow.

"Yeah. Same." I couldn't claim my conversational skills didn't need sharpening. I had no skills. I wasn't invited to birthday parties, or sleepovers, or girls' nights out.

Savvy swooped in for the save. "Hey, wanna see pictures from our trip?" She poked at her phone. A picture of a couple flashed across the screen. The guy had a lazy grin that reminded me of Dawson and the woman had dark hair and mischievous eyes. "These two are my best friends. I think the next time we go back will be for their wedding."

She thumbed through several more, rattling off details. A small cabin tucked in the woods that Xander had helped build after she had cleared the area of fallen trees. A tall mountain with a snowy peak. The hiking and camping business her friends ran and lived in was situated at the base of that mountain, a great place to gather selfies of her and Xander to post on any and all platforms.

Savvy tucked her phone away and went back to stirring the pasta dish. "Since I started doing videos of Xander outside working, we get crazy traffic."

Eva nudged her. "Does he have his shirt on or off?" She cleaned up the dishes Savvy and I were done with.

"Off as often as possible. I'm shameless." She stopped with her wooden spoon mid stir. "Think they'll work cattle with their shirts off tomorrow?"

Everyone giggled and I swore half of them groaned. The guys wouldn't take their shirts off, which was for the best. I'd have had to waste time starting profiles on all the social media platforms in order to see them. Dawson without his shirt was worth the time suck.

I cut the last strawberry. Kendall

dumped in blackberries and raspberries. I watched each one fall into the bowl and managed not to lick my lips.

"To be serious for a minute," Kendall said as she pushed the dish to the side, "I'm sorry about your dad."

I blinked against the onslaught of heat behind my eyes. "Th-thanks."

Savvy rubbed my back. I would've flinched, but I was frozen. There was true sympathy in Kendall's voice. Actual comfort in Savvy's touch. Kate crowded close. She wasn't touching me, but her emotional support was all but tangible.

"I'm really sorry," Eva murmured. "I wanted to send a card, but I wasn't sure what Beckett would say or how you'd feel about it. I should've. Fuck it. I should've and I'm sorry."

I rubbed my hands on my pants. Do. Not. Cry. "No. It's all right."

"I'm really sorry too." Kendall rounded the counter to stand on the other side of me. "I guess I left it up to Gentry, but

Dawson told him about running into you at the funeral home."

I winced. It hadn't been one of my better days. Same for Dawson. We'd been as toxic to each other as we'd always been. "Yeah. I just wanted it over with."

Kind of like now. If this was what a funeral for a well-liked person would be like, I'd happily pass. The idea of grieving publicly sounded as pleasant as getting my skin ripped off in inch-long chunks.

The guys wandered in, murmuring about plans for tomorrow. We stared at them from our huddle around the island. Our silence made Gentry and the brothers stop before they entered the kitchen.

"Steaks are done," Gentry announced, breaking the awkwardness.

Kendall sauntered to her husband. "Oh, baby. You know how to sweet-talk me."

"Yuck," Beck said and bypassed his dad to set his tray of meat on the table.

"It's not right," Xander muttered. "I don't care how old we are."

The easy atmosphere between them should've made me feel more like an outsider. But as each of the women broke off to walk to the table with their spouse, Dawson appeared at my side. "Did you find the lemonade?"

"I forgot to get it out!" Eva veered into the kitchen. "Good thing or it would've been gone by now."

I arched a brow at Dawson. "That good?"

"I don't want to brag . . . but I sweet-talk the lemons when I juice them. Then after the sugar, I add strawberries and a splash of cherry juice. There's lime garnishes too."

He wanted me to be impressed. I was. "Did you talk dirty to the cherries when you juiced them?"

Kate sputtered first and the rest of the girls dissolved into laughter. My cheeks bloomed. The first thing they'd heard me say that wasn't defensive or about cattle and it was lewd.

"It's not right," Gentry grumbled.

Humor gleamed in his eyes as he nudged Kendall. "I don't care how old they are."

We all settled into our chairs. Gentry was at one end and Dawson on the other. I sat next to Dawson and to my right was Savvy. I didn't see who passed the food, but someone started a dish and then it was like dealing cards. The dish was handed to the person on our left.

Ten people surrounded the table. I'd been in restaurants with a bigger crowd. But I'd been on the fringes. These people surrounded me. I was eating the same food they were. The room was closing in on me.

A glass of red-tinged lemonade appeared in front of me. I took a big gulp. When the sweet flavor hit my tongue, I kept drinking.

Damn.

When I looked up, Dawson was grinning at me. "Good, right?"

I scowled, but a smile played along my lips. The anxiety that had been building drained under the sugar rush. "You know it is. Everything you make is excellent."

Pride rippled across his expression, but there was a twinkle meant just for me that said, *It's the dirty talk that does it.*

Savvy handed me a basket of rolls that I'd had no idea existed. When had Dawson found the time for all this? "I know you haven't had much to do with the guys until now, but I'm all ears if you know of any embarrassing stories from when they were younger."

The table grew quiet, but the silence wasn't uncomfortable. An anticipatory air filled the room as everyone waited on me.

I wasn't brave enough to look at Dawson. It was Gentry's fatherly nod that broke the seal on my tongue.

"I started running over here when I was too young to be going off alone across the pasture. So Sarah would make Aiden or Beck walk me back. Only they didn't want to, so they talked Dawson into going with them and then ditched us."

Savvy's scandalized inhale was immediately followed by a laugh. "How chivalrous."

"Hey," Beck said as he was cutting his steak. "I was all of like, ten years old."

Which had meant a not-much-older-than-me Dawson running back with me, but always stopping at the fence. It was like we'd both known that Pop would chase him off like a rabid dog.

Yet Pop had never stopped me from going to the Kings'. Not until the funeral.

"What about Xander?" Savvy asked.

A touch of sadness laced Xander's smile. "I made sure to find somewhere else to be. If Mama was busy with Bristol, that meant she'd put us to work."

Aiden set his fork down, a line forming between his brow. "How did I not notice that?"

"Too busy kissing her ass, golden boy," Dawson said around a mouthful of food.

"I did not kiss ass." Aiden narrowed his

eyes and stunned me with an almost smile. "I didn't have to since I was perfect."

"Nah, not you. There was someone else who made sure he was a little better." Xander directed his gaze at Beck.

"Don't," Beck growled.

Xander's grin grew. "What's wrong, Gooder?"

Beck rubbed his temple—but with his middle finger.

"Anyway." Gentry's exasperation was apparent, but it didn't stop his smile. "Any of you coming back for the Fourth? I ran across Nelson Hammond and he said there's going to be a fair and a concert."

Nelson Hammond. The mayor. He was a man I actively avoided. Pop had been to several town hall meetings, raging about some vote or another.

"Would you be ready to have us back so soon, Dawson?" Kendall asked.

"Absolutely," he answered.

Well, that didn't take long. I was already looking forward to the Fourth of July when

Kendall and Gentry would be back. Would I be invited over for more grilling? More visits?

Because if this was how well-adjusted families acted, I was glad I hadn't known what I was missing.

"Want to go to the fair with me, Bristol?"

The fair came to town every year. This year was the first it'd be over the holiday weekend. I hadn't thought anything of it when I'd heard. When I was in seventh grade, Pop had actually let me go. The only stipulation had been that he wouldn't be able to take me home until he was done at the bar. The fair closed at ten p.m. and the bar closed hours later, but I hadn't thought of the logistics. He'd even given me twenty dollars.

A half hour after I'd gotten there, played a few games, and saved enough money for one ride and supper, I'd run across some high school boys. A scrawny Bristol all by herself had made a perfect target.

They'd followed me, relentlessly teasing

me about my tiny tits and a face only a mother would love—*Oh wait, is that why she left?* Even at that age, I'd been known to throw a punch for a strong enough insult, but I couldn't take on three fifteen-year-old boys.

I'd run and waited by Pop's pickup until he'd closed the bar down and gotten tossed out by the fed-up owner.

On the way home, we'd almost hit one of our yearlings that had escaped the pastures.

The remnants of the crappy memory must've shown on my face. Dawson squeezed my hand. "We don't have to go."

"No. It's fine." I couldn't sound more wooden if I tried. Damn it. I wasn't going to let my past with this town haunt my future. These people were more than tolerating me. And by all accounts, they should be the ones to shun me. So, yeah. I was going to that damn fair. "It'll be fun."

"Savvy and I could probably make it,"

Xander offered. I blinked at him, but Savvy nodded.

"I've never been to a fair." Her blue eyes sparkled, her excitement infectious.

Wasn't Savvy's family loaded? How could she have missed out on something as simple and common as a fair? I'd had an experience someone as sophisticated as Savvy hadn't. Weird.

"This is a small-town fair," Xander said. "Half the thrill is wondering if the Ferris wheel is going to hold together."

"Ooh, I can't wait." Savvy turned in her seat. "Xander and I are going to check on the progress of our house and then spend most of June camping in Yellowstone and doing some research for my company. We'll make sure we're back."

"I have an in with the CEO of King Tech." Eva might be smiling at Beck, but her eyes said they were going whether he wanted to or not. "I'm sure we can get off."

Beck wasn't fazed. "I haven't been to the

fair since I was a senior. Do they still have funnel cakes?"

"Yes," Kate answered as she was trimming a hunk of fat off her ribeye. "But eat them fresh. They don't age well." She looked up from her plate and blinked at the guys staring at her.

"You got Aiden to the fair?" Dawson asked, incredulous.

Her chuckle was nervous. "No. He had to work. I brought my nephews and tried to bring a funnel cake home for him."

"Aiden wouldn't risk getting powdered sugar on his laptop," Xander joked.

Kate's gaze dropped to her plate. Aiden lifted a shoulder. "It had dissolved by the time it got home. But it's the thought that counts."

From the forlorn look on Kate's face, it was the effort of getting off work that would've counted.

"The Fourth it is," Dawson said. "Anyone who can make it, come on up."

"The Fourth," Beck agreed. "Right

before your birthday. Could be a big weekend."

Dawson slanted a glare at Beck and everyone shifted. Once again, I was missing something.

I could enjoy the atmosphere of this family all I wanted. I could marvel over how different they were than how I'd thought of them growing up. I could be deliriously happy when I was with Dawson.

But I was the odd one out, and that would never change.

Dawson

I LEANED against the barn door. Kittens twined around my ankles. Staring at my phone, I gently shook my leg as one ambitious tabby tried to climb up.

Hey, kiddo. I'll buy you supper. Meet me at Hogan's.

It was the first of June and Grams was in town. Even worse, she was in town to meet with me. The countdown was on. It was T minus thirty-six days before I turned twenty-nine. I hadn't decided to do anything about the trust but enjoy my time with Bristol. Build her faith in me.

Wrong or right, the conclusion I'd come to, thanks to my brothers' help, was that the best course of action was to build a solid foundation of trust. Then no matter what shit show happened before my birthday, she'd trust me. She'd have faith in us.

The weekend we'd worked cattle had been a good start. She'd been around my brothers with no arguments. No barbs tossed back and forth. She'd come over both nights they were in town and watched the banter between my brothers and me like we were her personal TV show.

The last few weeks had been good. I did my job. She did hers. Sometimes we met up for lunch or dinner at my place. Other times we pitched in to help each other. I could spend every night with her, but I held back.

She hadn't stayed at my place yet. I had no idea why. Was she still unsure about us?

The message reminder buzzed on my phone. Damn. I had to let Grams know. If I didn't meet her, she'd come out here and I didn't trust her within a mile of Bristol's place. If anything could scare Bristol off, it'd be Grams.

There was a new message from Grams. *See you at 7.*

I hadn't answered yet, but to Grams, that didn't matter. I sent back a *K*. Grams wouldn't be deterred and I might as well face-off with her and tell her to butt out. The trust was mine to go for or not as I pleased.

I worked for a couple more hours. The horse trailer blew a tire. I replaced that, then filled in some large divots in the driveway. Running the big John Deere up and down it since March had taken its toll on the gravel. One good rain, and those holes would make their own mud pit, deep enough to pop a tire and wet enough to splash half the pickup with muck. After I was done, I went to the house and cleaned up. I put on black jeans and a navy blue polo. It wasn't like it was a date. Besides, I never had to worry about chasing Bristol off because I had a little dirt on my boots.

The drive to town went fast. I parked by Grams's SUV and went inside.

Skylar met me at the door. Her smile was tense. "How's it going, Dawson?"

"Good. You?"

"Oh. You know." She studied me. "How's Bristol?"

"Good, thanks for asking." Was this the turn we'd been hoping for? People understood the feud had died with us and would start accepting Bristol?

"Mm." That was all she said as she led me around the pillars that blocked the entrance off from the rest of the place. I thought we'd go to the main dining area, but she led me back to the meeting room. What the hell?

The door to the special back room was propped open. Grams's silver bob was easy to spot. My steps faltered. She wasn't alone.

My teeth ground together harder the closer I got. The person with Grams was a young woman.

Skylar stood off to the side of the entrance. She looked from the young woman, who wasn't dressed nearly as casually as I was, to me. "Have a good meal. Your server will be right in."

Yeah. I could see what this looked like. Over a month ago, I'd chewed Skylar out for how she'd treated Bristol and now I was meeting with a woman close to my age who was dressed in a tight black cocktail dress with impressive cleavage on display. Her style wasn't subtle. Not even Grams's presence could make it look like this was a casual setup.

"Grams." I went to the table, leaned down, and kissed her.

"Dawson." Grams beamed, her gaze going to the young lady. "This is Mallory."

"Mallory," I greeted politely. Grams could be a bulldozer. I didn't hold Mallory accountable for agreeing to whatever Grams had pitched. I turned to my grandmother. "You got a new assistant? Finally. After all this time."

Grams's gaze hardened. She didn't suffer fools. Just herself. "Sit. We'll talk. I already ordered."

I yanked a chair out and sat, my arms crossed. My appetite had vanished as soon as I realized what Grams was up to. Was she going to throw women at me until my birthday? "I'm not really hungry. I have some work to finish up at home."

"Dawson." Her voice cracked like a whip, its purpose to force me into compliance.

I was usually the easygoing brother. Not this time. "Grams, I don't know what you're up to—"

"Then let me tell you." Grams leaned

back and crossed one leg over the other. She was in one of her power suits like usual. Mallory shifted, her gaze dropping to her water glass. There was a bottle of wine chilling on the table. What the hell for?

A server swept in with a smile and friendly chatter. She dropped off dinner rolls and the salads that came with whatever Grams had ordered. Her pace picked up as she left. Had she felt the frigid air in the room?

"Your birthday is soon," Grams said as soon as we were alone again.

"I'm aware."

"You need to get married."

"No. I don't."

Grams's eyes flared. Real concern shone in her gaze. "You can't lose that money."

I leaned closer to her. Mallory's gaze was glued to me and Grams like she was watching a fistfight. "I don't need the money."

"Neither does Bristol."

"Bullshit."

Grams winced at my tone. "Dawson, don't be crass in front of our guest."

I smiled apologetically at Mallory. "I'm sorry you're in this mess. Whatever Grams is offering you, I won't agree to it."

"I'm offering you a marriage," said Grams.

I reared back, my horrified gaze connecting with Mallory's. Her cheeks flamed, but she squared her shoulders. I hadn't forgotten how much money was at stake, but I'd forgotten what a good influencer it was.

Grams put her hand on my arm. "Listen to me, Dawson. Mallory is willing to marry you, be as discreet as you want to be. Her NDA is ironclad. I will ruin her if she talks." She ignored Mallory like the woman was a heifer being auctioned off. "Then, when you turn thirty, you two can part ways. Or you two can stay together. You never know. It might work out."

"I'm seeing someone."

Grams's gaze lit, but the light went out a

moment later. She'd figured out who I meant. "You don't need to tell her."

"*What?*" I shook my head. How . . . What . . . How cold was Grams? "I'm not getting married before I'm ready."

"We both know there's no good way to break the news to Bristol. You, and this family, look like an ass either way. We've betrayed her three times already. Think about it, Dawson. Marrying in secret, fulfilling the terms of your trust, then dissolving the marriage when it's done is the only way."

"And if Bristol found out?" I'd never do it. "Wouldn't that be more of a betrayal? Oh, by the way, I didn't want to tell you about this shitty thing my family did, so I *got married* to keep from hurting you?" I pushed away from the table and tipped my head toward Mallory. "I'm sorry your time was wasted."

"I mean, my feelings should be hurt." Mallory's tone was breathless, but her eyes shone under the fluorescent lights. "But that's really sweet. You're, like, really dedicated to your girlfriend."

My stomach turned. Mallory couldn't be more than twenty-two. Probably had a lot of college debt and big dreams. And Grams had used her youthful innocence and promised her fifty million dollars to marry me.

"Dawson." There was the crack again. Grams expected obedience.

I rose. "No. I'm not . . . This isn't . . . you can't interfere with my life."

"I can and I will. I've always looked out for you boys. Did I bake you cherry pies or bounce you on my knee or make trinkets for you to clutter your shelves with? No. I made sure you all were set up *for life*. Life, Dawson. For all of you and your children, so you wouldn't have to work like me and your grandfather, like your dad. I trusted Sarah to take care of it when I gifted her the money. I had no idea that my hard work was at risk." Grams adjusted her suit coat and evaluated me, her face more drawn than I'd ever witnessed. "Fine. Go. But listen to me, kiddo. You go ahead and tell her. Test this relationship of yours. If she's anything like the rest of her family was, she'll ditch you in two seconds. You make one mistake and a Cartwright doesn't forget. They'll trash your name all over town."

"I'm not you and DB. She's not Danny and she's not her grandparents."

"Fine. Then tell her." My mouth tightened and she nodded. She rose and crossed to me. She gripped both of my shoulders. "That money can change lives and I'm going to make damn sure it doesn't change hers for the better."

The threat in her voice gave me shivers. Bristol was younger than me, and Grams wanted to see her suffer? Was Grams taking her anger at Mama out on Bristol?

It didn't make sense. None of this did. I couldn't be around Grams for one more minute. "Have a safe drive back to Billings." I spun on my heel and started for the door.

"If you don't tell her, I will."

I stopped. My hands clenched. Why did everyone assume that after the trust was revealed, Bristol would break up with me? Was it so hard to believe that we'd be strong enough to get through it? "I want you to stay away from her. She doesn't deserve the way you treat her."

"She already cost me my daughter. She's not getting the money that was meant for you."

I shook my head. My opinion of Grams before this had been that she was Grams. She was who she was. But this was a new low. "Grow up, Grams." And I walked out.

I passed Skylar by the front door. I must've looked like a funnel cloud on the loose. She hugged a menu to her chest and didn't speak to me as I passed. But her slight nod spoke volumes.

I slammed out the door and jumped in my pickup. I wasn't thinking about where to go. There were only two places on this earth I would want to go. To my place, or

Bristol's. Since Bristol was probably still working, my place wasn't the answer.

The large door to her shop was open. Since Tucker had helped me fix it, she'd been in the shop a lot. The haying tractor was inside. She must be working on it.

I parked by her pickup. She poked her head out of the open shop doors. Her quick smile died as she saw my expression.

I hopped out. The wind ruffled my neatly combed hair.

Bristol wiped her hands off on a rag she'd shoved in her back pocket. "Please tell me that your shitty mood after meeting with your grandma isn't about me."

"It's her problem," I said. I went straight for her. Like I had to wipe off the taint of an almost blind date by touching the person I wanted to be with. I wrapped my hands around her waist and buried my nose in her hair.

Faint scents of horse, sunshine, and tractor exhaust mingled together with her fruity shampoo. It was perfect.

"She tried setting me up. She even brought another woman along."

Bristol jerked back, her gaze raking my expression. "Seriously? She hates me that much?"

I'd told her most of it. Why couldn't I tell her the rest?

I couldn't tell her that my old-enough-to-know-better-than-all-of-us grams blamed her for Mama's death. We'd all been hurting for so long, I wasn't going to let Grams drag me and my brothers backward. And she wasn't fucking with Bristol's feelings.

"I don't know what she's thinking. I only know that I told her off and came straight to you."

"You told Emilia Boyd off?"

"Yeah." The feeling inside me wasn't righteousness, or pride, or satisfaction. I'd feel better if I could just tell Grams that I wasn't taking that money. I doubt Dad and my brothers would bat more than an eye after the talk we'd had. Grams was a different story. She wasn't one to let it go and walk away. She'd screwed over her best friends, Bristol's grandparents. She'd almost run the oil company into the ground, but she'd held on to enough shares to keep Dad and Aiden toiling away. She'd thrown money at a woman to get her to marry me, and she'd done the same with Beck before he'd met Eva. She would've done the same to Xander, but he'd made himself unreachable. Aside from that, Bristol would feel betrayed—by me, not by Mama.

"I'm sorry you had to do that." Bristol feathered her hands along my hair.

"You're worth it." Grams's threat stayed with me. I crushed my lips to Bristol's. I needed her to know how I felt. How much she meant to me.

My birthday was coming too damn quick.

ristol

His kiss was demanding, yet desperate. The argument with his grandmother had upset him. He might not know why, but I did.

Everyone liked Dawson.

That was probably why we'd mixed like oil and water until we'd come together like peanut butter and jelly. He hadn't been able to stand that I didn't like him when everyone else in King's Creek kissed the ground he walked on.

Being on the outs with his grandma was worse. She was supposed to love him unconditionally, and maybe she did—it'd be hard to tell with Emilia Boyd, but she wasn't entranced by his charm. And he'd had to lose his temper with her.

I met the strokes of his tongue with my own. It'd been a long day, and I'd been thinking about exactly what I wanted to do after my shower tonight. I'd planned to clean up and head to my hot neighbor's and let him work all the knots out of my tense body.

He excelled at getting me to relax. And making me laugh.

I hadn't known how little humor there'd been in my life until we'd quit being oil and water. Yet, I didn't have to tolerate other people to know that no one could get me to laugh like Dawson.

I wasn't good with words. He'd come to mean a lot to me in the last couple of months. My feelings for him terrified me. I wouldn't speak them. I couldn't. Not yet.

But I could show him. I could take away his tension, the way he'd done for me so many times.

I tugged his shirt from his pants and dipped my fingers under his waistband. He groaned against my mouth. My back hit the frame of the shop, but I didn't want to go inside. The warmth of the day lingered behind the sun that was setting on the horizon. Oranges and reds filled the sky.

I flicked open his fly. My fingers brushed over the broad tip of his erection. I wrapped my hand around his hot length and worked him free of his underwear and pants without stripping him down.

I broke the kiss, gazing into his hooded eyes, and lowered myself to my knees.

"Bristol, you don't have to . . ." He looked around, but we were alone. The cattle were in the pastures. Bucket was off grazing and Daisy was napping in the barn.

No one but Tucker and Kiernan ever stopped by and they were done for the day.

We were blissfully alone.

"Let me do this for you." I pumped his dick, loving how hard he'd gotten since I'd touched him. He pulsed under my hand.

I held his gaze as I licked across the tip. The shudder that traveled through his body vibrated into my hand.

I never would've guessed that one day, I would hold Dawson King captive with nothing but the tip of my tongue. From caustic comments to licking him senseless. That was the trajectory of our relationship.

My eyelids drifted shut as I sucked him into my mouth, as deep as I could tolerate. I fisted the base of his shaft and his groan was more ragged than before.

"Fuck, Bristol."

I hadn't done this for him yet. I didn't ignore this part of his body. He had a nice dick. Long and thick. Ropey with veins. Its bronzed color was a darker shade than even his forearms. I'd felt every glorious inch. But I hadn't put my mouth on him yet.

I pulled back, slicking my tongue down his length as I went. He buried his hands in my hair. My ponytail hindered him, but he remained gentle. His fingers would tense, but as I stroked up and down, he didn't push the pace faster.

This blow job proved that sex with Dawson didn't compare to anything else in my past. After high school and getting treated like I was either a tick on some unseen scoreboard or a bad call that was soon forgotten, I hadn't met anyone I'd wanted to do this for.

The few times I had, I couldn't escape the cringe afterward. The reflexive way my body drew into itself, waiting for the fallout. And it hadn't been much different than high school; only the feeling that they were somehow owed oral sex was new.

The way Dawson thrust his hips like he couldn't help himself. The reverent way he touched my hair. The awe that resonated in his moans. It all made me feel like he treasured this act between us. Just like when he went down on me, he made me feel precious. Like he didn't take for granted that I was opening myself up to him.

I wanted to make him feel the same, and it was easy. His reactions heightened the pleasure I received giving him pleasure. A cycle that kept on giving.

I cupped his ball sack with my other hand, lightly massaging them.

"Bristol. Fuck." Those two words seemed to be all he could get out.

I worked him faster. Satin-covered steel slid between my lips. He pulsed in my mouth and his hips jerked with each touch of my tongue.

He wasn't going to last long.

Taking a page from his book, I toyed with him. Backing off on the speed and pressure, I snuck a glance at him.

The hard planes of his face were shadowed. A hunk of his hair hung over his forehead and if I didn't know better, his expression looked like he was in pain. Exquisite agony.

I hummed against him and his eyelids fluttered. He caught me watching him. "You're killing me, woman."

I would've smiled, but my mouth was stretched wide. Retribution gleamed in his eyes. He was going to pay me back tenfold, and it didn't matter that he did this to me every time he touched me.

Pulling back, I let him pop out of my mouth, and I blew against his wet skin.

He shivered and his sides heaved. "God, that's just mean."

"I hope so." I drew him back into my mouth. The shock of my hot mouth on his cooling, sensitive skin sent another tremor through his strong body.

"Never mind. That's worse," he grunted and his head dropped back. "In all the best ways."

I worked him faster, then slowed, just like he had the first time he'd gone down on me. But I'd been on my back. If I kept it up too much longer, he'd topple and I was in no position to catch him.

Increasing the suction and speeding up my pace, I brought him to the brink. His balls tightened in my hand and he went rigid.

"Bristol." It was a warning, but I didn't pull away. For once, I didn't have to decide what the hell I was going to do when it came to this point. I sucked him in and he came with a long groan, his body jerking.

I swallowed his hot release and eased up on the pressure I was applying until he was done. His hands balled in my hair, but he didn't pull and tug. As soon as he tumbled down from his peak, he sagged, his hands brushing down my face.

I released him and rose, not bothering to dust off my knees. I wiped off my mouth as he tucked himself into his pants. He left his fly open and flipped his shirt over it.

He wrapped me in his arms and planted a kiss on my lips. I stiffened with my hands on his shoulders, unsure of how to react. Kissing him after he was done with me was no big deal, but this role reversal wasn't something I'd experienced.

"Thank you," he murmured against my lips.

"You're welcome?"

He chuckled and buried his face in my neck. His embrace tightened and I hugged him back. "I just want to take you home and stay in bed all night."

"I was finishing up when you arrived."

He straightened but didn't let me go. "Have you eaten yet?"

"I had a bite." A can of ravioli—cold. Supper of champs.

"Was it prepared by Chef Boyardee?"

I gave him a playful glare. "Food snob."

"I haven't eaten yet, but I can make something for both of us. What do you need done in here? I can help you wrap up."

"I was going to change the oil in the 8320, but I need to run to town for a new filter. And some lube for the baler."

"Filters and lube. Dammit. Thanks for reminding me. I guess I'll be running to town tomorrow too." He looked around. "Where's Daisy? I miss my girl."

"I don't think she'll mind sleeping at your place, but Bucket's going to get jealous."

He grinned and tipped his forehead against mine. "I have to let you go so we can get home."

My heart surged when he said home. I was home, but I missed his place too. I could get all sappy and think that wherever he was had begun to feel like home, but at his place, he could move around without bumping his head and shoulders. And at his place, I could find the peace that I'd never known.

When I was in his home, even after my leg had healed, I was taken care of. For the first time in my life, I had help. Each time I went back there, I was reminded of what my little RV, and the cabin I was putting off moving to for the summer, couldn't provide. Security. Shelter from my financial problems. All I had to do in the RV was open my eyes. Would it stand up to the next big thunderstorm? Would the patches I'd made to the cabin's roof hold in the next downpour? How did I demolish the trailer when I needed its bathroom?

Those worries didn't touch me at Dawson's. I could get real sleep without staying half alert the whole night, waiting for a gust of wind or the whack of hail to pound through my shelter.

It wasn't the sturdy house that Gentry had built. It wasn't that Dawson had the know-how and money to fix any minor or major problem that arose. It was Dawson. It was not being alone all the damn time. It was having support.

My stomach picked that moment to disturb my thoughts and stop the words that wanted to tumble out of my mouth. Words I'd never told anyone before.

Dawson chuckled at the low rumble in

my belly and twined his fingers through mine. "I've got something for that."

"You always do." I let him lead me to his pickup. I usually drove myself if I stayed at his place, but like him, I didn't want to be apart.

Dawson

MORNING SEX WAS A DOUBLE-EDGED SWORD.

I kicked my hips forward, loving the low moan I earned from Bristol as her body clamped around me.

It wasn't like an early workout. With one of those, I'd get done, feel better, wash up, and bounce out to work. A workout felt good. I damn well felt better each time I got Bristol to lose control around me. But I didn't want to go to work when I had a naked redhead with long legs and perky tits in bed.

I pumped faster. She was close to another orgasm and I couldn't believe I was ready to go again after last night. But all I'd needed was to see the fall of hair over her face and feel her tight body against mine and I'd been ready to go.

And I'd wanted to blow her mind as much as she had mine in the entrance of her shop.

Goddamn.

It'd been a while since I'd gotten head, and it wasn't like it'd ever been a common occurrence in my life. It wouldn't have mattered. What Bristol had done to me was unparalleled. She didn't drop to her knees to get 'er done and get it over with. She'd strung me along and enjoyed it too.

I changed my angle to one I knew was sure to drive her nuts and was rewarded with her body convulsing around me. Pulsing heat surrounded me and her fingers curled into my shoulders, the bite of her nails enhancing my own pleasure.

I hissed and thrust hard, losing myself

inside of her. I managed to keep my weight off her as I shook through my release. Good thing I was already on my knees.

This woman.

I collapsed and rolled to my side, sliding my hand down to rest over her rounded breast.

Her hair was spread around her, fiery like a sunrise. She ran her fingers up my stomach, tracing my abs. "I'm going to be too sore to work today."

"Leftover pizza will help." I'd made enough last night for breakfast. I didn't want Bristol to leave this house without one decent meal today.

"Mmm. I happened to work up an appetite."

We both rolled out of bed. I let her use the bathroom first, gave her a kiss when she walked out, then ducked in. By the time I was out, she'd let Daisy out and had the pizza in the microwave to heat up. My coffee cup was filling.

She still didn't drink coffee, but that

didn't stop her from making my morning dose.

"Thanks." My phone buzzed. It was a message from Tucker. He was working early today to get out in time for his daughter's softball game. "Damn." He'd found a hydraulic leak on the main tractor we used for feeding. "Looks like my day is going downhill from here."

I rotated the phone to show Bristol the message. "Need anything from town? I'm going there first."

"I'll message you if I do, thanks."

We chowed down on our food and put our dishes in the sink like we were a synchronized team. Then we went outside and were rushed by Daisy.

I bent down to get my special greeting from the excited dog that'd seen me just an hour ago. "I'll give you a ride back," I told Bristol.

"No need. I remember the way."

I straightened and looked at the path between the pastures we used to run when we were kids. "You're taller than the fences this time."

I gave her a long kiss before she left. When I turned around, Tucker was exiting the shop. I crossed to meet him in the middle of the drive.

Tucker adjusted his hat and squinted in the direction Bristol and Daisy had disappeared. "She's getting to be a pretty common fixture at your place."

"Yeah."

He cocked his head. "Don't mean to be a downer, but what happens if this thing doesn't work out between you two?"

"It'll work out."

"I hope so. You haven't acted this way with anyone else."

"What way?"

Tucker screwed his face up, like he couldn't believe I had to ask. "Like you thought about them longer than a half a second after your date."

"I wasn't like that." I made sure I wasn't a callous dick. Most of the women I'd been out with were still on friendly terms with me. I was invited to weddings and shown pictures of their kids.

He lifted a brown brow. " 'Hey, Dawson. How was your date last night?' " He turned like he was continuing the conversation with himself. " 'Fine. Did you get the pallet of mineral moved or do you need me to do it?' "

"I'm not one to kiss and tell."

"From the talk I've heard, you're not one to kiss much at all."

I scowled. "I . . . did things."

"Maybe with a select few. But if someone asked you out, you didn't want to hurt their feelings telling them you weren't interested, so you said yes. You'd have a nice old meal, you'd pay, and then you'd keep seeing them until they got the message there was no future or met someone who gave a shit."

"It wasn't like that." It'd been exactly like that. I had fooled myself, thinking I'd fooled any of them.

"Whatever. My point is, it's not like that at all with Bristol. You've actually missed her. She's sleeping over. But you're still neighbors. I get the relationship is young, but other than that one time you two went to Hogan's, you've kept it quiet."

"It's no one's business."

"No, but we all know better. You said you've been dating since she was almost out of her cast. That was, what? A month and a half ago? Where have you gone?"

Tucker knew what had happened at Hogan's, and that I'd taken her to Billings. What was he getting at?

"You can't hide out here and pretend you've got a good thing going. The town loves you. They love your family. They hate her. You tried to champion her and then you quit. Maybe she wanted you to, hell, I don't know. I never thought I'd be sticking up for Bristol Cartwright, but either you're with her . . . or you're just stringing her along like everyone else."

Because I was a nice guy. Wasn't that

what Bristol had said? Tucker certainly had. "I'm not doing it on purpose. I don't want to see her hurt."

"I get it. But you know why I got divorced?" Tucker never talked about his marriage. He'd talk about being a single father, and that he'd been married, but he didn't speak about the specifics. "She was a people pleaser on steroids. She'd do whatever anyone else needed until she ran herself into the ground and inside a bottle of pills. Couldn't have anyone dislike her. Wouldn't talk about her issues. Had to put on a show. You can do that for Bristol until you implode or she starts to feel like a dirty secret. Your choice. But the cost comes out of somewhere."

"Jesus, Tucker." What he said resonated, but I lashed out anyway. "I had a really good night and you're making me feel like shit."

"I get it. I do. But I've also never seen you . . ." When I arched a brow, he leveled me with a steady gaze. "In love."

I wasn't about to admit something like that to him. Bristol would be the first to know after I admitted it to myself. I'd told one other girlfriend that I'd loved her and I hadn't meant it. I hadn't felt it, but I'd wanted to. I had thought I should.

What I felt for Bristol diminished the puppy love from college. Swamped it. Trampled it.

So, yeah. I'd fallen in love with Bristol and it'd been inevitable. It was right. If Mama hadn't died, would we be married with kids already? Would we have been childhood sweethearts? Would we have snuck around on her pop? Would we have been friends, seeing others, until we came to our senses and realized the only half to our whole was each other?

That was what had happened, but rockier, so much rockier for her. I might've pulled her out of a frozen pasture, but I hadn't saved her from anything else. I hadn't taken her out again to show the town the girl I was crazy about was one of our own.

Except for the day she'd hurt herself, she didn't need saving. I'd been conscientious of that. But I'd swung too far the other way.

I adjusted my hat to keep the sun out of my eyes. "I'll think about what you said."

"Good. Cuz I need you to move that pallet of mineral while I help Kiernan fix the feeding tractor."

"I'm still not telling you about my dating life."

"Don't want to hear it, man. I think Bristol would gut both of us if you spilled too much." He swaggered around the shop to where Kiernan's truck was parked. The back end of his pickup was weighed down with mineral for the cattle. He'd back up to the shop. I'd get it from there.

I wandered into the building. Cool air hit me, along with the faint scents of exhaust and oil. Large ceiling fans circulated the air. In the hottest part of summer, it would stay pleasant inside.

I hopped in the little electric forklift and whizzed to his pickup. He'd already dropped the tailgate. By the time I was done maneuvering the pallet to the other end of the shop, I'd decided where I wanted to take Bristol.

We needed to go to the bar. I usually went a few times a month when my brothers weren't around. I didn't need to troll for women. I had friends that I hadn't seen in months—since I'd brought Bristol home.

My friends should know I was seeing someone. Tucker was right. Part of the reason I avoided town with Bristol was because I didn't want to deal with the bullshit. I didn't want her to deal with it either, but nothing was changing if I didn't go anywhere with her.

The crap I didn't want to shovel wasn't just how others treated her and the way they might act around me because I was seeing her. It was the damn trust. Last night, we'd connected on a deeper level than ever before. She trusted me.

I loved her.

No question she was the one for me. We were making progress, and after so many years of feuding, we'd gone this far despite our past. What Bristol and I had wasn't ordinary. She was special. We clicked together like two links of a chain. The two of us were stronger together.

But in town, there'd be more than the two of us and I'd have to work harder to keep her from withdrawing. I didn't have time to deal with the doubts others might put into her head.

She trusted me. Did she love me? I didn't know. But I needed all the time we had to add links to our chain before it was tested by the damn trust.

ristol

A COOL BREEZE blew through town, wicking the heat of the afternoon sun off my skin. June was the perfect month. Not too hot yet. Not too cold. And the snow was gone. Cattle were in the pastures they'd stay in all summer. Since it was just me, I didn't have as many head as the land could hold. They could stay in the same pasture all season and have enough to graze. My biggest concern was keeping my haying equipment running.

I wouldn't have to hay until the middle of July, but thanks to all the help from Dawson and the guys last month, I had time to check on all my equipment before a rainstorm barreled down on King's Creek and forced me to rush baling.

Which was why I was in town in the middle of the afternoon.

I needed an oil filter for the pickup. I tossed my sunglasses on the seat next to me and slid out. The hardware store was in a new building on the opposite end of town from my place. Nelson Hammond, the town's mayor, had built it a few years ago. The farm and ranch industry around King's Creek, and the hour-plus drive to either Miles City or Billings, kept the store in the black.

Inside, I went directly for the filters— and stopped when I saw Emma. I rounded the end cap and stared at oil plugs in the next aisle. I didn't need any, but I wouldn't have to make nice with the nurse who used to date Dawson.

It wasn't that I was jealous. It was that . . . I didn't know how to act. She'd been kind to me. She'd seemed to care and it hadn't been an act to impress Dawson. Did I just say hi? Did I nod? Or since we weren't at her work, she could act differently and I'd realize she'd only been nice because it was her job.

I didn't *people* well. I only knew how to be a Cartwright, and I didn't want to default to that.

I peeked down the aisle to see if she'd moved on yet. A man curved around the other side just as Emma selected a box from the shelf.

"Whaddya need, Emma?"

My stomach dropped. Ugh. I knew that booming voice. Creeper Hammond. His real name was Crawford or something that was supposed to be cultured enough for the son of Nelson Hammond, whose father had also been mayor. But every female under the age of thirty called him Creeper. He'd embraced the nickname like it was Bruiser or Maverick.

Creeper strutted around town like he was a gimme for the next election his daddy didn't run for. In high school, he'd tried to pin me against the lockers and feel me up when the hallway was empty. I'd shoved him away, late for class, then gotten detention because he'd told the teacher I'd punched him.

I had. I'd kneed him in the balls too.

So Creeper didn't mess with me, but I'd heard enough murmurings over the years to know he hadn't changed and he was body positive in the worst way. Several pictures of his privates floated around the internet and landed uninvited in women's inboxes. *When in doubt, whip it out* had become his motto. I wouldn't be surprised if he had some date-rape experience under his belt that his daddy had swept under the rug.

"Uh, nothing," Emma said cautiously. "I'm just getting some oil."

Creeper's voice dropped a few octaves. "You have a leak that needs to be plugged, Emma?"

I could've gagged. How could a grown man not hear how gross that sounded?

"No. I'm finding what I need. Thanks, Creeper." Emma held strong, but that wasn't going to be enough to get Creeper to leave her alone. It was coffee time. All the old ranchers that shopped here in the morning would be at the diner on Main Street. Everyone else would drop by during their lunch hour or after work. Creeper thought he had Emma to himself for a few minutes.

"Come on," he coaxed. "Tell me what you need. I bet I've got it."

"Actually, if you could just move over a

few inches, I can find what I need and be on my way."

"A few inches," Creeper purred and a shudder raced down my spine. Ick. "Let me show you that I have more than a few—"

I charged around the end cap and strode down the aisle. Creeper saw me first and dropped his hand from his fly. His face lost a few shades of color before annoyance took over.

"Hey, Creeper." I didn't slow. Emma's eyes grew wide. "Do you still have my footprint on your nuts?"

"Cartwright." His mouth twisted like I'd shoved a lime between his thin lips. "Go on about your own business. We don't need—"

"But you're going to show your junk to Emma? I didn't hear her ask for it. In fact, she asked you to back off."

"What are you talking about? I'm not dropping trou in the middle of the store."

Emma spoke up. "I heard that you like to flash, and I wish I could continue not believing it. Should we call you Flasher instead?"

Creeper flushed a blotchy red.

I cocked my head. "I agree. Creeper isn't strong enough to describe how you shoved your hand up my shirt."

He sneered. "Why would I do that? You ain't got no tits."

I was about to tell him that he was an asshole who should be in jail, but Emma beat me. "You open your mouth and insult Bristol one more time and I'm going to be the one to kick you in the balls, Creeper. Don't talk to me. Don't touch me. We all know that you won't get in trouble cuz your daddy swoops in to save you, but I will stomp on that little dick if I see even a shadow of it. Do you understand?"

He reared back, glaring at me as if the words had spilled out of my mouth instead of hers.

Emma shoved a finger in his face. "I've dealt with irate drunks. I've been vomited on. And I've had old ladies try to bite me.

I'm not afraid of you, Crawford Hammond, and more importantly, I don't get paid to put up with you. There's no other place in town to get some oil, so get out of this aisle and leave me and Bristol alone."

She stuffed her hands on her hips and glared at him. She was several inches shorter. Not even her messy top bun reached his nose. But she loomed over him.

I snapped my mouth closed and tried to look fierce when I was actually astonished. I'd never seen anyone tell Creeper off. I crossed my arms and tapped my boot.

Creeper's lip stayed curled. "Didn't realize it was PMS week." He spun and charged away.

Emma turned toward me and bit her lip. "Thank you so much."

My eyes went wide. "What? I didn't do anything."

"I thought I was alone, other than the cashier who isn't going to risk her retirement job to stop the owner's son from being a sex offender. Then you were there, telling him off." She shook her head and the steel in her spine was gone. Her steady gaze wavered and she worried her lower lip. "I wasn't going to let him tell everyone that you were a bitch when you were tough enough to stand up to him. I just stood here shaking in my shoes like a scared rabbit."

She'd tried being nice to him to keep from being accosted. I'd never had to do the same. For the first time, I was grateful for my reputation. "If he ever bothers you again, I've got a shovel, rope, and a lot of land."

She giggled and snorted, then put her hand over her mouth and laughed. "Oh my god, we'd have so much help hiding the body," she whispered. "And no one would tell. We'd be heroes."

I looked around. The joke was morbid, but I couldn't stop from laughing with her.

She saw my conflicted expression and waved it off. "Sorry. You get a sick sense of humor working in the medical field. How's your leg?"

I kicked out my right leg. "Getting better."

"PT went well?"

I hadn't been around Emma much, but I was learning that I couldn't hide anything from the nurse.

"You didn't go. I understand. It's a lot after all the doctor's visits," she sighed and glanced at the shelves of oil. "How about I get my oil and we get coffee next door?"

"I don't drink coffee." I froze like I'd been asked on a date by the most popular guy in school. Only I was already dating the most popular guy in school and I was way more chill around him.

"You can watch me drink." She giggle-snorted again. "Sorry, that sounded like a Creeper invite."

I snickered. "I won't kick you in the nuts if you don't try to grope me. I need a filter, then sure."

She selected a two-cylinder oil for a new lawn mower she was excited to try. I grabbed my filter and a package of root beer barrels.

"I haven't had one of those in forever," she said as we were leaving the store.

"I don't usually buy them. But Pop used to get them when I was little."

"It's hard, isn't it?" When I glanced at her, she shrugged. "When addiction steals our loved ones. It's like pieces of them get taken so slowly you don't realize how little of them is left with you."

We reached the coffee shop at the edge of the parking lot, far enough to have their own independence from the Hammond-owned hardware store. "You have experience?"

"Some. Not a parent. But I see it a lot at work. There are a lot more alcoholics in town than people would think. Your dad wasn't the only one, but I think he took the outrage for them all."

Fitting. Pop had gotten the shit for what his parents had gone through, and then for what everyone else went through with their loved ones. He'd taken the blame for a lot he hadn't done in life until eventually he'd earned all the blame.

The smell of coffee greeted us as we entered. A group of older men surrounded a little table in the corner, playing pinochle. The young barista, Taya, was the owner of Creek Coffee. It'd been downright scandalous that she hadn't used King as the moniker instead of Creek, but she wasn't native to town. She'd moved to King's Creek and wasn't afraid to buck the trend.

"Morning, Emma," she called, her gaze going from Emma to me. I expected the usual flash of derision in her gaze, or at least some superiority. But other than a hint of curiosity, I couldn't detect anything negative. She smiled in greeting. "Welcome."

Did she seriously not know who I was?

"Hi, Taya," Emma replied. "This is Bristol. She doesn't drink coffee. What do you have other than water?"

Taya pushed her dark hair off her face

and propped a hand on her hip. "Let's see, do you like really sweet, or more mellow like tea?"

Pop used to say that tea was nothing more than weeds someone had pissed on. I couldn't drink it without that imagery. "I like sweet."

"An Italian soda coming right up." She tapped a placard by the cash register. "Pick a flavor, any flavor. I can mix and match too."

I was digging out my wallet while I read the list. Emma put her hand on my arm. "You saved me from Creeper. Let me treat."

My inner being rebelled. I didn't want charity. But I'd seen how Tucker, Kiernan, and Dawson treated each other. Some days, Tucker arrived with a carafe from Creek Coffee for the three of them. Other days it was Kiernan with donuts or bagels. Also supplied by Creek Coffee. And then there was Dawson's Sunday night Bake-Offs. I'd helped him prepare extra coffee for the guys that morning.

It was what friends did. Acquaintances even.

"Okay, but only if you let me buy next time." Oh, god. Had I just asked her out? It hadn't been this awkward to ask a guy out.

Emma grinned and handed a twenty to Taya. "Deal."

I ordered a strawberry cream Italian soda and followed Emma to a table.

After we sat, she looked straight at me. "At the risk of being nosy . . . you and Dawson, huh?"

Her mouth twitched like she was holding back a grin. I didn't sense jealousy or the need to gather gossip to spread around town. "Me and Dawson," I confirmed.

"He finally wore you down?"

"I guess you could say that."

Her eyes crinkled as she smiled. "Good. That man needed to work for it. After you two came into the ER that night, I hoped you'd give him a good run for it."

"You're not upset?"

Her brows popped. "Because we dated? No. I think most of us ladies want to know what it's like. He's hot. He was nice enough. But . . ." Her forehead furrowed. "I want the guy I end up with to do anything to be with me. No coasting. No humoring. No hemming and hawing." She leaned forward. "I want the chemistry you two had in the ER. I mean, he would've carried you to town to get you to the doctor."

"He would've done that for anyone." And I meant it. That was the thing about that day. He'd done it for me when I would've been voted Most Likely to Be Left in a Ditch by Dawson King.

"He would've. Then he would've tipped his hat and been on his way. He wasn't leaving your side. I crossed my fingers for you."

I winced. "I might disappoint you."

She laughed and the pinochle players glanced at us. Taya dropped off our drinks and I tried not to down mine in one pull after the first taste. "Well, I'm glad it's working out. And I'm glad I got to know the real you. You were always so quiet in school."

I arched a brow. "Quiet? I was always in the principal's office."

"Because the other kids wouldn't quit fucking with you. They knew you'd take the fall. It's why they kept doing it."

I stared at her. The second time in twenty minutes she'd made my jaw drop. "I mean, I knew that, but I didn't think anyone else noticed." Or cared.

"Yeah, we noticed. But none of us had your balls." She put her hand on her chest in a faux dramatic gesture. "Speak up in a small town? Side with the infamous Bristol Cartwright?" She dropped her hand. "It would've been social suicide for a cheerleader who could barely name the fifty states. Anyway, I felt like shit for it. I'm sorry."

"Why? You weren't teasing me."

"No, but I could've said something."

"I appreciated your help in the hospital."

Her smile was quick. "I use my position to speak up now. You weren't treated very well and I reported it."

Third time my jaw hit the ground. "What? Really?" Her determined expression confirmed it. "He was a dick."

"He's always a dick. He needs to get fired, but not many doctors want to come to a small town and take calls at all hours." She took a sip from her foamy coffee. "Did I steal you away from work?"

I shrugged. "If the sun is up, then I should be working." But since I'd met Dawson, I'd taken more time off than ever. I couldn't depend on him and his workers to bail me out. I'd have to figure out how to grow. How to afford my own help. How to ranch more like a business than a hobby. And to do that, I'd have to work hard enough to earn the money. But I couldn't bring myself to end the coffee date.

"I won't keep you long. I have a lawn to mow and you have cattle to do whatever it is you ranchers do. But we'll have to do this again. Without the harassment first."

I polished off my Italian soda. "Sure." I had the same attitude as when I'd start dating someone. They could reach out if they wanted to see me again. I wasn't going to go begging for company.

"I have another Monday off in a couple of weeks. I usually only work three twelves but we have a nurse out on maternity leave and two more on vacation. I picked up a ton of overtime, and all the weekends." She rolled her eyes. "The single life."

"Want to meet here again?" I'd pencil it in, but I'd make sure I came to town for another errand. Just in case.

"Yes, and we'll make sure Taya can join us. You'll love her. Oh, give me your number. I'll send you a message so you don't forget."

"I won't forget." My social calendar was nonexistent. But I exchanged numbers with her.

My phone buzzed and I took a quick

peek. Dawson. *Wanna go to The Tap Friday night?*

I set my phone facedown.

"Is something wrong?" Emma asked.

I had a couple of bulls I planned to sell. I could check with local sales barns. One of them might be having a bull sale. That'd give me some extra cash to put back into the ranch—and into myself. "Dawson wants to go out this weekend, but I only have work clothes." I didn't want a repeat of Hogan's. This time I wasn't dressing up for anyone else, not even Dawson.

I wanted to dress up for me.

Emma's eyes lit up. "If you don't have time to run to Billings, my friend has this cute little online shop, but she keeps a lot of her stock in her house. Want me to make an appointment with her?"

Why the hell not? She could dress me in a burlap sack and have a good laugh with her friend, but it'd be a step up from what I had on.

~

Dawson

I PARKED in front of Bristol's RV, whistling as I hopped out, leaving the engine running. I jogged to her door and knocked. Daisy raced toward me.

"Hey, girl. Your mommy around?" I cocked an ear toward the door but didn't hear anything.

"You're early," Bristol called from behind me.

I spun around and my world tilted. *Fuuuuck.*

Bristol sauntered toward me. The rolling sway her boots gave her hips was gone. So were the boots. I took her in from head to toe.

Simple sandals were on her feet, showing an amount of ankle that would've been criminal a couple hundred years ago. Cuffed blue jeans were damn near painted on her long legs, and a baggy striped shirt hung off her shoulders, hinting at all kinds of curves underneath. The outfit was simple and sexy as hell, but only because of who wore it. Her red hair was brushed in a smooth line and hung over one shoulder.

I narrowed my eyes. Was she wearing makeup? No? Yes? If she was, it was a touch around the eyes. Her bright green eyes were softer, but vivid.

"Hell," was all I said.

She stopped in the middle of the drive and looked down at herself. "Is it bad? I thought I could trust Emma, but—"

"You're smokin'." I closed the distance between us. "You were always hot, but this is a different look and it's stunning. It doesn't hide you."

She wrinkled her nose and a blush graced her cheeks. "I have eye shadow on. And Emma's friend Lizette showed me how to . . ." She waved a hand around her head. "The whole hair thing. With a round brush and a blow-dryer."

She'd probably had to buy both.

I wore crisp blue jeans and a clean polo with the logo of a golf course in Billings. I'd blend in just fine, but it wasn't like I'd put in the effort Bristol had. The only change in my routine was that I hadn't put a hat on after I'd showered. My hair was combed and I'd shoved a hand through it so it lay to the side. Boom. Done.

"You didn't have to do this," I said.

"I wanted to. For me." She went to hook her hand through her jeans, but her belt loops were covered by the shirt. "This is going to take some getting used to."

She'd done herself up for herself. My ego wasn't insulted at all. I couldn't wait to walk into The Tap with her on my arm. I held my elbow out. "Ready?"

"Not really."

"You look amazing. Really."

"I know. But people are going to be all weird about it."

"You wanna go change?" I'd undress her myself. The way those jeans caressed her long legs—I had plans for taking them off.

She lifted her chin. "No. Fuck them."

That wasn't just bravado. It was her motto, a mantra to survive on. "That's my girl."

I opened the pickup's door for her and trotted around to the driver's side. "You want to go to Hogan's first for a bite? The Tap has pizza and . . . pizza."

"Bar pizza sounds good."

"I'd be jealous, but I like their pizza too."

She propped her elbow by the window and watched the countryside roll by. Green pastures. Brown buttes dotting the hills. Glimpses of blue from the river valley. My AC blasted and the ends of her hair fluttered.

Times like these were addicting, quiet moments we enjoyed together. I didn't have to ask her to know that she loved what she saw as much or more than I did. We'd grown up running these ditches, riding these pastures, working this land. Our lives were rooted in this area, intertwined for generations.

The buildings on the edge of town came into view. The box hardware store with the coffee shop on the other side of the parking lot. A tidy neighborhood on the opposite side of the country highway. I drove through them on the way to the bar downtown.

Bristol watched it all out the window. Tonight was supposed to be fun for her, not nerve-racking.

"Are you sure you're okay with this?"

She blinked at me. "Yeah. It's fine."

"It'll be fun." I didn't pressure her. As much as I wanted to tell her to say the word and we'd leave, I kept my mouth shut. Bristol had been navigating this community and their attitude her entire life. I'd gone out with her for a few hours, once, and then given up on them.

The parking lot beside the bar was over half full already, but we didn't run across anyone until we went inside. I held the door open for her, my hand on her back as I walked in behind her. She slowed, searching the place for a table.

"Dawson, hey," Jamie, one of the guys I'd graduated high school with, greeted me at the door. "Been a while since I've seen you out—Bristol?" His gaze hung up on her, drifting over her hair, then traveling down her body. His expression grew more incredulous as it went.

"Jamie," Bristol said, her voice neutral.

"How's it going?" I asked, keeping my arm anchored around Bristol. She appeared relaxed, but her body was rigid. I sifted through memories. Had Jamie ever been a dick to her? "How's Natalie?"

He lifted his gaze off my girlfriend, but the disbelief had disappeared. "Good. The guys and I are here for Samuel's bachelor party."

Dammit. Was that tonight? I would've avoided The Tap if I had remembered. "Right. I heard Samuel was tying the knot." My wedding invitation was on the counter. I'd opened it, seen the RSVP, and set it down, forgotten. I put up with Samuel—had my whole life. He was my insurance agent, but that didn't mean I cared to socialize with him. His personality had rolled farther downhill as he'd aged.

Jamie cocked his head. "You're going to the wedding, right? They've reserved the entire block his insurance company is on for the dance. It's going to be a bigger party than the fair."

Samuel was having his wedding on the same night as the street dance the weekend before the fair, knowingly taking business away from a company that refused to do business with him. He'd bragged about it.

He'd been a little rough around the edges in high school, but then he'd gone off to college and joined a fraternity, and not the kind that nurtured young men into becoming contributing members of society. They might've tried anyway, but Samuel moved back to King's Creek with his head full of all the ways he was better than anyone in town.

He catered to me, the ranch was one of his biggest accounts, but he shit-talked almost everyone else. I couldn't believe he'd found a woman who'd put up with him, but then I'd heard he used a lot of dating apps. I had assumed he used them for sex and not to find actual love.

"I'm going to have some family in town that weekend." Thankfully. Otherwise I'd have to nut up and go to the wedding. I'd even be expected to go to the dance afterward.

"King!" I cringed at Samuel's deep shout. "You made it."

"I'm sorry. It slipped my mind, but I made other plans—"

"It doesn't matter if you have a chick with you." His blurry eyes raked over Bristol. "Fuck me. Cartwright?"

"I'll pass," she replied and his laugh boomed across the bar.

"Damn. You clean up good." He clapped

me on the back. "You got the magic dick or what?"

I didn't bother holding back my cringe. I tightened my hold on Bristol, but she didn't appear in danger of leaping the five feet between her and Samuel to deck him. Her gaze was steady, as if she was waiting to see how bad this would get.

She wasn't the only one.

"Come on." Samuel gave an exaggerated wave. "Join the party."

"Sorry to pass, but—"

"Not taking no for an answer, King." Samuel swaggered to a group of tables in the corner. "King is here. Check it out. Hell's frozen over. He's with Cartwright and she's cleaned up *gooood*."

More obnoxious laughter. Half the guys around the table laughed nervously. The other half shifted uncomfortably and studied the tabletop. I couldn't be the only one afraid of what would come out of Samuel's mouth. Maybe they were afraid of what would come out of Bristol's too.

So, this was a shitty start to our date. A little too reminiscent of our first date. I steered Bristol away.

"King. Wait." Samuel elbowed his way back to us. "The party's over here."

"I'm sorry to miss it, but we're just here for a bite to eat."

Samuel threw an arm around my shoulders and another around Bristol's, forcing his way between us. "It's my special night, King. I don't have many more nights left as a single man."

Bristol ducked out of his hold. I stopped, which was a feat with Samuel's inebriated weight hanging off me. "I've gotta go, man."

"You're not going anywhere. Drink. It's on me." He shoved his hands in the air. "It's all on me tonight, boys!" He snickered and loudly whispered in my ear. "Bristol's one of the boys anyway. Don't worry about it."

"She's not—"

He lurched away, beckoning to the server and yelling for a pitcher of beer.

Bristol lifted a brow and edged away.

I caught her hand. "I think it'd be easier to take our pizza and go."

She gave her head a little shake like she hadn't heard me correctly. "Just tell him no."

Samuel didn't do well with no. "Maybe we can sit for a little while." I nodded toward an empty tall table in the corner. The chairs had been taken, but we could stand and eat until Samuel forgot about us.

"Or . . . we could do what we came here to do and Samuel can fuck off."

"Samuel can fuck off," I agreed.

She folded her arms. "So tell him that."

I sighed and turned my back to the bachelor party crowd. The rest of the bar was filling up with couples and groups. They were taking the tables the farthest from Samuel's crowd. "He's my insurance agent. I'm not going to his wedding. If I skip his bachelor party . . ."

"Then he still gets your business and . . . what? I don't see a downside."

"It's . . . rude."

Disappointment rippled through her emerald eyes. "And Dawson King is anything but rude."

My jaw tightened. "I'm not stooping to his level." To Bristol, I must look like a spineless ass. I tried to clarify. "I have to do business with him, Bristol. I don't want to call him up about a claim and hear about how I skipped both his wedding and bachelor party for a half an hour. Then he'll tell the whole office and we'll have a good laugh and he'll try to guilt me into higher premiums." I'd seen him do it to others. Clients would agree to anything to get him to shut up. Hell, I'd done it myself. It was why my deductible was so low when I could afford to pay for a higher one. "Look, if I play nice now, it saves me a helluva headache in the future."

She studied him. "Why not switch somewhere else? My insurance company is online."

"Support local."

"What about when local doesn't support you?" Her question rang with curiosity. "He's purposely screwing you over."

I had no argument. Our experiences in King's Creek were different. The locals supported me and I tried to do the same. "Can we just grab a bite?" My question snapped out harsher than intended. This night couldn't be over with fast enough. I hadn't wanted a repeat of Hogan's but this time I felt like I was the one ruining it.

Her expression blanked. "Sure."

How could I save this night?

As we went to the table, I nodded at a couple more guys sitting around Jamie. Broden Haggins from the gas station. Shelb Old Rock from the grain elevator. Guys I would've liked to talk to on an ordinary night at the bar. Guys who'd probably be decent to Bristol after they got over their shock. Without the bachelor party, tonight would've been the night I'd planned.

We stood at the table. I tried leaning against the wall, but the window frame bit into my shoulder. I straightened but then it looked like I was conducting an interview. I scanned the bar, looking for the server Samuel had no problem flagging down.

"She probably won't be by to take our order."

"Danika? Why?"

Bristol ran her bottom lip through her teeth. "Because Darren Morrel brushed her off to go out with me seven years ago."

"But they're married now."

"She holds a grudge. I didn't know he'd been seeing someone or I would've steered clear of that drama. Thankfully, nothing but a few beers happened before I figured out she was prone to drama and would fight to the death for Darren." She lifted a shoulder. "At least she hates me for something other than being shit poor with an ornery dad."

Danika should brush off her husband, since I'd heard he'd seen a few back seats since saying *I do*.

Bristol stepped away. "I'm going to go to

the bathroom. Maybe she'll come over while I'm gone."

As she wound her way through the bar, her back straight, her chin high, my hopes for tonight shriveled.

ristol

I FINISHED DRYING my hands under the blow-dryer. The silence of the bathroom seeped into my bones and I let my head fall back. The bar was so loud. Samuel's yelling had put my nerves on edge. He was an egotistical jackass and his shouting wasn't aimed at me, but it didn't mean I liked it.

Taking another look in the mirror, I

paused. If someone came in here and saw me checking myself out, I would melt into a pool of embarrassment. This wasn't me. I never cared if my hair was just right or if my clothing was just so. I barely had enough makeup on to worry about smudging, but I verified everything was in place anyway.

Before I could get busted, I stepped into the hallway. How slow could I walk back to the table that was too close to Samuel's party?

"Bristol, a word?"

My entire body tensed at that voice behind me and the gotcha tone that went with it. Errol, the owner and manager of The Tap, loomed under the red glow of the exit sign. He'd never cut Pop off. I'd tried talking to him, but he'd claimed Pop was an adult and it was "only business." It hadn't mattered if Pop couldn't see straight enough to hold his pickup key, Errol had kept pouring.

I didn't spare him a glance. "Not tonight,

Errol." I didn't owe him a minute of my time.

"Then leave."

I stopped and tipped my head. How could he think he had a right to kick me out? "And why would I have to leave?"

"Danika ain't going to serve you."

If Danika didn't serve all the women that Darren made googly eyes at, hit on, or messed around on her with—just since they'd been married—she'd have male-only clientele. He'd married her, so now he couldn't blow her off when another pair of legs caught his interest. She deserved better than him, but I'd pointed it out years ago when he'd acted like she didn't exist and she'd done everything short of covering her ears.

"Then Danika's costing you business," I pointed out.

"I told her not to serve you until you pay your tab."

When would I have run up a tab? Oh.

Right. "Pop's debts aren't mine. Do you need to see his death certificate?"

"Danny's debts are yours when he charges them to the ranch."

My mind whirled, trying to undo the wrongness of his statement. "And why, exactly, would a bar let a ranch start a tab?" Pop wasn't buying booze for the ranch. He'd been a party of one drinking his sorrows down.

Errol folded his beefy arms and stared me down. His handlebar mustache twitched under his nose as he sniffed. He held my gaze and the answer unfolded between us as if invisible words ghosted out of his lips.

It'd been a matter of time before Pop died. Car accident. Alcohol poisoning. Cirrhosis. Bar fight. Errol had wanted his money and he'd thought I'd be good for it.

"You let him run up a tab, thinking I could pay it off when he passed."

"Well, you're here." He looked over my

shoulder. "Danika says you're with a King. You must be good for something."

"Fuck you, Errol."

"You ain't never said that in all the years I've known you. Did I hit a nerve?" He rolled his shoulders, keeping his arms crossed. The red glow of the sign lit his bald scalp like a sinister halo. "Look, I don't care if you're sleeping with him so he can pay off all your daddy's debts, I only care that you find a way to pay for mine."

"You can't expect to get taken seriously for a bar tab you let an alcoholic take out against his failing business."

"You wanna get some legal counsel and find out? Because if I have to pony up a retainer fee, that's going on your tab too."

Suffocating frustration clawed its way up my throat. I ground my teeth together and glared at him. I couldn't pay. Danika wouldn't serve me or Dawson until my "tab" was settled. I didn't bother to ask how much the tab was. I wasn't wasting my hard work on this hole in the ground.

"Everything all right here?" Dawson said. He stopped next to me, his hand going around my waist like he'd done when we'd entered.

I held my glare on Errol. "No. But then I don't expect anything less out of a shithole like this."

"I can do a lot of renovations with what your ranch owes," Errol countered.

"You took advantage of a sick man. You're a piece of shit."

A young girl just past drinking age shot a wide-eyed look at me before she slipped into the bathroom. Guess I'd be keeping my mega-bitch reputation.

Errol's mustache twitched. "Tell yourself what you want to. I'll send the bill in the mail." He disappeared into the storeroom.

"Asshole," I growled under my breath and pivoted to storm down the hallway. I was done with this place. "I want to go."

"Bristol, what—"

"I just want to go."

I sped out of the hallway and crashed

into Danika. Her tray of drinks clattered to the floor, glass shattering and liquid spraying my feet.

"What the hell?" she shrieked. Her eyes narrowed on me and she slammed her hands on her hips.

"It was an accident," Dawson said, angling himself between us like I'd waste my time getting into a fight with her.

I skirted past the mess. "Put it on my tab," I called over my shoulder.

I didn't care if Dawson was behind me. I stormed out, and after the mess I'd left behind, no one got in my way.

Breezing outside, I finally let myself wonder what I'd do if Dawson didn't follow me. I couldn't say I'd blame him. Where I went in town, chaos followed. I attracted the idiots and assholes and I refused to put up with them.

"Bristol. Dammit. *Wait.*"

Any relief I felt at his voice died with his words. I whirled on him. "For what? To get humiliated some more? So Errol can hand me the bill he charged to the ranch because Pop said it was okay?"

"He did what?" He shook his head. "That's dirty."

Yeah. And I was sick of it. I was sick of this town and feeling like I wasn't a part of it when I'd been born and raised here.

Jamie came out of the bar with Shelb and Broden. His eyes lit up when they landed on us. "Hey, you two going to Miller's instead?"

The other bar in town had cut Pop off. He'd never visited there, and since he'd stayed away, I'd had no reason to go.

"We're not staying," was all Dawson said.

"Us either." Shelb snorted and grinned at me. "Jamie and I left a couple of twenties for the drinks that got dropped. Thank you."

I couldn't detect sarcasm in his tone and my confusion grew. Why would they pay and then *thank* me?

Broden bobbed his head and scratched at the stubble lining his thick jaw. "Yeah. It was the perfect distraction for Samuel. We made our escape."

"I have a sitter for a couple more hours," Jamie said. "My wife's almost done with work. Want me to have her meet us at Miller's?"

Shelb checked his phone. "My wife's bartending. I'll have her save us a table." He grimaced. "It'll be quieter."

Dawson met my gaze. "Want to go?"

His question was simple, but there were several questions inside of it that streamed across his whiskey eyes. *Are you still so pissed off that you're ready to say fuck this whole town? Do you want to see if the third time is the charm? Can you trust me that this entire town isn't full of people out to hurt you?*

The last unspoken question resonated. I trusted him, but did I trust my own reaction the next time someone pissed me off? I wasn't diplomatic like Dawson. A large part of me didn't want to be.

I knew the other guys, but I'd never had

a reason to interact with them. I'd have to find out. "Sure. Let's go."

Dawson didn't say anything until we got into his pickup. "Say the word, and we'll leave."

"Even if you have to do business with them?" My reply was snippy and I regretted it. I understood what Dawson meant. But at the same time, I didn't. I let out a sigh. "What if I can't go anywhere without the same thing happening?"

"I get it, but this town isn't just full of idiots. You have to deal with a deeper pool of them because of your dad. Samuel is obnoxious to everyone. He told me once that it was too bad the ranch kept me in town like a mouse dying on sticky paper. Said I should gnaw off my own foot in order to be free."

"But he moved back here to sell insurance."

"Yep. And Errol has a bad reputation for tacking on fees to every bulk order, but he's the only off-sale in town, so people just grumble behind his back about stocking fees and special-order costs instead of driving to a liquor store in Miles City."

I leaned my head against the headrest. Streetlights flashed through the cab. Couples and groups wandered up and down Main Street, going between Hogan's and Miller's and a wedding dance at the Eagles' club.

Dawson lifted his fingers off the steering wheel to wave every couple of seconds. "See all these people? They aren't at The Tap. I know my family goes there a lot, out of habit. And if your dad went there, it makes sense there's more people there that'll start shit with you." He curled his hand around mine. "I know I shouldn't have given in to Samuel on our date. But not everyone's bad."

"The bad ones get away with it. I think that's what upsets me. I can't do anything about it." I didn't have Dawson's money and reputation. I couldn't afford to take my business elsewhere. Standing up for myself cost me opportunities and I didn't always have the means to find new ones out of town.

"It'll get better, Bristol."

I wanted to believe him, but my mind churned over Errol's announcement. How was I going to pay for that?

Pondering the cost kept my mind off the group of people we were meeting. I knew who they all were. Jamie had ignored me in school, which was the most I could have asked for. His wife was a few years younger than me. Shelb was older than all of us, same for his wife. I had no idea who Broden was married to.

Dawson parked along the street. Miller's looked smaller than it was. The brick two-story building, longer than it was wide, had been around as long as the town. When we walked in, the hardwood floor echoed under Dawson's boots.

The other guys piled in behind us. The woman behind the bar glanced over, her gaze stopping on Shelb. Her curls bounced as she nodded toward a large round table in the corner. The middle of my back didn't burn with stares like it had at The Tap. Our group earned perfunctory glances as we passed. A couple of women reclined in front of video gambling machines. Tables with two or three people around them were scattered through the main floor, but for having as many people as The Tap, it was quieter.

My shoulders inched down as I relaxed. Dawson pulled out my seat before he sat in his own.

Shelb's wife came over and doled out small, square napkins with quick, efficient movements. "I didn't think you'd last that long," she said to her husband.

Shelb snorted. "It was going downhill fast. The more beer got poured, the more I worried what would come out of that kid's mouth." He shook his head and feathered his fingers over his dark hair. "Cass, have you met Bristol Cartwright?"

I tensed at the intro. The knowing look

would be next. Or the loaded "Oh" as my last name registered.

Cass rounded the table and rubbed my back. "Sorry to hear about your dad. What can I get you to drink, hon?"

Her touch catapulted me into the past when Pop would take me to the diner on the corner, the one that'd open at five a.m. to its crowd of regulars with their eyes on caramel rolls the size of their head. One of the older waitresses used to float around me, patting my back and squeezing my shoulder like I'd seen grandmothers do all over town. Cass was probably the same age that waitress had been, and she also didn't care whether anyone wanted her to mother hen all over them or not.

I managed not to stammer. "A Sprite, please."

She switched her hand to Dawson's shoulder. The woman was a toucher. "Been a while, Dawson. How's it going?"

"Thought I'd keep Shelb out of trouble while you were working."

Shelb leaned back. "He was going to bail on the bachelor party and walked right into it."

Jamie and Broden snickered, earning a rueful glare from Dawson.

Cass clucked. "I can't stand him. I keep telling Shelbie to switch our policy over. If the guy has to recruit his own clients to have a bachelor party, that should say something."

"Right?" I could've fist-bumped her.

Oops. Had I stepped out of line?

Cass winked at me. "Smart minds, hon."

As she got the rest of the orders, Jamie's wife, Natalie, showed up. Then Broden's girlfriend arrived, gushing about how she'd been home in her pajamas. Both women smiled when they were introduced to me. They didn't handle me like Cass, but I didn't sense anything other than friendliness.

This was the side of town I'd never seen. Before tonight, it'd felt like an exclusive club that I'd never learn the secret handshake to. Now, Dawson was my invitation.

Dawson

THE SLAP of air-conditioning on my face was welcome after the sun baking me on the sidewalk. I'd had to stop and talk to Samuel about raising the deductible on my pickup. Bristol's reaction toward how I dealt with him had left a bad taste in my mouth. I'd caught him on the way out to lunch and—shockingly—he hadn't had time to talk to me. He'd claimed he had to run an errand for his wedding.

I had my doubts.

If I had to make an appointment and push for a lower-priced policy because I didn't need to be covered to my earlobes when I could easily cover the cost of a higher deductible, then I would. I would just because he was being cagey.

Then I'd walked to the bank for my appointment with Richard Lang. I wouldn't forget the way he'd treated Bristol at Hogan's.

The night at Miller's had turned out better than I'd imagined the night going when we'd first gone out. After what had happened at The Tap, I'd thought I'd lost Bristol for good. That she was done with me, with the town, and with people in general.

But the guys and their wives had helped redeem me. I'd had nothing to do with it, but I owed them all. Not just for paying for the drinks that Bristol had accidentally knocked out of Danika's hold. They weren't nice to Bristol because she was my girlfriend. They were just decent people, and it showed in how they treated her. Same with their significant others.

The receptionist at the front desk in the

bank grinned as I approached. "Dawson, he's waiting for you."

I wandered through the desks on the main floor of the bank. Richard was behind his desk, a pair of reading glasses on as he scrutinized his computer screen. I tapped on his doorframe.

His gaze popped up and he took his glasses off. "Come on in. Shut the door."

Once I was sitting across from his wide desk, he slid a folder across the top. He was old school. If he could print it, he made five copies. Richard wasn't just the bank president, he was a savvy financial planner. He'd taken over the bank but kept some financial planning accounts as clients. King Ranch was one of the few.

"Haying yet?"

He asked that whenever I was in. Didn't matter if it was November when all the plants were going dormant or March when they hadn't started to grow. "Soon."

He brushed invisible crumbs off his chest and folded his hands across his belly.

"I've had a look at everything. Your investments are growing nicely. I don't think we need to move anything around. Your income continues to grow steadily." He adjusted his hands. "It's your call. What are your plans? We can make it happen."

"I'd like to take on another employee."

He sat up, interest gleaming in his pale blue eyes. "Oh, yeah? You're thinking of expanding?"

"Eventually. I'd like more time off. The guys and I are making do, but I don't want to burn them out. Maybe we'll start with a part-timer and see how it goes."

His interest changed to calculation. "I thought you'd be considering expanding. Like to a certain neighbor who's struggling to get by."

My blood ran cold at his suggestion, but as my irritation crept up, heat swept through my veins. "Bristol is quite capable of successfully running her ranch."

"Or she could sell to you, move somewhere else, and have a fresh start."

"Bristol's not going anywhere." That was her home. It'd been in her family for generations. I didn't want her to go anywhere, but I didn't have to worry. She wasn't leaving. "That ranch is hers. To say it's in her blood is putting it lightly."

Richard tapped his fingers on his gut. Soft thumps filled the office. "It would be a good move on your part. The oil wells aren't active; you can pasture that land. Expand your business. Hire more people." He sucked his lips against his teeth. "It'd be a good move."

"Regardless, it's not for sale."

"It will be. Just give it time."

My eyes narrowed. He didn't know that by next month, Bristol wouldn't have to sell in her lifetime if she didn't want to, but I couldn't use that to make a point. "It wouldn't be if companies in town quit making her pay for her dad's illness."

"Illness?" Richard scoffed. "Danny made his choices, none of them good. Bristol's done the same."

"But she hasn't—hasn't been given choices, I mean." I leaned forward, put my elbows on my knees, and folded my hands together. "If she were to walk in the door right now, would you treat her fairly?"

A faint flush spread across Richard's cheeks. "I didn't think you were the type to get drawn into that stuff."

"What stuff, Richard?" I enunciated each word and settled my weight into my elbows. And I waited.

He tipped forward in his chair, keeping his arms across his gut like a seat belt. "She's a pretty girl. Despite all the . . ." He fluttered his fingers up and down his body. "You're young. She's been forbidden for so long."

I barked out a laugh. "I'm young? Dad had four kids under the age of ten by the time he was my age. He worked on the ranch and for the oil company. I'm almost thirty." Too damn close to twenty-nine to think about. "I've had plenty of time to think about what I want. I've had plenty of time to be distracted by a 'pretty girl' and whatever else you're insinuating."

"Now, Dawson, I wasn't saying—"

"I don't care what you were saying. I don't want Cartwright Cattle. I want Bristol to have her place, and I'm willing to help her keep it. Not screwing over my neighbors is good business." I sat back. "Maybe you should reconsider what your idea of good business is."

The red blotches crept up Richard's neck. "I was merely suggesting your options for the inevitable. There's help and there's charity. You need to clarify what it is you're doing for her. That way you'll know if she's using you."

"Using me?" Bristol had spent her life pushing people away. How would she use me?

"Her grandparents thought yours should hand over all their assets. Her daddy thought the town owed him for what his parents drove into the ground. It's what Cartwrights do."

"It's not what she does." I gathered up the folder. We hadn't reviewed my accounts like we usually did. After the conversation we'd had, I couldn't talk business like nothing had happened. "I'll talk to you later."

I strode out of his office. He didn't bother to stop me. He had to know he'd overstepped, had to realize I'd called him out.

On the drive home, I tried to forget my interaction with Richard. One detail that he hadn't mentioned, because he didn't know, was that I would be helping Bristol a whole lot more than anyone in town. But to do that, I'd have to hurt her. I'd done that enough when she'd been all by herself and I'd been surrounded by family and town support.

The money in my trust was life changing, but not necessarily for the better. My brothers and I hadn't doubted that had Danny gotten some of the money, he'd have been like one of those lottery winners that takes the windfall and blows it, ending up more destitute than they were before. The only thing the money had done for them was ruin everything good in their life.

A what-if niggled at the back of my brain. What if he'd done everything we thought he would've, but what if he'd given Bristol some, free and clear? He'd known he had issues, yet he'd done what he could in his diseased state of mind, with his meager means, to protect his daughter.

And that daughter was so dedicated to him, she might've burned her good fortune to keep her dad going just a little longer.

In the end, it wasn't for me to say. We'd never know. We'd never given the Cartwrights the opportunity.

I pulled into my drive, my dust cloud dwindling with my speed. I stopped in front of the house. Bristol was laughing with Kiernan by the barn. A kitten squirmed in her arms. She set it down when she spotted me and waved. Kiernan lifted his chin.

I wiped all the disgust from my meeting off my face and hopped out. I was returning their grin by the time I reached them. "How's it going?"

"Better," Kiernan replied. His jeans were muddy and he had dirt smeared across his face. "Bristol and Bucket came to the rescue."

Kiernan looked like a mud-dipped lollipop, but Bristol only had a little dust on her clothing and the comforting smell of horse sweat surrounding her. No wonder the kitten was so cuddly. I'd cuddle them after a ride, and the little critters associated horse sweat with petting and treats.

Kiernan squinted into the sun and wiped off his face, leaving a larger smudge of grit behind. "After last night's rain, the little water hole in the pasture closest to the river was able to fill and not quite dry."

I groaned. We'd talked about fencing that portion off, but most of the time it functioned as an extra water source. Other times, it was a death trap. "And after today's heat, some cow thought it was a great way to cool off."

He tipped his head toward Bristol. "She spotted the calf this morning, lowing away, up to his rump in muck and tipped sideways." He held his hands out and looked down at himself. "So, roping him was out."

So he'd waded in and hooked the rope around the calf and Bristol and Bucket had pulled it out. Not only had they helped rescue the calf, but Bucket was trained. Bristol had probably positioned him between the calf and its worried mama so Kiernan could work safely. User? Fucking Richard. Human safety aside, Bristol had saved me more than a few thousand dollars I would've lost if we hadn't seen the calf in time. "Thanks to both of you."

Bristol's grin stretched wide, her emerald eyes glittering under the sun. "It was nice to bail out a King for once." She lifted a shoulder. "Even if it was by proxy."

"I owe you a lunch." I'd come up with any excuse to spend more time with her.

"What about me?" Kiernan cried.

I swatted his shoulder. "You need a shower and a change of clothes."

"Eh, Tucker's almost back from his daughter's softball game. I'll head home and change when he returns." He wandered into the barn, the kittens following him.

Bristol hooked her hands in her back pockets. "You don't owe me lunch. I'm serious. It was nice to be able to help someone out."

"You mean after you saved Emma? You're going to need a cape soon."

She rolled her eyes. "I'll borrow yours. How was your meeting?"

"Fine." She didn't have to know what Richard had said. "I'm thinking of hiring a part-timer."

Her eyes brightened. "This summer?"

I twined my fingers through hers and started toward the house. "Maybe." I didn't mention that I'd discussed it before with

Tucker and Kiernan months ago. We'd hoped to have someone training by now, but Cartwright Cattle had soaked up the extra time needed to hire and orient a new employee. "They'd have time to train and learn where everything is before we're deep in winter work."

"Good plan. So what food are you going to reward me with?"

I tugged her close. "Did I say we were going to have food for lunch?"

Her laughter rang through the yard. A joyous sound that originated from deep inside of her. A sound that I wanted to spend the rest of my life coaxing out of her.

CHAPTER 13

ristol

THIS WASN'T MY LIFE.

The group of older men I was starting to know by name were circled around the big table in the corner of Creek Coffee. They'd started with four guys but somehow managed to play pinochle no matter how many others showed.

Taya had taken her break when Emma and I had arrived. We'd grabbed the smaller table in the other corner while her summer college student worked the counter. She had tables set up on the sidewalk, but they seemed to know that I enjoyed soaking up the AC.

"Ugh," Emma said. She rubbed her eyes. "Switching from nights to evening shifts sucks."

Taya took a drink of her caramel something or other. "I'll remember that the next time I wonder why I went into the coffee shop business. I don't know what teenage Taya would say if someone had told her that she'd be getting up at four a.m. every day by choice."

Teenage Bristol wouldn't believe this either. A coffee date? I took another pull off my straw. Today's Italian soda was coconut cream. I really didn't care what the flavoring was as long as it paired with cream.

Friends. Fancy drink. And a break in the middle of the day. The only time I'd taken a break when Pop was alive was when he'd needed someone to watch over him in case he vomited while he was passed out. The work hadn't diminished since his death. Without Pop around to help what little he could, the duties had multiplied.

The pressure from the magnitude of the work that needed to be done was still there. But the worry of what Pop would do to create an even longer to-do list wasn't.

And this was important. A social network, however tentative. My friendship with these two didn't feel superficial. Emma talked about how she'd love to get a dog, but with her schedule, she couldn't let the poor thing sit alone in the house for twelve or more hours. And that she was sure she wouldn't find love in this small town, or that she wouldn't have the tolerance to put up with anyone if she did. Taya talked about how she'd left Wyoming right after graduation and thought she'd have to hitchhike to California so she could be homeless someplace warm. These two skipped the superficial bullshit and I liked them more for it.

"Everyone's excited for the fair," Emma said. "I work evenings that weekend, but I have the first night off that it's in town."

"Girls' night?" Taya asked, sitting straighter. Her body vibrated with energy that I was coming to recognize wasn't from the caffeine she peddled. She needed the coffee shop as an outlet.

"I think I'm supposed to go with Dawson and his family."

"Oh." Emma propped an arm on the back of her chair. She waggled her eyebrows. "Getting serious?"

"Maybe?" I'd dated Marshall twice as long, and it hadn't felt as serious. There was no comparison between my time with Marshall versus Dawson. A five-minute chat with Dawson blew my entire time with Marshall out of the universe.

Emma gave me a lopsided smile. "I think it's safe to say you two are the real deal."

"I'm new to long-term relationships." Ones that had potential to be long term.

"So is he," Emma replied.

I lifted a shoulder. Not entirely, but I wasn't going to spout his private life. "We managed to have a decent date last Friday. It ended decent, anyway." I told them about The Tap.

"Ugh, I wish there were more places in town," Emma said. "I like Miller's but it's a little sedate. But then I'd have to deal with the crowd at The Tap, and well, you know exactly why that's a bad idea."

"You two have had issues there too?"

Taya wrinkled her nose. "You mean with Danika's single-minded attempt to screw over every woman Darren has flirted with?"

I ran my bottom lip through my teeth. "And here I thought I was special."

Emma let out a wry laugh. "Where Creeper strays across the line of legal, Darren's smarter. He's a shit husband and he's not ashamed of it. I don't think Danika knows better."

I twisted the cup of creamy white soda in my hands. "You know . . . I thought it was just me. Because of Pop and how I act."

"I won't compare my experience to yours, Bristol," Taya said. "But adult bullies are the same as playground bullies. They can sniff out who'll give them a satisfying reaction. It's a game."

"But Dawson—"

"Has a lot of power behind his name," Emma finished. "And a lot of charm. Pair both together and he's—"

"King's Creek royalty." Taya took a sip of her coffee.

"I . . ." I debated what to say. I instinctively held in personal topics with Dawson, but this was about me. The other two waited for me to finish. "I grew up seeing how the Kings were treated compared to me and Pop. I didn't hear about other experiences."

Taya nodded knowingly. "And you thought all of us were treated the same as him."

I dipped my head. I was on the far side of my twenties and this social-life thing was new to me. Deep down, I was still that hurt kid getting teased on the playground. Most days, I didn't think there was another person in town more miserable than me. But when Emma rattled off what she experienced at work . . . Well, I'd never been so drunk I tried biting anyone.

"You and Dawson are polar opposites," Emma said. "And being with him, it's going to feel like a bigger gap than maybe it would for you and someone else."

"He said he has to do business with people. Thus the charm."

"I can see that," Taya said. "It's not always how much pride I'm willing to sacrifice to keep crappy customers. I also have to work with other businesses in town, and smiling a little extra reduces the friction."

"That's the part I get wrong." I was usually the customer and my cash was too hard earned to put up with idiots. Dawson had proved me wrong, but I held on to lingering disappointment in the way he wouldn't refuse Samuel.

Emma rested her hand on my forearm. "Bristol, don't quit standing up for yourself. No one's going to screw over a King. The rest of us, though . . ."

Taya lowered her voice. "Just the other day, the grocery store manager tried telling me that since she only stocks roasted cashews for my shop and my homemade turtle candies, that she'd have to raise the price. Premium shelf space and all that. I said, 'Aw, I'm sorry, I don't want to cost you money. I can just order them online,' and for a whole lot cheaper, but I didn't add that part. I know damn well that she carried them before I opened my doors. I went in there to figure out if I had to order them or not, so she was trying to play me. She was guaranteed sales from me. 'Premium shelf space' is pure bullshit."

Dawson probably would've paid the

extra. But I would've said what Taya had, just not as sweetly or diplomatically.

"Thanks, guys." My phone buzzed. The number was local, but not one I recognized. "Excuse me."

I rose and stepped closer to the door. "Hello?"

"Bristol? This is Richard Lang."

I continued walking right out the door. Emma had told me to stand up for myself, but that didn't mean I wanted witnesses. The pinochle guys were probably an anchor in the town gossip hotline. The door squeaked as I exited. I didn't know if Richard realized that I was on the move, or if he thought my silence meant I didn't want to talk to him. I wasn't sure myself.

"It's, um, it's been brought to my attention that now that you're the sole owner of Cartwright Cattle, you might want to meet and discuss your options."

"Do I have options?" My question sounded as incredulous as I felt.

"There are several programs available

for those in various forms of agriculture. I can give you information on farm loans, even housing assistance due to how rural King's Creek is. You might even qualify for a first-time rancher loan since your name is on Cartwright Cattle now."

That wasn't what I'd meant. I could walk into any bank or loan office and I'd be pounced on, a starved bunny in need of a carrot. Only that carrot would come with a ton of interest and I'd be so overloaded in payments that I'd have to take out another loan to live on.

Just because no one had wanted to do business with Pop didn't mean I hadn't done my research. Reading articles online didn't suck up a lot of data, and in my RV, Pop hadn't known what I was researching. All my plans for the ranch were in my head, but they were there.

"I can meet with you this week," he pressed.

"I'll give you a call back if I'm interested."

"Uh . . . okay?"

Big Dick Lang wasn't used to waiting and that wasn't my problem.

I disconnected and called Dawson. When he answered, I jumped right in. "Big Dick called wanting to meet with me."

"Really?" Wind blew across the line. I pictured him leaning against one of the fence posts he and Tucker were pounding in around the murder pit.

"Did you tell him to?" Would I be mad if he had? Big Dick was the only surviving bank in town. The last one had closed its doors when I was in high school. Miles City and Billings were too close and online was easier than another errand to run.

"No. But we had words."

"About me?"

"About how unfair he was. He thought —fuck—he thought you'd fail and I'd buy you out." Rage swept up. Not at Dawson, but at the thought that everyone was waiting for me to fail—and that without Dawson's help, they would've gotten their wish. "What'd he want to talk with you about?"

"Loan programs."

"I told him he should think about his business ethics. That's all." He paused. "You gonna meet with him?"

"Maybe. I don't know."

"You can at least get the information, and take it somewhere else."

"Dawson King, that's downright scandalous."

He chuckled. "Big Dick doesn't deserve one cent of interest he'd make off you. But it's nice to think he's actually going to do his job. You have time to make him think he has to work for it."

Why had Big Dick called me and not one of his loan officers? Had Dawson rattled him that badly? I might have to find out. Have Big Dick scramble to work for me for once. "He wants to meet this week."

"Everyone will be on vacation next week for the Fourth."

"Okay, I'll meet him."

"Let me know when. We can grab a sandwich in town afterward."

"Will do." I hung up and called Big Dick back. I patted myself on the back for calling him Richard when he answered. "Friday at eleven sound good?"

Friday was the best option because Big Dick probably took off every Friday of the summer.

"I . . . Yeah. No, it should be fine."

"See you then." I hung up and ducked into the coffee shop.

I soaked up the cool air as I crossed to the table. Emma and Taya were shooting me curious looks. I got to tell them the bank president was actually going to treat me like a real person—and I wasn't going to let him get away with anything less.

~

Dawson

.   .   .

ANOTHER MESSAGE BUZZED on my phone. *Are you ignoring your grams?*

Grams had been relentless today. She'd tried calling, and I hadn't legitimately ignored her. The baling tractor needed a new radiator hose and I'd been elbow-deep in replacing it. But I hadn't called her back.

Then the messages had started. She didn't say anything other than *We need to talk.*

I knew Grams's form of talking, and it wouldn't turn out any better than when I'd met her for supper.

I wiped grease off my hands and was thinking about what I wanted for lunch when my phone buzzed again. *Have you told her yet?*

Grams's threat ran through my mind. Time was running out. Would she tell Bristol? Would Grams throw me onto the train tracks and think that would help? That if she screwed things up with Bristol for me, I'd shrug and marry some stranger just to keep the cash?

That was what my brothers had done, so yeah, that was what she thought. Ignoring her would only antagonize her.

Ignoring my protesting belly, I called her back.

"Dawson." Warmth infused her voice as if the arranged-marriage date hadn't happened. "How's it going?"

"You tell me."

She chuckled. "Did I catch you at a bad time?"

"No," I sighed. "Can we skip the pretense? I know why you're calling."

"It's an important issue."

"I'm not talking about this with you, Grams."

"But have you talked to her?"

"I will."

"When?"

I rolled my neck, tiring of our back-and-forth already. It wouldn't be for much longer. "I'm sorry, but it's none of your business."

"Be an adult about this, Dawson.

Ignoring the problem isn't going to make it go away. It's almost like you want me to deal with it."

Was that how she justified her meddling? "I've gotta go, Grams. Hundred million or not, this cow-calf operation doesn't run itself." I hung up without waiting for her response.

"Goddammit!" I took a wrench from the work bench and flung it across the shop. The clang soothed my frayed nerves and I spun around with my hands on my hips.

Bristol had just stepped through the door and hustled back out.

"Hey." I jogged toward her. "Sorry, I didn't mean to scare you."

She lingered outside the door, her arms crossed and her eyes tense. "No, it's fine. Sorry I didn't send a message first."

"It's fine. You can pop in anytime."

She nodded. A sheepish expression crossed her face and she dropped her arms and crossed them again like she didn't know what to do with her extremities. The moment when Marshall had yelled at her on my porch ran through my mind. She'd flinched. She'd done the same thing once when I'd raised my voice.

"I didn't mean to scare you," I said quietly.

She flattened her lips and scowled. "I'm not scared."

"Brings back memories?"

She let out a long breath and wandered to an old pallet I hadn't broken down for the fire pit yet. She sank onto a corner, bending her long legs and resting her arms over her knees. "Pop never hit me. No matter how drunk he was. But he'd rage. Rant and throw things, like people do when they're pissed. But in true Pop fashion, it'd grow out of control. I'd find him working in the shop, ask him how his day was, and he'd spin on me, hollering about whoever had done him wrong." She fell quiet and stared across the yard to the red shop at the end of the long loop through the property. "Then when he got so sick toward the end, I almost missed those outbursts. I think that's half the reason why I jump."

"You think you should hate them, that they should bring up bad memories."

The corner of her mouth lifted. "They do that too. I used to dread his fits. I'd just stay out of the way and regret whatever question I had approached him about. And when he got so weak he couldn't throw a wrench more than two feet, I realized that the end was near."

I lowered myself next to her, careful to balance on the pallet to keep from tipping her off. "I don't usually throw my tools, but I can whenever you want me to."

She smirked and nudged me with her elbow. "Thanks for the offer, but I don't miss cleaning up the mess and fixing whatever he broke during his tantrums."

"Good. As a rule, I don't like to make more work for myself."

She rewarded me with a quick smile. "So how did that wrench do you wrong?"

"Oh, uh . . ." Now was the time. I could

tell her everything. I could explain what Mama had done and the bind it'd put us all in. And how flat would that explanation land between us?

Oh, I'm sorry your family had so much money that they didn't want me to have any.

Big ol' chicken, right here. I couldn't bring myself to ruin a beautiful June day in Montana. Goldilocks weather. Not too hot, not too cold. The bugs were out but hadn't grown to obnoxious levels. Green pastures surrounded the buildings. Bursts of yellow sweet clover brightened the countryside.

Today was too beautiful to waste on family drama. "Grams thinks I'm ignoring her."

"And you're still seeing me."

"That's all she needs." My chest burned from the pressure of staying quiet. I'd have to tell her. Soon.

But not today.

I stood and held my hand out. "My stomach's going to mutiny if I don't get some lunch. Hungry?" I pulled her up but held on to her warm hand.

"I owe you a meal."

"You don't owe me a thing."

"No, let's go to the diner on Main. My treat."

The local diner wasn't an expensive meal, but I hated wasting her hard-earned cash on food for me. I had a fridge and freezer full of food. But if she stayed with me, and if she forgave me when I finally came clean about the trust, she could buy the whole damn restaurant.

CHAPTER 14

ristol

I SAT in my pickup and rubbed my clammy palms on my jeans. It was time to meet with Richard Lang about the options for my ranch. My business. I had to run it like a business, and as Dawson said, like it or not, I needed to know what my options were with regard to financing and agriculture programs.

Pop hadn't been good at this stuff and he'd played it off like he was a lone wolf that didn't need any help. He'd also bitten the hand that had tried to feed him. I'd learned nothing from Pop other than what not to do.

But I'd learned one more thing on my own these last several weeks. My land was good, my cattle would bounce back, and I could do more with my life than just try to survive one season at a time. Once the ranch was in the black, I could grow, and I could give back to the world. Maybe not to the people who'd shunned me my whole life, but I could be in a position to aid those who felt helpless to help themselves.

So that was why I was here. I wasn't going to antagonize the only people in town that could help me. They didn't want to work with me, but the last few weeks of dressing a new way and showing my face in a town I'd lived in my whole life shouldn't be for nothing. This was me. I wasn't Pop, and I wasn't the Bristol Cartwright they'd all stereotyped me as. I decided who I was.

Pep talk over, I gave my palms one more swipe and got out. The heat of the sun kissed my face. Dawson was going to meet me at the deli two blocks from the bank after the appointment. I'd parked closer to the restaurant than the bank. It was a beautiful day and these sandals kept me cooler than heavy boots.

I passed the vehicles parked along the curb, not looking at any too close. I was nervous enough without wondering who I knew that would bear witness to this show. I was willing to do business with Big Dick Lang, but if he insisted on being an asshole, then I could burn an afternoon and go to Billings.

I wasn't powerless. Dawson had ingrained that into my head. The bank had the money, but they also needed clients like me to make money. Inhaling a steadying breath, I opened the glass door to the bank.

A wall of frigid ozone-laced air smacked me in the face. Goose bumps spread over my body. In my boots and work shirt, I wouldn't have been fazed.

An older woman smiled at me over a tall desk at the entry. "May I help you?"

"I have an appointment with Mr. Lang." I'd called the man Big Dick my whole life. *Mr. Lang* left a sour taste on my tongue. Depending on how today went, I might never call him that again.

She smiled. "You can go on back. They're waiting for you."

They? My heart sped up. I could face Big Dick. I was ready for him. Who else would be in there?

If Dawson had snuck in on this meeting, I'd be irritated. His support was everything to me, but I didn't need to be coddled through town. I'd lived here my whole life just like him. If people treated me like shit, then—

I approached an office with glass walls.

Big Dick sat behind a desk. His black suit coat gaped open to reveal the buttons straining to hold the panels of his shirt together. He looked up and spotted me. Lifting his chin, he slanted a glance across his desk.

As I neared, I slowed like I was walking through fresh concrete.

Emilia Boyd was the other person in the office. Had she come to testify against me? Was she the opposite of a good reference? Did I even need references for some of these programs?

Big Dick rose, opened the door, and stuck his hand out. "Thanks for coming, Bristol. Have a seat."

I ignored the hand and went to the chair by Emilia that was angled so we'd be a happy little threesome in the office. I remained standing. I didn't plan on talking about my ranch's business around her. "What's this about?"

He shut the door and scooted around

his desk to sit in his ergonomic throne. "Please, have a seat."

"No."

His bushy brows rose and guilt laced his expression. He shot a disapproving look toward Emilia and attempted a friendly smile.

I didn't like him, but if he hadn't wanted Emilia here either, then she'd browbeaten him into it. Her accounts probably fueled his winter vacations to Cancun and his summer golf trips with his buddies.

He rubbed his temple. "Well, uh, Ms. Boyd asked me for a favor."

I planted my hands on my hips, wishing I'd worn boots and dusty blue jeans after all. I was out of my element in too many ways. "Am I here to talk business or not?"

"Of a sort," Emilia replied.

"My business isn't yours."

"You'd be surprised."

I hated that she'd hooked me. But my animosity was greater than my curiosity. "Nope." I turned for the door.

"Dawson can't marry you. Or he won't. I'm not sure yet which one he'll choose."

"My business with Dawson is also not yours."

"That's where you're wrong. You're going to cost our family a lot of money if you keep seeing my grandson."

Walk away, Bristol. But I asked, "How?"

She waved to the empty chair but I only arched a brow. This situation was spiraling out of control faster than a panicked herd of cattle, and refusing to sit in that damn chair was my only power move.

Emilia looked down on me. From her chair. "Fine. When DB and I sold some shares of the company, we gifted it to Sarah. For the boys." There had to be some advantage for her and DB if they'd gifted the money. Either that, or Emilia's only soft spot had been Sarah. "She made it into a trust, for each boy. For when they turned twenty-nine."

She waited for me to understand. "Yes, I get it. Dawson's birthday is in two weeks."

"Mmm. But if he doesn't marry by then, he'll lose it. One hundred million dollars, Bristol."

I scoffed. What an absurd amount of money. Was she embellishing? Who had that amount of money?

She tilted her head, still looking down on me while she was sitting. "Has he proposed?"

I didn't answer, but gave her a *you know he hasn't* look.

"Right. If he doesn't marry, that money goes to you."

I chuffed out a laugh again. This lady was unbelievable. Should I warn Dawson that they might have to worry about her mental health?

Unease curled through my belly. What if it was the truth? What did that mean? "Okay, so he's not marrying me so I'll get the money."

"Wouldn't he have told you if he wanted you to have the trust?"

"I don't know." And I didn't know. Hurt

wedged a toehold into my heart. He hadn't mentioned a thing about this trust. Emilia's gaze was steady, her expression determined. She wasn't fucking lying. She wasn't showing signs of dementia. We were in the middle of a bank. With the bank president watching our exchange. Emilia wouldn't lie in front of him. She'd planned this.

The one thing I knew for certain about Emilia Boyd? She was motivated by money. And her family was in danger of losing money. To me.

And Dawson hadn't said a thing. I swallowed hard and tried to stop shock from spinning my thoughts out of control.

"Do you realize," she said in a light tone, "that all of his brothers married days before their birthdays in order to keep the money from you?"

I opened my mouth to say something smart, something that would make it seem like I wasn't buying what she was selling, but I couldn't. The King brothers were all about a year apart. And for the last three years, each of the three older brothers had gotten married. If I asked Dawson when their birthdays were versus their anniversaries, what would he tell me?

"Each boy married so the trust wouldn't revert to you. Each. One." She studied me as if willing me to comprehend the magnitude of their actions, right here, this second, so she could witness it.

I clamped my teeth together. Three hundred million dollars. Three guys had gotten married so I wouldn't get a dime. It wasn't my money, but that didn't stop the sheer rejection coursing through me.

"Dawson's stuck, Bristol." Emilia's tone was softer, but her eyes brimmed with determination. "He can't ask you to marry him without telling you about how the rest of his family kept the money from you. And if he doesn't ask you to marry him, it's like he's saying you're not worth it."

Her words seeped in, severing what I thought I knew about Dawson and me. "Why do you think I'd believe you?"

"Bristol, please. You've never played stupid in your life. Don't start now."

I reared back like she'd slapped me. "You don't know me," I hissed. "All I know of you is that you're a liar and a cheat. You lied to my family and cheated them out of quality land and oil money."

"Then ask Dawson yourself. Ask Aiden. Beckett." She spoke slower as she ticked off names. "Xander. Gentry."

Five King men. Guys I'd barbequed with. Socialized with. They'd all kept this from me? They'd had to get married to keep me from getting some mysterious payday.

"If it's true, why did Sarah do that? Why have an option where I get the money?"

"I can't begin to understand her reasons behind this silliness." She aimed her disdain-filled gaze at me. "And because of you, we'll never know."

Anger snapped the last of my tolerance

for Emilia Boyd. Emilia could heap the blame on me. She needed a target, but I didn't have to stand still and let her aim. "Whatever. You can lord around town like you're the queen of goddamn King's Creek and get people to dance at your command." Big Dick had the humility to look ashamed. "But you mean nothing to me. And I'm not going to dance for you."

I stormed out. But her words followed me. The details of everything she'd said.

Was Dawson going to lose money if he didn't marry me by his birthday? Was he waiting until the last minute before asking me so we'd appear in front of a judge and I'd love him so damn much I wouldn't question it?

Was he willing to give up all the money because he wasn't ready to settle down with me?

I stomped through the bank. The slap of my sandals only angered me more. Boots would've been more satisfying.

"Bristol," Emilia called from behind me.

I couldn't believe it. I had to out power walk my boyfriend's grandma. "Are you going to talk to Dawson?"

I ignored her. I refused to air my dirty laundry in the middle of the bank. Thankfully, no one was coming inside. I banged out the door and aimed straight for the deli.

Dawson's truck pulled into a spot next to mine. He got out and rounded the hood, a grin on his face, his eyes squinting under the sun. His smile faded, his concerned gaze shooting down the sidewalk toward me, then behind me.

My stomach lurched. This trust bullshit had to be true, but I wouldn't fully believe it until his soft lips crushed my world. All the ways his family had screwed mine over. Money. Land. Friendship. Support.

One hundred million rang through my mind. That was Monopoly money. Fake. That much money was absurd. How much would my grandparents have gotten if things had been different? Would our lives have changed? Would they have bought a nicer plot of land and settled into a calm life with better neighbors than the Kings? Money meant a lot to me, but the way I'd grown up had shown me what I truly treasured. People.

People who treated me decently. People who took the time to get to know me. People who were honest with me.

The Cartwrights had had enough of the Kings' lies.

Dawson was still several feet away when he asked, "What's wrong?"

His face was pale and anxiety rippled in his eyes, answering many of my questions. He hadn't wanted Emilia to tell me. He'd been keeping it from me.

Damn. "I think you know."

His jaw clenched. "Grams, what'd you tell her?"

Emilia pulled up next to us. Her face was flushed and she was breathing heavily.

She shouldn't have trucked behind me so fast. She should've stayed in the bank and out of my life. "The truth. Like you should've done."

"It wasn't your—" He shook his head and shoved a hand through his hair. "Bristol—"

"There's a trust and rules about when you marry and your whole family has been trying to keep the money from going to my family."

"No. Well, yes, but no, Bristol. Dammit, Grams."

"I warned you, young man." Emilia gulped in air. "I tried helping you. You could've married Mallory."

The woman she'd tried to set him up with? And he'd come to me afterward—and still hadn't told me.

I'd given him everything that night. If I hadn't been in love with him by then, I'd have cartwheeled over a cliff as soon as he held me in his arms.

People were watching us. I had to get

out of here. The bank was bad enough. It was close to lunchtime and customers were coming and going from the deli, their lingering glances taking me in at my lowest. All those embarrassing moments with Pop in town had nothing on getting my heart ripped out in public. "I've heard enough. Go ahead and get married. Keep the money."

"Bristol—"

"Let her go," Emilia rasped.

Her interference was the last straw. I whirled on her. "What do you have against me? Why do you hate me so much?"

Her eyes flashed and her nostrils flared as she leaned forward. She raised a shaky finger and stabbed it at me. "Sarah stayed home because of you. I talked to her that night and she said she was staying home in case you needed help. Because you said you were scared of the new guy your dad hired." She swayed closer. The blazing specks of yellow in her brown eyes flashed under the sun. "I lost my daughter because of you."

Horror replaced my anger. "What?"

I didn't remember telling Sarah I was scared. But I'd talked to her about everything. She'd been the closest thing to a mother I'd ever had.

"My . . . daughter . . ." A strangled cry ripped out of her and her knees buckled.

I lunged for her but Dawson was there first. "Grams? Grams!"

A couple in their fifties who had been lingering outside of the deli rushed toward us. The woman got on her phone. "I'll call an ambulance," she said.

Emilia's head lolled. Dawson lowered her to his lap on the sidewalk.

I backed up. The scene was too much.

My fault. It was all my fault.

I snagged my keys from my pocket and ran to my pickup. I'd done enough to Emilia.

Dawson

. . .

GRAMS HAD JUST BEEN SETTLED into a hospital room. I'd sat with her in the ER, where they'd run tests on her. The doctor was different than the one who had treated Bristol, but it wouldn't have mattered for Grams. She'd have gotten better treatment regardless. I'd stayed by her side in the ER and then followed her cot to a room down the hall.

The last time I'd sat at a bedside like this was when Dad had had his heart attack. My brothers had rushed to town and we'd rallied as a family.

Today, I was alone, torn between the pain that had ripped through Bristol's eyes when she'd learned the truth, and the lingering worry of watching my indomitable grams collapse. Seeing her weak and shaky had set my world off-kilter. She wasn't the warm, nurturing grandmother who crocheted blankets and sent me birthday cards with five bucks, but she'd always been there. Always. Even when we'd avoided her.

Worry aside, fury simmered inside of me like a ditch fire ready to jump the road and spread uncontrolled through acres of pasture. She'd set up Bristol. Recruited Richard Lang to help corner Bristol and spill the beans.

I peeked at my phone. No notifications. I'd tried calling. I'd sent messages. All had been ignored.

The only place I wanted to be was by her side. To tell her that it wasn't her fault. To tell her that Grams was hurting and she hadn't meant it. She shouldn't mean it.

Dad appeared at the door. His charcoal-gray suit coat hung open and his tie was loose. He'd come straight from the office. Kendall wasn't with him. He'd left during a big meeting I'd interrupted him in, and she'd probably stayed behind to finish up.

He went to Grams's side and carefully pushed the IV stand out of his way. "She asleep or did they sedate her?"

"She fell asleep as soon as they moved her to this room. They think it was stress or some shit, but they want her overnight at least." I glared at the white square tile floor. I should stop, but I kept talking. "I guess driving up from Billings, cornering my girlfriend, and destroying my relationship, then blaming an eight-year-old girl for the death of my mother took a lot out of her."

Dad blinked at me, then looked back at Grams. His gaze grew pensive and his jaw tightened. He'd know better than to accuse me of overreacting. "Want to tell me what happened?"

"I can only guess most of it, but I'm sure it's pretty damn accurate. Richard Lang called Bristol. Offered to meet with her." I propped my elbows on my knees and rubbed my temples. "And I encouraged her."

Dad walked around the bed and perched on the vinyl-covered recliner in the corner. I hadn't wanted to sit there, choosing the office chair instead. The recliner had seemed too long term.

"Richard is a pompous ass."

I bobbed my head. How much of Richard Lang's behavior had I tolerated because it was what we'd always done? "Grams was there. She told Bristol about the trust."

"Shit." Dad adopted the same pose I was in, pushing his fingertips into his temples.

"Yeah. Bristol and I were going to meet for lunch, so I was close by when Bristol stormed out of the bank. Grams followed her and then . . ." I blew out a long breath. "And then Grams told her that Mama stayed home that night because Bristol was afraid of the guy her dad hired. Mama wanted to be around if Bristol needed to go somewhere safe."

Dad didn't respond. After a few moments, I glanced at him. His head was in his hands, but his eyes were closed. Yeah. It was a lot.

He lifted his head. "Well, damn."

"Yeah."

"We all know it wasn't Bristol's fault."

"Grams doesn't."

"She's hurting. She and DB took Sarah's death pretty hard, as would any parent. Then she lost DB, and I doubt she's gone to a damn bit of therapy."

I chuckled without an ounce of humor. "That seems to be on brand for our family."

The corner of Dad's mouth lifted. "What are you still doing here?"

"Didn't feel right leaving. Didn't feel right to stay either." I stood. "Thanks for coming so fast."

"Sorry I couldn't get here sooner. Xander and Aiden are coming down after Aiden's done with work. Beck will fly out tomorrow morning. Emilia's going to hate the fuss, but I don't want her driving to Billings. Aiden can drive her home in her vehicle when she's discharged."

"Thanks for getting it arranged."

I was almost to the door when he said, "Dawson."

I stopped. Dad glanced at Grams, then

rose and crossed to me. With a hand on my back, he guided me into the hallway. People buzzed around the nurses' station, but we were four doors down. Our section of the hall was quiet.

Keeping his voice low, he said, "I know she's your grams. But the next time you're caught between her and taking care of someone you care about like you care about Bristol—choose differently next time. Your grams's first priority is herself."

He wasn't telling me anything I didn't know. Bristol wouldn't hold it against me, staying with my grams until she got to the hospital. But she wouldn't realize the depth of my feelings now that I'd stayed by Grams's side for hours instead of making things right between us. "I've gotta go."

He nodded like, *Yeah, you do.*

I managed not to run to my pickup or speed through town or on the highway. Once I hit gravel, I kicked the pedal down. A billowing dust cloud followed me as I turned into Bristol's drive. Her pickup was parked outside of her trailer. I killed the engine but left the keys in and went to the RV.

Tapping on the door, I called, "Bristol, can we talk? Please?"

No answer.

I knocked again. "Bristol?"

I couldn't have fucked this up that bad. What we had was too special.

Then you should've told her, dumbass.

Birds chirped. Happy-sounding shits. The wind rustled through the tall weeds along the fence posts and around the other two RVs. Crickets. But no human sounds.

I pounded harder. I didn't want to sound irate, but the need to talk to her, to see her, pumped adrenaline through my veins. She was the hurt and angry one and she had every right to be. Grams could argue that the money was ours all she wanted, but it didn't feel right. If it had felt right, I wouldn't have had an issue telling Bristol about it.

I crossed to the trailer. My boots kicked

up small puffs of dust that mimicked my race here. I knocked harder on the trailer door in case she was in the bathroom. "Bristol?"

The same sounds of nature were my only answer.

I sank onto the metal stairs outside the RV. They cut into my ass but I didn't budge. Should I recite my *I'm so damn sorry* spiel anyway? Just holler it so she could hear it in the RV or the trailer?

More birds sang. A hawk soared over the pasture behind the trailer, waiting to attack its next meal. I hadn't eaten lunch. Dinnertime was passing.

Had Bristol eaten?

Probably not. She would've come home and thrown herself into work. She would've retreated into the giant, solid shell she'd built for herself. And she'd be thinking that what Grams had said was true. That Mama's death was her fault.

Twenty minutes went by. Her pickup was here. She had to be too.

No Daisy. I got up and went to the barn, checking inside. No Bucket.

Right. She had cattle to check and the four-wheeler wasn't running reliably, and even if it were, nothing could beat horse therapy when the world turned to shit and you felt like you were alone.

It wasn't something I did. But I'd asked Xander once in high school why he disappeared so long when he got upset at Dad and that was what he'd said.

Would she come back? I toed the ground.

I'd wait.

I parked my ass on the weathered stairs to the trailer. It was more comfortable than the RV steps. And I waited.

An hour went by. Then another.

Was she hurt again? Maybe Daisy was at my house wondering where the hell I was.

My phone rang and I answered without looking at the caller. "Hey."

"Hey, Dawson," Xander answered. "Aiden and I are leaving the hospital with

Dad to pick Beck up at the airport. We can get a room if you need the house to yourself."

"Dad told you what happened?"

"Yep. And we all feel like shit. You talk to her yet?"

"No. She's not home. She's out riding, but I've been waiting close to three hours."

"Is there anywhere else she can go?"

"On horseback?" I smacked my palm against my forehead. "The cabin. Dammit."

"The old hunting cabin out by the wells?"

I'd spent the evening on my ass. I could've walked there by now. How was the reception? Was she getting my messages?

Of course, asshole. She probably went to the cabin so you couldn't reach her.

"Yes. If she's out there, then she doesn't want to talk to me." I blew out a breath. "You might as well stay the night, but I'm not going to be good company."

"You don't have to be. We'll try to help you figure out what to do."

There wasn't much I could do if she wouldn't talk to me. She might want space. She might need it, and that was why she'd gone to the cabin.

I'd respect that. It was the least I could do.

"I'll be right there."

"We'll grab some pizza at the gas station."

"That's crap pizza, don't bother. I'll make dinner. It'll get my mind off today." Nothing would get my mind off today, but I'd rather be cooking in the kitchen than sitting on the couch, staring at the wall, and ruminating over everything that had happened.

"See you there." Xander hung up.

I dropped my arm and stared at the RV. Then I looked around the yard. Tidier than it'd ever been. Bristol had gotten the Weed Eater working, sharpened the lawn mower blades, and tuned up the riding lawn mower. She'd removed old car parts, sold an old John Deere 4450 that hadn't run in twenty years, and used the money to buy nicer matching posts for the section of fence that bordered the yard.

Signs of her were everywhere. But she wasn't around. Because of me.

CHAPTER 15

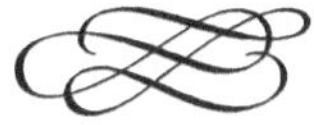

ristol

I PUT the arc welder down and took off my helmet.

This motherfucking piece of— I kicked the workbench. The chunk of metal I was using to make a new hay tine for the raking fork clattered to the floor. Nothing was going right today. I didn't have to be a genius to know why.

First off, I'd slept like crap. No, that

wasn't the first thing that'd gone wrong, but I didn't want to think about yesterday. Emilia Boyd's words had run through my mind on a loop last night. The crickets and frogs hadn't drowned the memory out.

My stomach cramped. I hadn't packed more than a couple of peanut butter and jelly sandwiches to take with me. They'd comprised lunch and dinner yesterday and breakfast this morning. I'd made sure Daisy and Bucket had enough to eat, but I didn't care about myself.

I wiped sweat off my forehead. The shed door was open, but the wind had died during the night. It wasn't stifling, but I was hot and cranky.

If I kept working without fuel, I was going to hurt myself. The last thing I needed, but what I really wanted, was Dawson riding in to save the day again.

I tossed the helmet on the counter and swiped at more sweat with my forearm.

I turned around and jumped. Dawson was leaning against the door of the shop, his long, lean form outlined by the sun. He wasn't wearing his hat and that damn lock of hair had fallen over his forehead. My fingers itched to brush it aside.

"I was worried about you," he said.

Why hadn't Daisy barked? I would've known it was him by the joyous sounds she made when he idled down the drive. But she was probably passed out in the barn. I wasn't the only one that had slept like shit.

"I stayed at the cabin." I'd needed the peace. I hadn't found it.

"I would've come, but I didn't know if you'd want to see me."

I lifted a shoulder. I didn't know either. "How's your grandma?"

"She's getting discharged. They didn't find anything wrong. She was put on blood pressure meds and refuses to take the anxiety meds they gave her."

Sounded like Emilia Boyd. "Don't you need to be there?"

"Xander and Aiden rode up. Aiden will drive her back."

"Did all your brothers come up?"

"Yeah. Dad too." A furrow developed between his brows. Here it was. The talk I didn't want to have. "Bristol, about the trust . . ."

"It's not my money. I get it."

"I didn't know how to tell you. No matter what, you would've been hurt and that was the last thing I wanted."

"So, what exactly is this trust about?" I wanted to hear it from him. My traitorous mind wanted to defend him. He had to be the one to tell me that he didn't want to marry me. That he didn't want to give up the money.

He wandered in. I stayed where I was. Getting closer to him was a bad idea when my heart hurt this bad.

"Mama set it up so that we'd each get an equal share if we were married for a year by the time we turned thirty. After that, if we got divorced, our spouse would get half. It couldn't be touched by a prenup."

I waited. That wasn't the part that hurt

so much. Oh, it was its own knife through the gut. My logical brain didn't care that we'd only been dating for a couple of months. Too early to get engaged or married in most relationships. But my heart ignored the major details.

His lips flattened, but he continued. "And if we weren't married by the time we were twenty-nine, or we got divorced before we were married a year, then the trust went to you and your dad. But since your dad's gone, it'd go to you." The last sentence was a whisper.

I shoved my hands in the pockets of my jeans. I'd stuffed my clothes from yesterday in my dirty laundry pile and didn't care if I touched them again. "I guess Pop would've blown it all."

"My brothers love their wives."

"But they only married them to get the money."

Regret rippled through Dawson's features. "Yes."

"And the woman Emilia lined up for you?"

"I wasn't interested."

"It's a lot of money."

"I want you. I want to be with you." He inched closer. "I want you to get the money."

So why hadn't he talked to me? I hugged my arms across my waist. "Don't."

"Bristol—"

"No, Dawson. I don't know what to think."

"I didn't want to hurt you."

"But you did." Tears burned the backs of my eyes. I did not want to cry in front of him. If I cried, he'd be the one I yearned to hold me. I blinked, but the tears won. "It hurts a lot."

"I didn't know what to do."

I licked my lower lip trying to keep from sobbing. "I think that's what hurts the most. You didn't know what to do. You didn't know what to do about me."

"What we have is—"

"Special. Yeah, you've said that. But you couldn't be honest about something really fucking important. You weren't honest about your grandmother trying to bribe you with another woman while we were dating. Instead, you came here and we . . ." I shook my head. Tears tracked down my cheeks. "I trusted you." *I loved you.*

I still did. I didn't think I could quit. But how could I move on? His grams had spilled the beans and he'd still come not knowing what to do or say.

"If we marry, it should be—"

"Leave." I couldn't stand talk of marriage. Not now.

His mouth snapped shut and he studied me. "I thought we could talk through this."

"You missed all your chances to talk."

"Bristol—"

"You need to leave." Because I didn't know what to do either. I'd been through breakups. They stung, but I came home, went to work, and forgot about them. I got on with my life.

Yesterday, it had felt like my life had imploded, only I was alone in my little snow globe of destruction.

"We're stronger than this."

I sighed. My tears were slowing. He'd come to make it better, but we were spinning our wheels in a big damn mud pit. I couldn't see any way out. His birthday was in two weeks. He wasn't dropping to one knee.

"Look, if you don't get married by the fifth, I'll write a check back to you." If I could even spell an amount that large. "It's not my money. Your brothers worked really hard to keep it in the family."

"No, that's not what I want."

There was enough room in my heartbreak for anger. "You know what really gets me?" Other than Dawson's role in all of this. And his brothers'. "It's your mom. She made the rules. What did she think would happen?"

His gaze was steady, sadness emanating

from his whiskey eyes. "She wouldn't have wanted you to get hurt."

"That's what it seems like. That's what Emilia's hated me for. For most of my life. But if your mom really wanted me taken care of, then she could've just left a trust for *me*. So, I can't accept the money. She didn't want me to have it either."

"That's not what—"

"I'm not taking anything more from your family."

"We don't blame you for Mama," he whispered.

I doubted that was true. How could they not? I was here and she wasn't. Sarah's death had become just another thing I'd been left behind to take the blame for.

He opened his mouth again, but I couldn't let him get another word in. When it came to Emilia's claims, he didn't know how everyone in his family felt and it wasn't like I could say *fuck them* like I did with the rest of the town. I blamed myself more than they did. And when it came to the trust, his words echoed in this big barn.

"Goodbye, Dawson."

He let out a breath and stared at me, a crease across his forehead. He studied me for a moment and I lifted my chin. I clenched my jaw to keep my lips from quivering. With a shake of his head, he left.

I watched him walk out of my sight. Every step. Each boot strike drove a wedge further between us. I hadn't given him a choice, but I couldn't help but want more. I'd been nothing but a temporary distraction in my other relationships. No one ever planned for a future with me. I hadn't been important enough to think of beyond the next date, the next way I could fulfill whatever they'd been looking for. I couldn't bring myself to accept more of the same from Dawson.

I knew what I wanted from him. I wasn't using him to make myself feel normal, to feel like I mattered. Being with

Dawson had made me feel like myself for the first time since I was eight.

I hadn't moved by the time he pulled away.

I sniffled and swiped at my nose. Back to work.

Wait, I'd been planning to eat.

I wasn't hungry.

I yanked my helmet off the workbench, but my phone buzzed.

A message from Emma. *I know we were supposed to meet for coffee next week, but I had the shittiest overnight at work and could vent. You free tonight?*

I didn't think before I messaged back. *I'm free every night now.*

Oh, shit. What happened?

Everything. Nothing? I don't know.

I'll be over with Taya. You mind?

My place isn't . . . A real place? It'd be crowded with three of us in the RV and the trailer might be okay to use for the bathroom and laundry, but it wasn't fit for entertaining. There wasn't enough Febreze in the world for that. I settled for *My place isn't presentable.*

Then we'll tailgate. I don't care if you live in a tent, it's fine.

I didn't have the energy to argue. Would it really hurt to let my friends know how I lived? If my trailer and RV combo scared them off, then they weren't good enough to be in my inner circle. I was desperate for friends, but I wasn't desperate to get treated like crap. I'd had enough of that.

Dumping the helmet back on the bench, I walked out of the shed.

My friends couldn't listen to my sob story if I burned down my shed trying to weld. I was too tired and hungry and distracted to keep going.

I could only take care of two of those three obstacles. I could eat. I could nap if I needed to. But I was afraid that I'd never get Dawson off my mind.

Dawson

DAD HADN'T GONE BACK to work by the time Grams was discharged. It was only the two of us at the house. Aiden had driven Grams to Billings. Xander had taken Beck to the airport in Billings the day after Grams had gone home. Between my brothers, they'd checked on her. I had stayed away.

I entered the house after it was dark enough to hurt myself if I kept working. Dad had quit before sunset, which wasn't early this time of year, but I couldn't go back to my place and think about how I'd love to wind down with Bristol in my arms, watching a show.

It couldn't be over between us. It'd been so abrupt.

Toeing my boots off, I hooked my hat in its usual place. Dad was in the kitchen. Savory smells filled the house.

"You cooked?"

"I still have some skills." He shoved a plateful of crispy hash browns and sausage toward me.

I sat on a stool and dug in. My stomach thanked me for the food but my heart hurt too badly to feel the hunger. "I thought you were supposed to be eating better."

Dad hardly talked about his heart attack, but his meals had more fruits and vegetables than they had when growing up. And I was diligent about offering him heart-healthy items when he was home.

He went to the fridge and withdrew a bowl. He slid it across the counter. Salad greens tossed with tomatoes, cucumbers, onions, and avocado. "I am eating better. But a guy can still have sausage and hash browns," he grumbled.

I smirked but dug in. Telling a rancher he had to cut back on red meat and potatoes wasn't always successful. But Dad and Kendall had done their research. They wanted to be together for a long time.

My smile died. That was my dream too,

but I'd messed it up and Bristol didn't want to talk to me. I shoveled food into my mouth out of habit.

When I was done, I shoved the plate and salad bowl away. "I'm going to Billings tomorrow. I'm switching banks."

Dad leaned on the island, his gaze unwavering. "Your grams called today."

"Worried she missed too much business while she was in the hospital?"

"That too." Dad didn't sugarcoat it. Grams would always have her priorities and her family wasn't always at the top. "But she wanted to know how you were doing."

"Did you tell her I was shitty?"

"No, I said that you'd have to be the one to talk to her, if you wanted to. I also told her that none of us condoned what she'd done."

Dad didn't stand up to Grams too often, but when he did, he made it count. "I want to be so angry at her. And I am. But . . . I can't help feeling like it would've turned out the same because I waited too long to do what I had to do. Except for Bristol getting blamed for Mama's death."

"Bristol was a kid. Your mom was worried about her when the rest of us should've been too. Hell, I can kick myself until the end of days, wondering what I could've done for each of them that night, and I will. But that won't do Bristol any good today."

"She doesn't want to talk to me. We could discuss it, work through it, but she doesn't want anything to do with me."

"Doesn't mean you need to give up."

I glowered at Dad. "I'm not a teen that needs advice."

"No, you're a grown man who might be smart enough to think your old dad still has something worth saying." The look he gave me made me feel like a teen getting a lecture at the dinner table all over again. I slumped onto my elbows, ready to listen. "Think about it, Dawson. No one's stuck around in her life. Her mom left. Sarah died. Her dad was around but he wasn't. Now he's gone. Workers. Boyfriends. Friends. Neighbors. We all left her to do whatever it was she did. To handle whatever came at her all by herself. I think the guy who's in love with her, who wants to spend his life with her, should do a little more than try to talk to her once."

Fatigue swamped me. I hadn't slept well for three days and it was late. Dad thought he had all the answers, but it was almost ten at night and I'd put in a fifteen-hour day. "What exactly do you think I should do, then? Go over there every day until I wear her down? When does winning her back become harassment? She doesn't want to talk to me."

"Maybe she doesn't know what to do either. You're both circling each other like dogs, hurt and wary of anyone else." He circled the island and sat on a stool next to me. "So you're on the right track. Figure out exactly what you want. Get over your hurt and how it makes you feel when she tells you to leave."

"Get over myself, is that what you're saying?"

"That's part of it." He drummed his fingers on the counter. "You know, when I have to fire someone, or sever ties with a company, I have to get over myself. I can't send an email at five o'clock on a Friday and hope they forget about it by Monday. I made the decision, so I have to own it. I don't want the conversation any more than they do, but I made the decision and I have to stand by it. I have to tell them in person and list my reasons why. I have to be available for questions and explanations because my decision affects their life."

"Okay? I might be too tired to get the connection but what does firing someone have to do with Bristol breaking up with me?"

"The trust. You decided not to talk to her about it because you didn't want to hurt her. But how much of that decision was about saving yourself from a hard conversation?"

Goddammit. I sank my head in my hands. Dad and his fucking wisdom. "If your goal was to point out how I fucked up even more than I thought, you succeeded."

"Get over yourself, Dawson. You asked what to do. You need to figure out what you want, with Bristol, with the money, and you need to tell her. Then you need to be available for her. You don't get to smile and joke and say something charming so everyone likes you. You need to stay for the hard conversation. Once she realizes that you're not circling the issue and that your apologies are genuine, then maybe she'll talk to you."

He patted me on the back, then slid off the stool and went to his room upstairs. I was alone with my thoughts.

As much as I wanted to feel sorry for myself and slink off to bed, Dad's words were sinking into my brain. Slow, like a warm cup of coffee resting on a snowbank.

I wanted Bristol to trust me, but I had to prove I was trustworthy. To do that, I had to tell her the truth. To talk to her, I had to get her to let me hang around long enough to listen. And before I said a damn word, I had to give her more than an excuse about not wanting to hurt her.

She didn't think I'd stick around. She might think that I was done with her.

I wasn't. Not by a long shot.

So, what'd that mean?

I went to the office and grabbed my laptop. First, I logged in to my email and sent a message to our lawyer. Then I searched businesses in Billings and scribbled out a list. After that, I brought up a list of businesses in King's Creek. I ran through all my conversations with Bristol since I'd found her shivering in the pasture.

It was time to back up my words with actions. Tomorrow, I'd ask Kiernan to cover for me while I ran to town. I might need him to fill in for me for a few days while I worked on proving to Bristol that I wasn't abandoning her.

Once all that was done, I would be ready to find Bristol. And I'd back up everything I told her, starting with how much I loved her.

ristol

IT WAS OBNOXIOUSLY NICE OUTSIDE. Birds chirped in the bushes a hundred yards from my trailer. Their cacophony was worse than living next door to frat boys. There wasn't a cloud in the sky and I was sweating before ten a.m.

I put on the sunglasses that Emma had given me the night she and Taya had come over. I'd told them the bare-bones story about the trust and asked for their discretion. I needed someone on my side in town, but if they told the world what had happened, it wasn't like my life would change.

Everyone thought I had done something to make Emilia Boyd collapse. Taya had heard I yelled at her. Emma said the gossip was that I'd pushed the woman. Both of them claimed to have defended my honor.

I believed them.

So, that night, we tailgated. I warned them about the trailer and they didn't let it stop them. They used the bathroom several times and didn't comment on the state of the rest of the space. Since Taya brought over a couple bottles of wine and I didn't drink, both women had to crash in the RV for the night. Taya took the couch and I made Emma sleep on the bed instead of on the floor by Taya. I slept in the back of my pickup with Daisy after they each fell asleep. An impromptu campout. Otherwise, they'd have argued, and I couldn't share a bed with anyone but Dawson. Too soon.

They'd begun the next day hungover and I had started work late. But it'd been worth it.

I'd felt lighter the next morning. Tired and worn out, but not holding in everything that bothered me, not letting it eat away at me. I had even gone to town for mouse traps and rodent stations and managed not to lob off a sarcastic remark when I was asked if I needed more than one. A trailer, three RVs, a shop, and a barn. Yes, I needed more than one.

I missed Dawson every second of every day, but I remembered to eat when I was supposed to. I had even cooked a small meal in my RV. Spaghetti didn't take much, but it had tasted better than something out of a can.

The Fourth of July was tomorrow. Taya and Emma had tried to talk me into going to the concert after the fair closed and staying for the fireworks. Some country singer I'd heard on the radio was performing, but I didn't care if I ever heard them again, much less saw them in person. I hadn't committed.

Dawson and I had planned to go to the fair with his family and I hadn't heard from him since the day I'd chased him out of my shop. I hadn't seen increased traffic at his place—not that I'd caught myself staring across the pasture that separated our houses one or a hundred times. I doubt they'd come up for the weekend.

Two weeks. Felt like months.

I hadn't gotten any new messages from him. The fences were strong, so there was no need to contact me about my wayward cattle. I might have had fantasies about cutting a hole in the fence just to see if he'd message me or leave it to Tucker or Kiernan.

That wasn't all I'd fantasized about. Working all day by myself ran long. Hours and hours in my own head. Dawson centered in most of my fantasies. And that money. It was hard not to think about it.

What would anyone do with that much money? What would *I* do with that much money? Move out of town? Build a fresh life where no one knew me?

It wasn't mine, didn't matter. But it was natural to wonder. To ponder all the possibilities.

The countdown to his birthday was on. Tomorrow. The town would spread word if he married, but if he didn't, he was going to lose the trust in a matter of hours. Less than a day.

Curiosity ate at me, but the hole it made wasn't bigger than the one Dawson had left behind.

I looked at my phone. It was early for lunch, but my stomach protested and I was hot and uncomfortable.

I brushed out Bucket and put him into the pasture. Daisy barked and sped off. An engine rumbled moments later.

As I crossed through the barn, I missed

who was driving by. Daisy wasn't going wild, so it could only be a handful of people.

It hit me. People, as in more than one. Daisy was comfortable around multiple people. Shit might've happened between me and one important person, but I had others I was learning to count on.

I exited the barn. The sun hit my eyes the same time I saw the pickup. Dawson shut his door and came straight for me.

He wasn't stopping. His strides were long and his expression determined.

I frowned and fought the urge to retreat. "Is something wrong?"

"Yep, but I'm here to change that."

His hard tone stalled me. Had I done something I didn't know about? Were ten of my cattle romping through his yard? Damn, I'd just checked on them.

He stopped close. We weren't touching, but I had to look up at him. His hair was finger combed off his head. He hadn't put on his hat yet. Wasn't he working today? It was a holiday but he usually gave one of the other guys the day off.

"I have to talk to you. Are you going to let me, Bristol Jane?"

"I didn't think you had anything left to say."

"I have a lot to say. But I wanted to make sure I had my shit together before I did."

Daisy raced around our legs, then shot for the barn, something else catching her eye. It was only me and Dawson in the middle of my drive.

So he had his shit together. What did that mean? "Should we go inside?"

"The money's yours," he blurted.

"I'm not taking it."

He scowled and shoved his hand through his hair. "Dammit, that didn't come out right. I mean, it's what I wanted to say. But here—I want you to have the money. I'm not getting married. To anyone. And you're getting the money. Then I'm going to ask you to spend the rest of your life with me. That way, if you say yes, it'll be because you want to. It won't be because of the money. It won't be because you have to. Or because you don't want the ranch to fold, so you need to marry money. You'll be stinking rich. You won't need me, or my help, or anyone's help. You can buy what you damn well please and you'll tell me yes because you're in love with me, just as I am with you."

His words bombarded me. Information overload. My mind looped and rounded back on details until it snagged on one it couldn't shake loose. "You love me?"

"I was too afraid to say it when I knew I wasn't being honest with you. I screwed up, and when my world exploded, you didn't know how I felt."

"It's been two weeks," I whispered.

"That's because"—he flourished papers I hadn't noticed were in his hands—"I had to get some arrangements made, and with a summer holiday, a lot of damn people were on vacation."

He swiped the paper off the top and held it out. I couldn't concentrate to read it.

"First, this is the trust. Simple. Defined." He handed me the sheet and I numbly accepted it without looking. He shuffled another piece to the top. "And this is the letter stating that you're receiving the trust. All our lawyer needs is your info. The account will be switched to your name and you can choose what you want to do with it. He listed several contacts who can help you decide. While I support doing business locally, I made sure he included people outside of King's Creek. Which brings me to the rest of the reason why I took so long to come beg you to take me back."

Dawson King was going to beg me? I shook my head. Was hunger making all this hard to follow?

"I changed banks. The King family no longer does business with Richard Lang."

My mouth dropped open. "But your grandparents helped that bank get off the ground."

"And maybe we'll go back when Big Dick steps down."

"Dawson, that's going to piss off a lot of people."

"Yep. It did. I also switched mechanics since Buck assaulted you. And there's a new insurance agent that moved to town. I gave her a call and I think I made her year. With Samuel pissing all over his territory, she was afraid her firm would have to shut down the satellite office in King's Creek." His grin was lopsided. "Now, she won't have to."

"Why? Why do all of this?"

"I've coasted on my family's name long enough. I can make a few waves. I don't need everyone to like me, I just need you to love me."

"But the money . . ."

"Is yours. I'm serious. I'm not touching it, so don't let it go to waste. You can put it to better use than I can."

"You mean like a sobriety ranch?" I bit

my lower lip. Oh, yeah. I'd fantasized about that too.

His grin spread wider. "Exactly like a sobriety ranch." He stepped closer. "You been thinking about how that would work?"

"Maybe."

He dipped his head down. My chin lifted. We were painfully close but not touching. "You been thinking about me?"

"All the time," I answered raggedly. "What about your family?"

"They're on standby. The trip to the fair is still on if you're willing to put up with us." He brushed a finger down some stray strands of hair that evaded my standard ponytail. "I love you, Bristol Jane Cartwright. I don't want to waste one more day, but I'm wasting today. Tomorrow, I'm asking you to marry me. Two weeks without you is too fucking much."

Sinking into him and forgetting all of my questions would be too easy. "Your grandma?"

Concern rippled across his face. "I think she actually feels bad. Speaking what she'd thought all those years out loud made her face reality. You were a kid. Mama's decisions weren't yours, and Mama wouldn't have changed what she did. That guy would've hurt you and your dad if he hadn't broken into our house."

He cupped my face. "But I went to talk to her. I told her my plans and said that if she interfered, that would be the end of my relationship with her. I also told her not to talk to me if she didn't apologize." Sorrow seeped into his gaze. "I don't know if that'll happen."

"You can't burn relationships all over town because of me."

"If people don't support you and me, us, then fuck 'em."

Happiness welled inside me. Was I scared? Hell, yeah. But Dawson and I had been through too much to think that we couldn't work. "Dawson Preston King, I love you. And when you ask me tomorrow, I'm going to say yes."

He whooped and picked me up, whirling around as I laughed. He captured my mouth and strode toward my RV with me still in his arms. "I need to be inside of you."

"I'm dirty and sweaty." Would it take too long to drive to his place and jump in the shower together?

"Damn right. We're both getting real dirty."

I giggled. "That's not what I meant."

"I'm going to lick every drop of sweat off you," he growled.

Paws scrambling on the gravel broke up the sound around us, but Dawson didn't hesitate. "Sorry, Daisy. You're going to have to wait out here for the rest of the afternoon. I've got some catching up to do."

Dawson

· · ·

THE LAST DAY of July started out the opposite of how the month had begun. Two sections of chairs had been set up in the yard, just like we'd done for Aiden's wedding and Dad's. And like both of theirs, Bristol and I hadn't invited a lot of people. My brothers and their wives were in attendance. Tucker and Kiernan. Emma and Taya. Jamie and the rest of the crowd that Bristol and I hung out with at Miller's. Someone named Lizette, who had helped Bristol with her wedding gown.

Grams sat with Dad and Kendall in the first row. Her chin was lifted, proud as ever, but the hostility was gone from her expression. The rigid tension that had sat like a rod strapped across her shoulders that last couple of years was gone too.

The King–Cartwright feud was being laid to rest today. Grams'd had two choices. She could've missed the wedding. But she'd chosen to drive up a couple of nights ago and talk to Bristol and me privately. Her apology had been succinct, but the sincerest I'd heard from Grams. She'd said she was happy for us and she meant it, and she'd given us her blessing on what Bristol planned to do with the money. It wasn't her choice and we hadn't needed her permission, but Grams was Grams.

My bride walked down the makeshift aisle, alone. Any of my brothers or Dad would've escorted her down the aisle, but she wasn't anyone's girl to give away.

My grin widened as she got closer. She bit the inside of her lip but ended up grinning at me. Our unspoken exchange was about one thing. The dress.

The biggest drama about today had been what she was going to wear.

I've never worn a damn dress in my life had been heard several times, in several tones. I'd caught hints of despair. Then a pissed-off attitude at people's expectations. And finally, excitement that she could pick whatever the hell she wanted, and she could afford it.

I didn't care what she wore. As long as she said *I do,* I was a happy man, and I'd be happier when I stripped her out of it. To give her something to strip me out of, I'd ordered a tux.

Her gown was simple, a little lace diamond pulling the material tighter at her waist. A long V-neck with a softly flowing skirt, the dress hugged her body in all the best places. The cream color brightened under the sun and gave her an ethereal glow. Her long red hair shone in one long wave over one shoulder, and she'd even put on a touch of lip gloss I planned to kiss off as soon as we were pronounced man and wife.

This woman. My wife.

I'd never been so nervous in my life. So elated. So happy.

We breezed through our vows. As soon as the words *You may kiss the bride* drifted in the wind, I wrapped my arms around

Bristol and claimed her. My brothers' whoops mingled with the ones from Bristol's friends.

I released my wife from my kiss but didn't let her go. I gazed at the intimate crowd of family and friends and said, "Let's eat!"

The next few hours were filled with laughter. We hadn't planned a large reception, or a dance. The only music Bristol wanted at the wedding was the mooing of the cows in the pasture with the occasional whinnies of the horses. Bucket was at my place—*our* place. He had been ever since I'd convinced Bristol to come back. After we'd made all the love our bodies could handle, I'd helped her pack her meager belongings and moved her into my bedroom. Our bedroom.

Daisy was back in her bed in the living room. Bucket was with the other horses, but we'd kept the cattle separate. We were in the middle of interviewing new ranch hands to help with the combined King–

Cartwright herd until we finalized plans for the sobriety ranch.

Bristol spent the evenings when we were relaxed in front of the TV gathering research on how those ranches operated. The next step would be to find a financial advisor to make sure the money lasted as long as possible and helped the highest number of people possible. Then we'd hire developers and search for staff.

She even had a name: Sarah's Recovery Ranch. Bristol intended the ranch to be a working ranch, supporting itself so the money Mama had left behind could support the people.

As guests filtered out, my brothers and their wives cleaned up the food, then left. They'd all gotten motel rooms in town. Bristol and I had assured them that they could stay in their bedrooms like normal, but all of them had shuddered, claiming they didn't want to be under the same roof as us on our wedding night.

Kendall caught a ride with Aiden and

Kate. Dad lingered behind. The last guest. He finished up what was left of the dishes and bagged the garbage. The house didn't look like it'd had twenty people roaming through it all day.

He put the bags by the door, then stood with his hands in the pockets of his black slacks. "I have something for you two, but . . ." His brows pinched together. "I wasn't sure when I should show you. If I should show you."

He pulled a folded sheet of paper out of his pocket and held it out. "It's from your mother. She asked the lawyer to hold on to it until the trusts were all distributed. You both should read it."

I stared at the paper. A letter from Mama?

My hands were unsteady as I opened it.

Dear Gentry,

· · ·

I HOPE *this letter doesn't see the light of day and that I'm around to watch the amazing things our boys do with this money. But I just have a feeling, and you always tell me to go with my gut. So, honey, if you're reading this, it's your one and only I told you so.*

You're all probably wondering why I set up the trusts the way I did. I can't say for certain either. I never liked what Mom and Dad did to the Cartwrights, and as the company grew, I watched Danny struggle. And because of it, Bristol is going to have a tough life.

I love that little girl. You and I both know Danny can't be trusted with that much money. I'm afraid to leave it for Bristol. If I'm not there, who'll tell her that her dad has no right to drain her of one single cent?

And the boys. God, I love our boys. But, Gentry, they're wild and they have the world at their fingertips. You and I settled down so young and my gut says they won't. This money? It's a privilege, and I trust us to raise them to do good things with it. But if I'm gone, if you've moved on, and I hope you have, then I want them to have someone to share their life with. They can suffer a little mama interference even if I'm not there.

I also know you. If Danny is still around and if he wouldn't be a good steward for this money, I know you and the boys will do what's necessary to keep the trust in the family. But if it's just Bristol, and she grows into the bright, capable young woman I think she will, then I know that one or more of the trusts going to her won't be the end of the world no matter what my parents say.

I also admit to hoping she ends up with one of the boys. A mama can dream, right? (It's Dawson, isn't it? They're so cute together, and the way he watches out for her melts my heart.)

But if it doesn't work out, if all the boys marry and get the trust, can you make sure she's taken care of? She'll be stubborn like her dad, and proud, but everyone needs a little help sometimes.

So, I guess that's it. I hope I'm around long enough to change the trust into an inheritance. But if I'm not, then I won't be around to deal with the repercussions. I'm going with my gut, Gentry. I love you. And make sure the boys never forget how much I love them. After this, I'm writing a letter to each of them. They'll be tucked away in their baby books in my office.

ALWAYS YOURS, even if you're cursing me out for what I did,
Sarah

I PRESSED a palm against one leaking eye, then the other. "Shit."

"Yeah," Dad said, his eyes gleaming.

Bristol sniffed and handed me a napkin from the counter. She gave one to Dad and the three of us dabbed at our eyes without saying a word.

"I guess that answers that," I finally said and carefully folded Mama's letter. "The baby books are packed away in the closet in the office. The others didn't want theirs until they'd settled down. I never thought to look inside them." I hadn't wanted to. Packing up Mama's office had been hard enough when I took over the house.

Dad took the letter back. He stared at it for a moment, then reverently tucked it into his pocket. "This was such a Sarah thing to do. Figuring out a way to say goodbye even after she's been gone for so long."

"Did you show Kendall?"

He nodded. "She thought it best to give us privacy." His gaze touched on Bristol. "You both did what two generations couldn't and got over yourselves." He started for the door. "By the way, Kendall left a gift box in the mudroom from all of us. She said you two didn't have time to plan a honeymoon. So if it works for you, Xander and Savvy will stay the whole week so you two can get away. Aiden has the plane ready to go tomorrow when you are, and Beck left instructions for how to get to his cabin in the mountains after you land in Denver. Congratulations."

I twined my fingers through Bristol's. Dad went out the front door and I faced my wife. "I guess we're getting a honeymoon."

"I've never left Montana." She squeezed my hand. We'd talked about getting away on short notice, but we'd been too impatient to marry and left it as a conversation for later. My family had our backs.

I pulled her into my arms. "Are you doing okay?"

She pressed her lips together, emotion heavy in her eyes. "I thought I was fine not knowing, but . . . I needed that. Your mom was a really special person."

I tugged her toward me. "It just so happens that I married a really special person today."

Faux surprise widened her eyes. "No way. Me too."

I pulled her in and pressed my lips to hers. "I love you, Bristol Cartwright King."

"I love you, Dawson King." She brushed

her lips along my jaw. "You're pretty hot in a tux, did you know that?"

I skimmed my hands down the back of her silky dress until I cupped her butt cheeks. I gathered the material of her skirt, hitching it higher and higher. "I want to peel this dress off you with my teeth, but first I'm going to take you against the counter in it. What do you think about that, my dear wife?"

She tapped her chin. "Hmm. I think there's no better way to put the King–Cartwright feud in the grave than fucking on the island in a wedding dress and a tux."

"Time to make it official."

ate

I PARKED OUTSIDE of Creek Coffee. I'd messaged everyone for their order. Except for Aiden. He had the same drink everywhere. Coffee. With cream. He didn't drink coffee often, but when he did, it was the same.

Breezing in, I nodded at the table of older men who played cards most mornings at the coffee shop. Taya grinned from behind the counter.

"Kate! Nice to see you. That time of year?"

I laughed. "Sure is."

Grabbing coffee on the morning the guys worked cattle had become tradition. Dawson provided the early-morning brew, and I picked up the midmorning stash. It gave me an excuse to get out of the pens.

I didn't mind working cattle. It wasn't like I did more than wave my arms to keep cattle from escaping the group and avoiding the corrals. An entire day of being with Aiden, except we didn't get to really talk. An entire day of that dragged on.

I enjoyed chatting with Kendall, Eva, Savvy, and now Bristol. But the coffee shop offered an escape. A way to feel like I contributed more to the family than waving my arms around.

Regardless, coming to King's Creek to hang out with the rest of the family during the spring and fall were my favorite times of the year. Aiden and I tried to drive together. An entire hour with my husband.

Often he drove, which meant he wasn't working. Almost as often, he fielded phone calls, but when he wasn't immersed in business, I prattled on about work. He listened.

For a woman who'd spent her youth and adult years listening to others, it was like someone yanked my plug out and nothing but rambling spewed out. The people I dealt with at work. Cool facts I'd looked up during my shifts for the patrons. Gushing over my coworkers' vacation stories. I was a reference librarian. I had more interaction with patrons than my coworkers, and if any career could compete against the medical field for TMI, it'd be mine.

"Yeah, I have some, um . . . discharge, coming from . . . Do you have books on STDs?"

"Can you help me apply for a job? I got fired from the gas station last week because my boss thought I stole money from the till. They think I did it for drug money. But I've been clean since

my husband caught me in bed with his brother, who's also his cousin . . ."

"I need to buy a plane ticket and the print's so small, can you read it off for me? Here. Here's my credit card. Just put that in."

So, it was nice to have someone listen to me for a change.

Taya was ready at the register by the time I reached the counter. There was a younger girl behind her, making a smoothie for a drive-through customer.

"Ready?" I asked, holding my phone with the list of everyone's request. It was substantial, but I never called ahead. The coffee shop was my solace. It wasn't that I was a city girl—the trailer park I'd grown up in could hardly count as urban sophistication. It was just that I accepted I wasn't cowgirl material for more than a couple of hours. I wore the boots for practical reasons, and I'd used them enough that they made me look legit. But the jeans, the hoodies? They weren't me.

Or they were more me than I cared to

admit. But I'd worked hard to blend into an environment that wasn't crass and rambunctious and unrefined. I worked hard to remember where I'd come from and to keep from going back. And to convince myself that I didn't miss it at all.

I rattled off the orders, paid, and went to sit in the corner opposite the card players. The hazard of a job that was so quiet: I required more solitude during chaotic days. And working cattle with eleven other people was busy, sometimes boisterous, and just *a lot*.

Scrolling through my phone, I enjoyed the sunshine streaming through the window. Taya skirted around the counter and sat at the table with me. She slid my mango smoothie over. "Giselle's getting the rest of the order ready."

"No problem." I pocketed my phone, enjoying one-on-one conversation with someone I didn't see often but had become friendly with. "How's it going?"

"Things are well. Not exactly exciting,

but that's okay when it comes to business." She crossed one long leg over the other. If only I had half Taya's grace. But I'd need her graceful body to go with it. Not my padded, sturdy one. "Is everyone in town?"

"Yes. There's a big cattle sale and they're sorting. Getting the rest into winter pastures." I pressed my lips shut. Dawson's business wasn't trade information. I'd start rambling if I kept going. Most people's eyes glazed over when I spoke too long about a subject. I'd learned the hard way to shut up well before I was ready.

"I'm so glad things worked out between Dawson and Bristol. After that trust drama, I wasn't sure."

"What trust drama?"

Taya's brows shot up. "You don't know?"

Apparently not. I switched to business mode. Sometimes I worked with individuals who were too proud to admit what they didn't know, or were too ashamed to admit what they'd done. The opposite of TMI made my job harder. I couldn't help them apply for jobs or fill out resumes if they weren't forthcoming with all the information.

I used the roundabout method. "You mean with Emilia?"

Aiden had raced to King's Creek with Beck last June. He hadn't said more than Grams had collapsed. Then during the Fourth of July fair, Aiden hadn't been sure plans were still on since Dawson and Bristol had briefly split up. But when I'd asked him why, he'd said he didn't know the details.

Taya knew something. What were the chances my husband had lied?

I swallowed hard, willing Taya to talk.

She did. "Yeah, it was shitty how she cornered Bristol and gloated about the trust Dawson's mom had set up."

I knew about a trust that Aiden had received when he turned thirty. We'd been married a little over a year. He'd stuffed it away, said we were doing fine and didn't need it, and I'd read between the lines. It wasn't my business, and Aiden rarely discussed anything to do with his mom.

"Right." My mind sifted through ways to get more information. I took a long pull of my sweet smoothie while thinking, but Taya wasn't done.

"It also seems really weird that his mom would set up a trust like that. Maybe she was afraid her wild boys would never settle down and bribing them with money would do it. I don't know if I'd make my kids be married for a year before I gave them the payout. But then I don't have kids. Maybe it'd be different if I did. And I certainly don't have a hundred million to pass out."

I choked on my drink. Sputtering, I grabbed for a napkin. "Sorry. Swallowed wrong. How much did you say?"

"Sorry. I shouldn't be talking about stuff that's not my business."

"No, it's fine. The trust. Right. All the boys got one." I didn't know for certain. But Aiden had gotten one. Dawson, apparently. One hundred million? Was she *serious*? Split between the four brothers—that was a staggering amount of money. Why hadn't Aiden told me? And what had Taya said about being married a year?

"I can't imagine that amount of money, just having four hundred million to split up."

I sucked on my straw. Long and hard.

One hundred million. Apiece.

Aiden and I were well off. Aiden had been well off when I'd married him. But I'd assumed he worked hard for every penny.

We were legit millionaires?

"But Bristol will do good things with that money. Her plans for Cartwright Cattle are admirable."

"Yeah. Totally." The dude ranch. A sobriety ranch. Yep. Good things. My mind circled back to how much my husband hadn't told me.

"I'm so glad the rest of you married for love and not for the money though. I know it seemed suspicious at first, that they all married before they turned twenty-nine, but here everyone is, married over a year, and Dawson wanted his trust to go to Bristol."

The pieces clicked in my brain. Married for a year. Married before twenty-nine. The money going to Bristol. The drama with Emilia.

Emilia Boyd wouldn't want one cent to leave the family. They were all she had left without Sarah. But Sarah had—what, figured that if the boys didn't want to marry and live happily ever after, that Bristol should be stinking rich? Or would the money have gone to Danny Cartwright? He'd only passed away seven months ago. That would've made it more urgent to marry before the deadline.

Which was their twenty-ninth birthday.

Aiden's thirty-third birthday had just passed. We'd met for dinner and then he'd gone back to the office. How. Romantic. But that also meant we'd just celebrated our fourth anniversary. Because we'd married before he turned twenty-nine.

Same with Beck. And Xander.

Dawson hadn't. Had he wanted his marriage with Bristol to mean more?

What did that say about my marriage?

My stomach twisted around the cold drink.

"Everyone got happy endings." Taya's grin radiated happiness. Four couples. Together for love instead of money.

Giselle appeared with two carriers full of drinks. "I'm all done. Want help carrying them to your car?"

No. I wanted to run out of the coffee shop and find a corner to cry in. I wanted to track down my husband, pull him off the cattle shoot right onto his ass even if it did look chiseled from a perfect slab of marble, and demand answers.

But I was married to Aiden King. A man who didn't share more details with his wife than necessary. Not even critical details that affected our marriage.

"Yeah, I'd love some help, thanks." The foundation of my world had cracked and crumbled. But I could act like it was just another Saturday.

Both Taya and her employee walked me to my car. I was parked out front and the card players would watch over the shop better than any security guard.

Giselle rushed back in. Taya lingered. "Hey, I'm sorry if I was being nosy or gossipy." She shrugged, her expression chagrined. "It's not often I get some girl talk, and I end up saying too much."

"No. No, anytime." Seriously. Otherwise I wouldn't know anything. "Please, don't beat yourself up. It's all right. We all care about Bristol."

"She married into an awesome family. Hey, next time you're in town, we need to meet up."

"Yes. Absolutely." I pulled off a friendly smile when all I wanted to do was sob. How could I hang out with Taya? What would I say the next time I saw her? BTW, you totally tipped me off and destroyed the fantasy I'd built around my empty, lonely marriage. My marriage lacking information. My marriage based on a lie.

Taya went inside and I got behind the wheel. I didn't drive far. I pulled off into the empty parking lot of the school and stared out the windshield.

I could go back and pretend nothing had happened. Sunday night, we'd drive home, and I could go back to the way it was. Only I wouldn't be able to delude myself any longer. About how I waited for scraps of affection from my cold, distant husband. About how a seven-figure salary —and nine figures in the bank from the trust—wasn't enough to make my husband slow down and spend time with me. I couldn't return to lusting after him like I had as a teen when he'd first wrestled my brother.

I'd been in ninth grade. Another introspective freshman had marched to the mat with that rolling gait all the hot wrestlers developed. Like they were stalking their prey, and if it was an opponent, they'd make him submit. But if it was a girl, they'd make her submit without moving a muscle.

I was that girl.

He'd looked over me that day. Through me. Most people had. A mousy girl who probably wore an expression that read the same as her shirt: *I'd rather be reading*. My hair had been down, nothing more than brushed, and my job had been to hover at the sides of the mat and toss down the towel when the time ran out.

But I'd watched him. The coiled strength. The quiet power. He hadn't boasted. He hadn't gloated when he'd dominated my brother, a promising candidate for state champ. Aiden had evaluated him until it was time to wrestle. Then he'd methodically worn my brother down and won. When it was over, he'd shaken hands and walked away. No boasting. No arrogant grin. He'd done what he'd come to do.

I hadn't thought much of boys until that

day. Before that wrestling tournament, I'd been a ninth-grade girl going on old spinster cat lady. But after that day? I'd catapulted through puberty and came out the other side with only him on my mind. Over a decade later, when he'd asked me out, I'd submitted without him moving a muscle.

How did I move forward with this new information? I couldn't ignore his behavior this time.

Because I couldn't be Kate King, librarian and overlooked wife of Aiden King, one minute longer.

ABOUT THE AUTHOR

Marie Johnston writes paranormal and contemporary romance and has collected several awards in both genres. Before she was a writer, she was a microbiologist. Depending on the situation, she can be oddly unconcerned about germs or weirdly phobic. She's also a licensed medical technician and has worked as a public health microbiologist and as a lab tech in hospital and clinic labs. Marie's been a volunteer EMT, a college instructor, a security guard, a phlebotomist, a hotel clerk, and a coffee pourer in a bingo hall. All fodder for a writer!! She has four kids, an old cat, and a puppy that's bigger than half her kids.

mariejohnstonwriter.com

Follow me:

ALSO BY MARIE JOHNSTON

<u>Oil Kings</u>

King's Crown

King's Ransom

King's Treasure

King's Country

King's Queen

Like hard-working men who are in control of everything but the one they fall for?

The Walker Five:

Conflict of Interest (Book 1)

Mustang Summer (Book 2)

Long Hard Fall (Book 3)

Guilt Ridden (Book 4)

Mail Order Farmer (Book 5)